ACCLAIM FOR AWARD WINNING AUTHOR BARRY FINLAY

SEARCHING FOR TRUTH
A JAKE SCOTT MYSTERY

"Don't let Jake's pipe-and-slippers persona fool you into thinking this is just a cozy mystery. It's not. It's merely a disguise for a sharp and compelling whodunnit." – **Cath 'N' Kindle Book Reviews**

"Searching For Truth is an intriguing whodunit that embraces much more psychological depth than most mysteries and will have readers both guessing and involved to the end." – **D. Donovan, Senior Reviewer, Midwest Book Review**

THE BURDEN OF DARKNESS
A MARCIE KANE AND NATHAN HARRIS THRILLER

"Thoroughly captivating, ingenious, and full of heart-pounding suspense, this is an action thriller done right…" – **The Prairies Book Review**

"Those who like their thrillers especially strong in interpersonal relationships and connections and character psychology and evolution will welcome *The Burden of Darkness* for its compelling blend of action and insight." – **Diane Donovan, Midwest Book Review**

D1278789

NEVER SO ALONE
A NATHAN HARRIS THRILLER NOVELLA

"Finlay constructs a convincing special operations plot, complete with high action to keep the reader on edge." – **The Prairies Book Review**

"Brilliant. Would be an amazing film!" – **Goodreads reader**

REMOTE ACCESS
AN INTERNATIONAL POLITICAL THRILLER

"Finlay paints a frighteningly realistic picture of two of the things people often fear today — terrorism and cybercrime." – **RECOMMENDED by the US Review of Books**

"While grounded in reality, Remote Access is a must-read with a singular sense of escapism rare in a political thriller." – **BestThrillers.com**

A PERILOUS QUESTION
AN INTERNATIONAL THRILLER AND CRIME NOVEL

"Written with a compassionate, knowledgeable voice, the book is an excellent story of mystery and intrigue." – **RECOMMENDED by the US Review of Books**

"A Perilous Question sizzles with international intrigue as the tension and suspense mount to a compelling pitch. Barry Finlay will keep you turning the pages." – **Rick Mofina, Bestselling Author of FREE FALL**

THE VANISHING WIFE
AN ACTION-PACKED CRIME THRILLER

"I had a hard time not just giving up the rest of my life and reading this in one sitting." – **Vaughan Hopkins, Amazon reviewer**

"The pace grabs hold. Whether the mild-mannered accountant Mason Seaforth could actually pull off what's at stake depends on the colour, the energy and dialogue of the story telling. The Vanishing Wife is convincing." – **Donald Graves, Canadian Crime Reviews**

KILIMANJARO AND BEYOND
A LIFE-CHANGING JOURNEY

"The book reads like a journal and the writing is warm, familiar and humorous. 'Kilimanjaro and Beyond, A Life-Changing Journey,' will challenge all who read it to consider how they too can make a difference, not only for others, but for themselves as well." – **Reader Views**

"...at once so inspirational and courageous, so human and humane, and so deeply personal that the reader feels they are climbing right along with this small and highly determined group." – **Reverend Dr. Linda De Coff, Author, Bridge of the Gods**

I GUESS WE MISSED THE BOAT
A TRAVEL MEMOIR

"This is an exhilarating read." –– **Grady Harp, Amazon Hall of Fame reviewer**

"I Guess We Missed the Boat is a fresh, ironic and jovial travel adventure novel in which each traveler can recognize himself or herself. It is a travel book that is amusing and practical at the same time." – **Reader Views**

SEARCHING FOR TRUTH

A JAKE SCOTT MYSTERY

BARRY FINLAY

Searching For Truth

A Jake Scott Mystery

Published by Keep On Climbing Publishing

Copyright ©Barry Finlay 2021

(613) 240-6953
info@barry-finlay.com
www.barry-finlay.com

Cataloguing data available at Library and Archives Canada.

ISBN: 978-1-7771395-2-0

Dedicated to Annika, Jaelyn and Isaac. May reading always bring joy to your lives.

ACKNOWLEDGEMENTS

Searching For Truth introduces a new character, Jake Scott, a retired, bored, and lonely former reporter needing someone or something to drag him out of the lethargy he finds himself in.

While retirement is the pot of gold at the end of the rainbow for many, it's not treating Jake very well. Most glide into it. Others, like Jake, find the transition rougher than expected. Experts will tell you there are pitfalls hiding in the pot of gold. Loneliness is one, as coworkers are no longer available to swap stories with five days a week. While it seems counterintuitive, not having something else to occupy the mind can lead to even more stress than work ever provided. Reduced physical activity can create health problems. While everyone dreams of retirement, a person must be prepared for the transition.

I enjoyed writing about the challenges Jake faces in his retirement, as he is failing miserably at adapting. He has also lost his wife and his only daughter has moved out of town, which makes his challenges even greater. I hope you enjoy reading as Jake finds something to do that may be more than he bargained for.

The setting for the book is Ottawa, Canada. While most of my books are set in locations that we have visited around the world, the pandemic ended that, at least temporarily, so there was no better place to set the book than my hometown. Many of the locations and street names mentioned in the book are real. I thought Jake should have to deal with the winter like the rest of us since Ottawa is the seventh coldest capital city in the world where snow and ice are prevalent for too much of the year. Most inhabitants embrace the cold with outdoor activities, except those who escape to warmer climates, which is something Jake dreams of doing.

Many people were involved in writing *Searching For Truth*. Of course, any errors in fact or detail remain my responsibility. Several readers worked their way through the early manuscript despite the grammatical errors and typos and I appreciate all of them very much. Jacques Tremblay and Steve Mitchell provided editorial comments and suggestions for which I'm very grateful. Constable Amy Gagnon, Media Relations Officer, Ottawa Police Service, was wonderful at filling in some blanks, and I'm very appreciative of her efforts. Thank you also to Books Go Social for designing the cover and providing the layout.

Thank you to you, my loyal reader. As much as I enjoy writing, it is your reviews and feedback that encourage me to make every book the best it can be. For those who help by telling your friends and family about my books, thank you very much. Making people aware of a book among the millions available is always a challenge and I appreciate everyone who helps.

Finally, a special thank you to my wife Evelyn, who always reads the earliest versions of the manuscript, and provides invaluable comments and inspiration.

Now, it's time to delve into the mind of Jake Scott in *Searching For Truth*

PROLOGUE

A SLIVER OF the moon was all that illuminated their spot at the end of the parking lot. A cave would have offered better light as the burned-out streetlamp hanging above the car provided nothing. The absence of light suited Matt Pawsloski and Melissa Thomas just fine.

They had arrived around nine o'clock and parked at the far end of the lot, relieved to see theirs was the only car. If Matt rolled down his window, they could hear the roar of Hog's Back Falls and the bravado of teenagers shouting somewhere nearby. He shut off the car but left the window down a crack. Just enough to provide a breath of air in the humid Ottawa night while muffling most of the outside noise.

Matt unknotted his tie. It produced a zipping sound as he yanked it from his shirt collar and tossed it on top of the light gray suit jacket draped across his briefcase in the back seat. He had removed the jacket earlier in the evening when he left the office. The suit and tie fit his upwardly mobile path at the legal firm where he worked downtown. Shortly, he would have his law degree, but by watching others of lesser capabilities progress in the firm, he learned that being seen in the office by the bosses after hours was almost as important as the work he produced. Besides, he needed to confirm the identity of the person responsible for an irregularity at the office and waiting until others left afforded the best opportunity. He had stayed late, which suited Melissa since she worked beyond her scheduled shift end of eight o'clock.

Matt reached for Melissa's hand as they sat in silence for a few minutes. She was jittery, shuddering at the sound of a sewer hole cover clattering as a passing car on the street drove over it. She leaned across the center console in the Camry to be closer to Matt. A mosquito buzzed around her head until it made a fatal miscalculation and landed on her arm where she swatted it.

She said, "I hate this, Matt. It's too dark and creepy, and this car is so uncomfortable. I feel like a teenager stealing a few minutes with her boyfriend."

Matt's annoyance showed as his lips scarcely moved.

"Well dear, I guess it's partly true. I *am* your boyfriend. What else can we do? We can't rent a hotel room every night, and there's no time to drive to my place. Your husband wouldn't appreciate it if we used *your* bedroom." His tone softened as he changed the subject. "Speaking of your husband, what's Gary doing tonight?"

Melissa gazed into Matt's eyes. Her hesitation signaled her discomfort with the subject. Finally, she said, "He went to a friend's place. Just a bunch of guys getting together like they always do. You're right, I can't be too long. Besides, you seem edgy."

Matt leaned to pull Melissa closer and brushed her lips with his.

He said, "I'm sorry, some things at work are bothering me. Things I'd rather not talk about yet. When are you going to leave him? You know he stormed into the office and threatened to kill us? *In the office!* Good thing I wasn't there. You've been talking about leaving him for weeks, but I don't think it will ever happen."

Melissa pulled back, saying, "It *will* happen. The time just has to be right. If he ever caught us, he *would* kill us. He's got a terrible temper when he's mad. You know that, right?"

"I heard about his temper when he came into the office. It's all the more reason to leave him. Does he have a job yet?"

Melissa shrugged and blew air through her lips before responding. "He says no one in town is looking for chefs right now. He's pretty picky, but eventually, he'll have to take something, even if it's in a fast-food restaurant. We had a tremendous fight about him not working the other night. It was so loud, the police came."

A fleeting smile crossed Matt's lips as he said, "That must've been something. Now, there isn't another car in the parking lot. It's just you and me, so let's make the best of it."

Melissa snuggled close to Matt again for a moment before jerking upright again, saying, "What if a police car shows up? They must patrol the parks."

Matt's head dropped back in exasperation. "Oh my God, Melissa. You worry too much." He pulled her closer to continue what they started. He found her lips again and kissed her intensely as he unbuttoned the top of her blouse. His words were a whisper. "The way I feel, we won't be here long. Let's get into the back seat. This console is in the way."

His fingers found the inside of Melissa's lacy bra as she draped her arms around his neck.

The lights of a car turning into the parking lot reflected off the facets of Melissa's diamond ring. The vehicle crept past their parking spot before doing a deliberate, meandering U-turn and pulling in on the opposite side. Shallow breathing was the only sound in Matt's car as he peered through his back window, but the other vehicle's tinted glass obscured the driver's face. Eerie shadows cast by the moon danced across the asphalt as tree limbs rocked gently in the breeze. Matt shivered involuntarily, but he tried to hide it from Melissa.

Melissa sat back and whispered, as if the other driver could hear, "I told you the police might patrol the park." Her voice was frantic. "We had better go, Matt."

"Melissa, it's not a police car and I have never seen them drive an unmarked Mercedes. That car is expensive. It's probably just some old guy hiding from his wife. Or maybe the driver stopped to make a phone call. Even if it is the police, we're consenting adults, so they won't do anything. Let's just wait a bit and see if he leaves."

They used the next few minutes to discuss their future, ever watchful of the other car. The tension in Melissa's body eased, comforted as she was by Matt's words. She wasn't a stunning beauty, but the smile that came readily to her face, and the dimples it created, attracted Matt from the beginning. She found the humor in anything, tonight being an exception. He found that incredibly attractive. The first time they met, when she patched him up in the hospital after a bicycle accident, the smile and her sense of humor drew him like metal to a magnet. She made him laugh by emphatically imagining a curb leaping in front of his bike at the last second. It took his mind off the pain. He noticed her wedding band only after he asked her out for coffee, and she accepted. He wondered if she took it off when she worked, but he never asked. The affair had been ongoing for months.

Her hands ran nervously through her hair as she talked about leaving her husband, but she continually glanced over Matt's shoulder to see if the dark car had moved. Matt listened as she talked. He had heard it all before, and he didn't actually believe it.

Melissa was too timid to walk out on her husband. She was too afraid of what her husband might do if she left him. But he listened, nodding at the right time, and deliberately, tantalizingly, letting his fingers wander under her skirt.

Melissa stopped him. She said, "Matt, listen to me. I have a plan this time. We *will* be together. I'm going to leave him."

Her voice trailed off as a sharp knock on the window startled them. Neither had noticed the man approaching from the black Mercedes. It wasn't a hand knocking. It was something metallic rapping against the glass that set both their hearts racing. Melissa gasped. Matt turned to peer at the intruder, but a piercing flashlight beam blinded him. He threw one arm up to block the light while he pressed the button to roll down the power window. Nothing happened because he had turned off the car.

It didn't matter.

The last sight either would see was the flashlight beam and the flash from the barrel of a gun. Melissa died first as the blast from the man's weapon pierced the glass and the bullet struck her in the forehead. She slumped against the passenger door. Matt died right after as the next bullet entered his heart, interrupting the scream forming in his throat. The gunman shot them each twice more for good measure.

The killer shoved the gun into his waistband and listened to the night as he strode to his car as if nothing had happened. Dogs barked in the distance, disturbed by the sound of the gun. The boisterous teenagers had gone quiet, either trying to identify the noises or running the other way. A smile danced across the man's lips. He started the car and drove away into the humid Ottawa night.

Two and a half years later

CHAPTER ONE

THE SOUND OF the newspaper thudding against the door registered somewhere deep in Jake Scott's subconscious. He pried one eye open to see the clock on the nightstand. After blinking the sleep away, he watched the luminescent orange numbers click over to 8:05. He wasn't sure, but he thought it must be Saturday. The days had become essentially meaningless since his forced retirement two years prior.

Saturdays offered some promise. He met his buddies for coffee every week at Brew and Buns on Wellington Street. They always teased the owner that with a name like that, if his coffee business failed, he could open a strip joint. The jabs never more than mildly amused the owner, since he thought the name cleverly advertised his superb coffee and cinnamon rolls.

Jake dragged himself into a semblance of wakefulness and wondered if the weather forecast was right. He doubted it, since a correct forecast was rare these days, and the newspaper had rattled off his door at the usual time. The forecast called for 30 centimeters of snow to bury the city during the night. Jake still dwelled in an imperial world, so for forty years he had been converting metric numbers to understand what they meant. In his hazy state, he calculated the estimated snowfall to be about 12 inches.

He lay in bed dozing for another half hour before telling himself to get up. The scheduled breakfast time was 10 o'clock, and besides, falling into a deep sleep in the morning always left him groggy. The breakfast may not even happen if Mother Nature gave the forecasters a win for once. He tossed the covers back, threw on his bathrobe, and shuffled to the bathroom. Returning to the bed, he sat with a groan and decided he must have twisted his arthritic knee in the covers during the night because it was protesting every move. If it didn't settle down, he would take an Advil, even though it wasn't something he liked to do.

Three events in the last few years had changed Jake's life dramatically. His high school sweetheart, Mia, his wife of 33 years, died abruptly from an aneurysm four years previously. It sucked the enthusiasm for life right out of him. Then he accepted early retirement from the *Ottawa Citizen* newspaper two years ago. He fought for less opinion and more news, but readers and social media influenced the market. His lack of enthusiasm, decreased resources, increased workload, and a decent retirement package nudged him out the door. He missed it. The pre-retirement course warned him there would be a transition, but he never dreamed it would be so difficult. Finally, his daughter Avery moved to Toronto a few months ago to be with her boyfriend, Nick. Jake supported his daughter's choice, but a feeling of melancholy dragged him down for days after she left.

The days merged since retirement with little to show for them. Offers to do freelance work came, but he ignored them. It became even worse during the pandemic. With the loneliness and boredom, he wondered some days if he would survive. He realized he had become lethargic, but he had difficulty digging himself out of the hole. Saturday coffee and a cinnamon bun with the guys and one lady was the bright spot on his weekly calendar.

He got up and pushed the curtain aside to peer outside. It had snowed enough that the plow service he hired would arrive later to clean out the driveway. He noticed the squirrels had successfully raided the bird feeder again. Large fluffy flakes still drifted down, draping a sheer curtain over the still-lit streetlights. He decided to go if the breakfast was still on. It was a short walk, and the street appeared to be navigable.

He wandered into the kitchen where his overweight and temperamental tabby cat, Oliver, greeted him loudly. The feline made his distaste for the tardiness of his breakfast delivery clear, but he threaded himself clumsily through his owner's legs as Jake poured food and milk into the bowls. Food always soothed the cat's disposition. Jake rubbed his head, saying, "So, who's in charge today, Oliver? Is it your turn or mine?"

Oliver ignored him as he buried his face deep in the bowl.

Jake took a leisurely shower and pulled on black jeans and a bulky worn red sweater as his mood brightened at the thought of meeting his friends. He wore the same outfit every Saturday during the winter and amused his friends by calling it his Sunday sweater since it was "holey."

He wandered into the second bedroom he had converted to an office and fired up the ancient desktop computer he used as little as possible. Since retirement, the computer's sole use had been to converse via email with Avery in Toronto. As usual, it took its time booting up. Jake thought it had some life left, even though Avery urged him to replace it. She wanted him to follow her on social media, but his old computer wouldn't handle it. He smiled as he opened an email from her that offered greetings and a political joke that she thought he might appreciate. The joke elicited a chuckle. Even from 250 miles away, Avery seemed to sense when his mood needed a lift. He would have to remember to reply later.

The email he was looking for was in his inbox. It was from Eric Jacobson, the oldest of the breakfast group and the organizer of the Saturday coffee get-together. Like Jake, Eric lived within walking distance of Brew and Buns, and his emails were always short and to the point. This one encouraged them to show up despite the weather. "Okay, Canadians. We aren't letting a little snow stop us, are we? See you at Buns." Eric loved to refer to the restaurant by the half of the name that got under the skin of the owner the best.

No one else had replied.

Jake hit "reply all," typed, "I'll be there," and tapped on the "send" button. That ended today's computer use, he thought as he powered it down. He puttered around the house, frequently checking his watch until it was time to go. He wandered to the front door and pulled on a puffy black nylon winter coat and bent to lace up his thermal winter boots.

He stepped out into the frigid air and stooped to pick up the cold newspaper from the doorstep. He glanced at the headline. In large black font, it read, "HUSBAND SENTENCED IN PARK SLAYING." He tossed the paper on the bench in the hallway as he closed the door. It bounced once before settling on the floor, accompanied by a shower of ice crystals.

CHAPTER TWO

JAKE LEANED INTO the wind as he slogged through snow up to his boot tops on the driveway. He decided walking on the street would be easier since the plow had already gone by. The sidewalk lay under a blanket of snow. He hadn't noticed the bitter wind, but as he moved away from the sheltered porch, it bit into his exposed skin. He tucked his chin into the collar of his coat to hide from the blowing crystals. Branches of forlorn trees in the mature neighborhood drooped, burdened by heavy clumps of snow.

He was already puffing from the exertion when the familiar whine of spinning tires cut through the wind. A car ahead rocked back and forth as the driver attempted to pull from the curb. Jake peered through the falling snow and instantly recognized two problems. The driver was applying too much gas to his older model Volkswagen, turning the snow beneath the tires to ice. Second, since the plow had gone by recently, a mound of snow surrounded the car, sealing it in its spot. Jake thought the driver fortunate he didn't receive a ticket because of the overnight parking ban that became effective with sizable snowfalls.

He tapped on the driver's window, startling the young man behind the wheel. The driver rolled down the window a crack and lifted his foot off the accelerator. He glanced anxiously at Jake with an exasperated expression, looking like he was already late for something. Jake motioned to the rear of the car.

"Just press the gas slowly. I'll push and we should be able to get you through that mound of snow."

Jake pressed his shoulder to the back of the car as the inexperienced driver sped up. Ice rattled against the undercarriage of the vehicle from the front tires. Jake's knee protested but held up as he put all his weight into pushing. The wheels spun at first, then the grips on the tires caught. The vehicle hesitated when it hit the mound, but with one last shove, it made it through. A padded thermal-clad arm waved through the open side window as the driver gunned the accelerator and the car slithered down the street.

Jake walked past shuttered businesses on Wellington Street, victims of the economic slowdown caused by the pandemic. It was 10:10 when he arrived at Brew and Buns. As he put on his mask, he glanced through the window to see two of the group sitting around their usual table: Eric Jacobson and Ryan Cambridge. He went inside, stamped his feet to shake the snow from his boots, and pulled off his toque as he wandered to the table.

Jacobson's bald head reflected the overhead light as Jake approached. Eric spent his entire working life in the government bureaucracy like many others in Ottawa. At close to 70, he carried several extra pounds and was the oldest of the bunch. Tight wrinkles surrounded his eyes, and his mouth turned down at the corners, leaving people with the impression he was always sullen or angry. It surprised Jake to learn as they became friends at school that the opposite was true. Eric Jacobson had a great sense of humor. He also played bass in a classic rock band.

Ryan Cambridge was the youngest and the athlete of the group. Tall and thin with a full head of jet-black hair and chiseled features, he played forward in a hockey beer league. He was 50 and a senior partner in the law firm of Cambridge and Tremblay LLP, downtown. He became part of the group because of a friendship that developed after he worked on a real estate deal for Eric.

Jake greeted them and draped his coat over the back of the chair as he thumped down, digging deeply for each breath. Each of his friends had coffee and a partly eaten cinnamon roll sitting in front of them.

Cambridge peered at him over the coffee mug he held in both hands in front of his face.

"Good morning, Jake. You're breathing hard. Did you run here?"

"Mornin' guys," The words rode out of Jake's mouth on an exhale. "No, I pushed some kid's car from a snowbank. He parked illegally on the street overnight. He had a heavy foot, so he wasn't gaining much traction. At the speed he raced away, I think he's probably in the ditch by now."

Jacobson recommended they give Daniela, the lone female of the group, the license number so she could give him a ticket. Jake reminded him it wouldn't do much good since Daniela worked homicide. She had risen to the rank of acting Staff Sergeant in charge of the homicide division after her boss retired. They decided laughingly that maybe Daniela could just shoot the kid.

The owner of Brew and Buns, Jason Pruitt, wandered to their table carrying a mug of coffee and a warm cinnamon roll that he set in front of Jake. The restaurant offered sandwiches, other pastries, and specialized deserts, but it gained its reputation for the coffee and cinnamon buns. Pruitt was in his mid-thirties and handsome in a Brad Pitt kind of way, but the mask that had become de rigueur since the pandemic covered half his bearded face. He recognized early in the pandemic that he could provide curbside service for his treats, and the sight of his customers using that option supported and encouraged him. Other neighborhood restaurants were not so fortunate. He admitted it was tough, but his quick response paid the bills and kept his business solvent.

Jake had the same order since the first day he started meeting the others for breakfast. He glanced up at Pruitt and thanked him with a smile. He regarded the mostly empty tables surrounding them. Customers typically filled the place by now, but the snow apparently convinced the usual patrons to stay in bed.

Pruitt turned and strolled back behind the counter, but he tossed over his shoulder for the benefit of the others, "So, you're late, Jake. Hot date last night?"

Jake searched for a witty answer, but Jacobson chimed in loud enough that everyone in the room heard. "He wouldn't know how to handle a woman if he caught one. He's kind of like a dog chasing a car. If he catches up to it, it's like 'what do I do now?'"

A round of laughs erupted from Cambridge and Pruitt and other customers tried to hide grins. Jake forced a grim smile onto his face. It wasn't far from the truth.

Jake removed his mask and inhaled the aroma of the restaurant as he cut into the gooey bun with a knife. The mixture of freshly brewed coffee and baking from the oven transported him back to the kitchen in his childhood farmhouse. The coffee pot was always on and fresh baking available without exception in case, as his mother said, "someone showed up."

He glanced at Eric and said, "No sign of the other two?"

Jacobson leaned back in his chair and touched his cheek. It was a familiar tic he used before speaking. "I haven't heard from Daniela. Pierre replied he couldn't make it. Unlike you, Jake, the others don't hit 'reply all' when responding to an email, so you wouldn't see their answers."

Jake was disappointed that Daniela wasn't there. Breakfast was more enjoyable when she showed up. Pierre Chevrier's absence didn't bother him. He was French Canadian, in his fifties, and drove a city bus. Jake sensed Chevrier didn't like him. He had even given Jake the nickname Gloomy Gus, but fortunately, it hadn't stuck.

The three friends sat around the table enjoying their coffee and rolls and discussing the weather. The conversation occasionally veered towards politics, and sports always found its way into the discussion. Some days the discussions could get heated, but today the group remained relaxed. Jason Pruitt brought refills for the coffee when Cambridge said, "Did you guys see this morning's paper about the husband who got life in prison for murdering the couple in the park at Hog's Back three years ago?"

Jacobson shook his head, but Jake acknowledged seeing the headline.

Cambridge continued his story, although the others had displayed little enthusiasm. He said, "The husband, Gary Thomas, received life in prison with the possibility of parole after 15 years. I remember it well. The couple was having an affair, and the husband didn't take kindly to it. He shot them both three times. The police found the gun with the husband's fingerprints all over it. Slam dunk."

Jacobson, who had been leaning back in his chair with one leg over the other, bent forward to pick up his cup with a disinterested shrug. Jake wiped his mouth with his napkin and eyed Cambridge. He said, "I saw the headline, but I can't say I read the article. No time. I hardly remember the incident. I don't know how you remember these things." Then recalling Ryan was a lawyer, Jake wondered out loud, "Were you involved in the case somehow?"

Cambridge shook his head as he said, "Not me. I handle real estate, as you would know if you ever sold your house and moved into a condo you could handle. No, I remember because I knew the man who died. He worked at our firm. His name was Matthew Pawsloski."

CHAPTER THREE

A CHILL FROM the outside air shivered through the restaurant as the door swung open, admitting the newest member of the group, Daniela Perez. She had joined the group a few months earlier when she arrested a drug-crazed man in the neighborhood one Saturday morning. A foot pursuit ended on the street in front of Brew and Buns. She had to tase the man, and after her colleagues took him away in a squad car, Daniela entered the restaurant to sit for a minute, apparently to calm her nerves. She sat at a table alone until the men asked her to join them. After some cajoling, she did, and an instant camaraderie developed.

Daniela sat in the empty chair beside Jake and greeted the group. Jake immediately noticed her eyes were heavy and red. It didn't detract from her Venezuelan beauty, which featured a small, turned-up nose, firm chin, and dark eyes. She had olive skin and a slim, toned body that was enhanced by the blazer and pant outfit she wore. She always brightened the room with her quick sense of humor. Jake enjoyed her sharp wit, but her eyes could quickly turn cold if something offended her. She shared her opinions and spoke her truth. Because of her job, she attended the coffee meetings sporadically. Jake was glad she showed up this time.

Pruitt, ever alert to his customers, brought Daniela a coffee and set it down in front of her. He hesitated to see if Daniela wanted her usual cinnamon roll, but she said, "I have to sleep when I get home. No sugar highs for me today."

Cambridge piped up, "We were just talking about the Pawsloski and Thomas murder."

Jacobson grinned as he said, "Ryan was talking. We were listening."

Daniela removed her mask, shoved it in her pocket, and poured cream into her coffee, stirring it slowly while making a face.

"Don't get me started about that case. My partner and I were the lead investigators. Let me just say it didn't turn out the way I expected." She examined the attentive faces around the table and abruptly stopped speaking as if thinking she had said too much.

Cambridge prodded her. "Tell us more."

"No, I can't. It's not something I should talk about."

Cambridge persisted. "C'mon, you can't leave us hanging. How did you expect it to turn out?"

Jacobson, sensing Daniela's discomfort, changed the subject by noting how difficult it is to keep a group of musicians together and that his band was auditioning guitarists. The conversation drifted to music for a while until they exhausted that subject.

Daniela turned to Jake saying, "So, how have you been?"

Cambridge and Jacobson started analyzing the previous night's hockey game, knowing that Jake and Daniela were about to have their own conversation.

Jake had noticed when Daniela came in that her hair was damp, and it still had not dried completely. She had it fastened at the back with a colorful scrunchie, and Jake thought it enhanced her beauty. The dancing flames of the restaurant's gas fireplace reflected off random droplets of water in the raven blackness of her hair. He assumed it was from the cascading snow, but for a moment, he imagined her stepping out of the shower. It had been quite a while since thoughts like that wormed their way into his brain. Since his wife died, in fact. He frowned and forced himself to concentrate on the question.

He said, "Ah, you know. Same old, same old. How are you?"

"I just finished investigating a death in Vanier. Took all night. But don't change the subject, Jake. I worry about you since your wife died and then your retirement and your daughter moving to Toronto. That's a lot for anyone to deal with. What do you do all day?"

Jake's heart fluttered at the thought of her caring.

"The days go by, Daniela. I admit, some days are boring. Believe it or not, I'm happy when I have a dentist or doctor's appointment because it gives me something different to do. Today, I'll be shoveling the walk. I'll take my time, so the job lasts." His attempt at humor fell flat as the concern remained etched in Daniela's face.

"Did you ever think of taking a freelance writing job? Didn't you say you had offers?"

"I've considered some, but I attended enough meetings during my career to last me two lifetimes. If the job demanded meetings, I just couldn't do that anymore."

Daniela blew on her coffee to cool it.

She said, "Well, what are your interests? You can't just retire and do nothing, Jake. Didn't they teach you that in one of those pre-retirement courses? I took one my department offered, and they spent half the time talking about it. You had staff when you worked, and you interviewed people. Now, who do you talk to? Your cat? You're going to drop dead from boredom, for God's sake, and when they call the medical examiner to investigate it, he won't even bother showing up. He'll just sit at his desk and write on the death certificate that the cause of death was ennui."

Jacobson and Cambridge had finished breaking down the hockey game, so they listened to the conversation between Jake and Daniela and snickered at her comment. Jacobson said, "Jake, you were a reporter at the *Citizen* for about 100 years. I know you loved to write. Write a book. Lots of people do that nowadays. Maybe you could write a steamy romance novel or something."

Pruitt, who leaned over them refilling their coffee cups, said, "I'd read it. I read everything. But since Jake wouldn't know what to do with a girl if he caught one, I'm not sure any steamy romance he wrote would be that interesting."

Jake's eyes widened at the thought as Eric and Pruitt slapped palms in triumph over their wittiness.

He said, "That's probably the last subject I'm qualified to write about."

Pruitt was on a roll. "Write a classic book. I love the classics. Especially classic crime novels."

Jake shook his head as he said, "Uh, I think an author has to die before their book becomes a classic. I'm not quite ready for that yet. Thanks, everyone for your advice, but after taking it under advisement for thirty seconds, I concluded writing a book would mean sitting in front of a computer all day. I had my fill of that."

"Hmm." Daniela clearly wasn't buying it as she rose from her chair, but she addressed the group. "Well, boys, it's been lovely, but I have to go home and get my beauty rest. My next shift isn't that far off."

Cambridge agreed, saying, "I have to shovel." He cast a glance at Jake. "Unlike some people, I don't have the luxury of hiring a plowing company to clear my lane."

Jake looked at him and said, "Hey, I shovel—the doorstep. And besides, if I had your money, I'd throw mine in the garbage."

As they put on their masks again, settled their bills, and pulled on their coats, Jake noticed Daniela staring at the floor while she donned her winter attire. He didn't want to pry, so he let it go. She was probably thinking about her case. Or maybe something else. Like Jake, she was going home to no one. She had confided in a moment of candor how her job ended her marriage a few years ago.

The four friends said goodbye to Jason Pruitt and walked out into the snow. Jacobson and Cambridge turned to their respective homes in the opposite direction, and Jake and Daniela walked together. Daniela's condo building was in the same direction as Jake's house, and he always enjoyed their time alone. Soft flakes created feathery designs on their coats, but the sidewalk plow had gone by, making it less treacherous. They walked in silence until Jake couldn't resist any longer.

"Is something bothering you, Daniela? You seem distracted. I'm not trying to pry. I'm just concerned."

Daniela peered at him around the hood she had pulled up to cover her already damp hair.

She said, "Actually, I'm thinking about you. Is writing a book something that would interest you? It would give you something to do. As Jacobson said, you're used to doing research. And obviously, you write well. You spent your career doing it. It probably wouldn't be that difficult for you."

The corners of Jake's eyes crinkled in amusement.

"I don't know. I never thought about it. What would I write about? I wouldn't have a clue how to get it published if I wrote it."

They arrived at Jake's house, and the detective hesitated, staring at the snowy sidewalk. Did he dare think she was hesitating to spend more time with him? Snowflakes glistened in the light on the fur surrounding Daniela's hood as she stood silently. Jake realized she was hesitating because she was debating internally about saying something. His body tensed as he waited. *What could it be?*

Finally, she put her hand on his arm and said with a seriousness Jake hadn't seen in the times they had been together, "Give it some thought, Jake. If you decide to write a book, talk to me first, please. I might have a story for you—something to do with the murders at Hog's Back Park."

CHAPTER FOUR

JAKE WATCHED CURIOUSLY as Daniela trudged down the street, her head lowered and her hands in her pockets. She seemed serious about him writing a book. He hadn't even considered it, but it *would* give him something to do. He enjoyed reading true crime novels and some fiction. But where to start? Should he take Daniela up on her offer to speak to her first? He climbed the three steps and unlocked the door to the house. Silence greeted him as usual. Oliver must not have heard him, or he was in a snit because he had been left alone. Jake interpreted one meow as a greeting, two meant the cat was hungry, and three informed him who was in charge that day. The silence just reminded Jake of his lonely existence.

The cell phone in his pocket buzzed as he was about to go back outside to retrieve the shovel from the garage. Jake turned and sat on the bench at the front entrance without taking off his boots or the rest of his winter clothing. He could clean up the marks on the floor later.

He removed his mask and opened his flip phone to hear his daughter Avery's voice.

Now 30, Avery moved to Toronto when a high-tech firm offered Nick a prestigious job he couldn't turn down. The move was a hard decision for her to make. She knew her dad was lonely and initially she said she wouldn't go, but Jake knew that would be impossible. Then she tried to convince her dad to move to Toronto. Jake responded that if he was unhappy in Ottawa, he would be doubly so in the much larger city. She finally left with her dad's blessing, but the moving day was full of tears.

Since then, they had settled into a comfortable routine of calling and emailing regularly, and it always delighted Jake when they connected.

He said, "Hi honey, it's great to hear from you. How's everything in the big smoke, or is it the center of the universe? I can never remember."

"Haha. It's great, Dad. Pretty snowy, though. Is it snowing there? Did you get out to meet your buddies for coffee this morning?"

"The snow just quit coming down, so you saved me from going out to shovel. We had our breakfast this morning. Everyone but Pierre Chevrier showed up and Daniela came in late."

"Daniela, she's the homicide detective, right? Is she married?"

"Now, why ask that question, as if I didn't know?" For the last two years, Avery had encouraged her dad to date someone, but he had no interest. "She's divorced, but she's just as fixed in her ways as I am, so no need to play matchmaker."

"You need some companionship, Dad. You're going to go crazy in that house by yourself."

"I'm not by myself. I have Oliver." The cat still hadn't shown up.

"I guess that's companionship on his terms. He'll be your companion when *he* wants to be. So, what was today's hot topic?"

"It was the usual, but Eric suggested I write a book. They even suggested I write a steamy romance. What would you think of your old dad being a published erotica writer? I would have to do some research and you're always trying to set me up." Jake burst into laughter, looking forward to his daughter's response.

"Eeeww, Dad, let's not even go there. But what about writing a book? It would be something to fill your days. I think you might have to buy a computer, though. At least we would be able to video chat without the picture crashing every two minutes. Seriously, though, is it something that might interest you?"

"Honey, I wouldn't even know where to start. I know how to write newspaper articles. That's different from writing a book. Well, fiction anyway. I don't know if I have a creative bone in my body."

"Who says it has to be fiction? You could write your life story, so there's a legacy for your grandchildren. It doesn't have to be a best seller."

Jake hesitated before saying, "Wait, a minute, did you say grandchildren? Am I going to be a grandfather?"

It was his daughter's turn to laugh.

"Whoa, cool your jets there, pops. And don't change the subject. I think you should give the book idea some thought. Do something, Dad. Otherwise, you'll go crazy."

"I'll give it some thought, honey. Really, I will. What have you got planned for today?"

"Nick and I are going grocery shopping. I think we might watch a movie tonight. It's been a while. Oh, and there's one more thing I wanted to tell you."

Jake sucked in his breath. "Okay, I'm all ears."

"I sent you something. It's a new smartphone to replace that antique flipper you have. Well, it's not new, it's refurbished, but then we can text. When it arrives, call me and I'll help you set it up. Or you can go to the store and they'll help you do it. Promise me you'll use it, okay?"

Jake shuddered when he thought of setting up a new phone. It's not that he was incapable. He just didn't care. He would not tell Avery, but he had just received a message from his service provider that they were about to discontinue support for his old flip phone. A new phone had become a necessity.

"You didn't have to do that honey, but I appreciate it and I'll try to figure out texting. Maybe it's possible to teach an old dog new tricks."

"You're not old, Dad, you just think old. I have to go. Love you."

"I love you too, honey. Thanks for calling. Stay safe!"

Jake hung up, closed the phone, and stuck it in his pocket. Oliver arrived as he finished his call and purred as Jake scratched the cat's ears. Oliver soon decided it was enough, so he wandered off to sit on his tower in front of the window where he could watch for intruders passing by on the sidewalk, or worse yet, squirrels invading the bird feeder. Jake always wondered if the birds flitting around the feeder entertained the cat or tortured him, but Oliver always went back for more. Maybe he dreamt of the day he would break through the glass and eat them all, including the squirrels.

The cat was approaching his tenth birthday. Jake presented him to his wife as a gift when he was a kitten. He tried ignoring

Oliver over the years, but that just increased the cat's interest in him. He read once that people who ignore animals don't pose a threat. Like Jake, Oliver had gained a few pounds since Mia died. Any thought of running somewhere had faded to a distant memory. The cat's thinking seemed to be if he had to hurry somewhere, it wasn't worth going. Despite everything, it was just Jake and Oliver now, and the cat was an agreeable companion when he felt like it. Jake always knew the house wasn't altogether empty.

As Jake descended the steps from the porch, he turned to smile at the cat who stared back, expressionless. He pressed the remote to open the garage door, retrieved the shovel, and pushed the snow from the side of the driveway leading to the house.

The book idea bounced around in his head as he shoveled, but it was more than that. It was Daniela's parting words about calling her if writing a book interested him. The book could be something worth considering, but calling Dani definitely seemed like an idea worth pursuing.

CHAPTER FIVE

THE PLOWING COMPANY never risked scraping the grass on the sides of the driveway or driving too close to the garage, so Jake always had to clean up the leftovers after a snowfall. Sparkling snow stood piled to Jake's waist on either side of the driveway when he finished. That is until the street plow went by filling the end of the driveway again. It was a common occurrence that frustrated every homeowner who deals with snow. Jake had to take a break before tackling the new mound.

The more he shoveled, the more breathless Jake became. He decided he had to sign up with a gym soon or he could end up having a heart attack. Either that, or he would have to hire some kid to do the shoveling. It seemed like there was more snow to deal with every year. Another option was to follow everyone's advice and move into a condo. The skyrocketing housing prices in the city meant he could buy something nice with a superb view with the proceeds from his house. The irony was that if he sold his house and became a homeless person, he would be a millionaire. He knew he would move someday, but he still enjoyed the outdoors while sitting on the spacious patio or in the backyard. A box in a high-rise building wouldn't offer that luxury.

He finished the driveway, stowed the shovel in the garage, and returned to the house. This time Oliver wandered out of the living room to greet him. "Hello Oliver," he said as the cat rubbed against his leg while he took off his winter attire. The cat wandered off again as Jake picked up the *Ottawa Citizen* newspaper and set it on the table in the kitchen. The thinness of the paper always surprised, especially since it was Saturday's edition; the paper's size had been decreasing steadily over the years. He glanced at the headline again quickly, but the details of the incident Ryan referred to eluded him.

He toasted two slices of bread, found a clean plate on the counter, and threw together a sandwich with tomato, mayonnaise, and a processed cheese slice. With all the effort of snow shoveling, he decided he had earned a beer, so he searched the fridge. One lonely can of Coors Light sat on the shelf at the back. He popped the top on the can, licked the foam off the top, grabbed the paper and his sandwich, and headed for his favorite chair, a recliner, in the sunroom.

The house was a bungalow that sat among mature trees in the well-established neighborhood. Jake loved the place, although he hadn't kept it as clean as Mia did. The kitchen sat at the front of the house with the large window overlooking the porch and front yard. The clean dishes he had removed from the dishwasher sat scattered across the countertop. He stood by his philosophy that he would soon use them again, so why waste the effort putting them away? A hall ran from front to back with rooms on each side. Two bedrooms occupied the main floor, and a stairwell led to a finished basement and another bedroom. Jake passed the living room, which had a sitting area with four large brown chairs where he could entertain guests if he ever had any. Because he rarely used the living room, it remained relatively spotless, except for a layer of dust on the side tables. No one would notice if he didn't turn on the light.

The sunroom overlooking the yard at the back of the house was where he spent most of his time. A spider plant, rubber tree, and other plants he couldn't even name had long ago succumbed to a lack of water and ended up in the garbage. Papers and magazines stood piled by the side of his beloved recliner, each featuring articles he planned to read someday. His dinner plate and utensils from last night sat on his footrest. A large screen TV occupied one wall and a picture of him and his wife on a cruise hung on the wall opposite his chair where he could see it easily. A bookshelf held his retirement plaque, assorted books, and a few of Mia's favorite knickknacks that he couldn't bring himself to discard.

Jake set his coffee on a side table and picked up the soiled dishes, depositing the newspaper in the vacant spot. He started the gas fireplace with the remote and wandered back to the kitchen where he deposited the dishes in the dishwasher. His knee hadn't appreciated the shoveling, and he limped down the hall. Normal activity didn't bother it, but it protested when he placed more pressure on it. He returned to the sunroom, picked up the newspaper, and settled into his recliner. Oliver followed him into the sunroom and jumped on Jake's lap, but he shoved the cat back onto the floor.

"Not now, Oliver. Can't you see I'm about to read the newspaper?" The cat meowed his displeasure three times and found a warm sunbeam where he promptly curled up and fell asleep.

Jake took a large bite from his sandwich while he picked up the *Citizen* and read the headline again. HUSBAND SENTENCED IN PARK SLAYING. Fascinating that Ryan knew the guy that was killed, but Jake needed to read the article to refresh his memory. The murder rate in Ottawa was low relative to other cities, but he didn't keep a compendium in his head, even though he had reported on a few in his day. Text surrounded pictures of the murdered couple in happier days and the husband being led away from the courthouse. He started reading.

A handful of friends and supporters gasped and wept as convicted murderer Gary Thomas was led away to serve a life sentence for second-degree murder with no chance of parole for 15 years.

The summer murders occurred in Hog's Back Park nearly three years ago. Justice Benjamin Chamberlain explained his reasons for sentencing Thomas for the "brutal killing" of his wife, 35-year-old Melissa, and her lover, 36-year-old Matt Pawsloski. He noted that the murder was premeditated but weighed that against Thomas's lack of a criminal record and supportive testimony from friends and former co-workers in ruling in favor of the possibility of parole after 15 years.

A second-degree murder charge carries an automatic sentence of life imprisonment. The crown prosecutor argued no parole eligibility for 18 years, while Thomas's lawyer countered by asking for no parole for 13 years.

Melissa Thomas and Matt Pawsloski were shot to death at close range in Pawsloski's car in the parking lot at Hog's Back Park. According to the facts presented at trial, each sustained three bullet wounds in the upper torso. The murder weapon was discovered in bushes nearby, and the prosecution established that Thomas's fingerprints were the only ones on it.

Thomas's lawyer argued that Gary, who visited friends the night of the killing, could not have committed the murders. The prosecutor pointed out in his arguments that there were gaps in the period Gary was with his friends, giving him time to drive to the parking lot, commit the murder and return. Witnesses stated Gary had been aware of his wife's affair for several months and testified that he was overheard saying he would "kill them both." Gary Thomas's fingerprints on the murder weapon provided sufficient evidence for the jury to convict.

The jury heard Thomas had a license to own the handgun that was found near the murder scene. He was often seen at gun ranges and in target shooting competitions.

Gary Thomas stated in his testimony that he was in love with his wife and proclaimed his innocence. As his lawyer walked him through his testimony, Gary swore his gun had been stolen. The jury didn't buy his arguments in finding him guilty.

Family and friends of the Pawsloskis attended Thursday's hearing in court and by video conference. Long-time friend Sam Uttman told the Citizen he was satisfied with the sentence. "It's certainly a relief to have an end to this long ordeal, finally. Family and friends should never have to wait this long."

Thomas stood trial nearly three years after he was charged. The trial and his sentencing were among many court decisions delayed by the consequences of the pandemic.

Jake set the paper aside and washed the rest of his sandwich down with the beer. He watched the flames dancing in the fireplace as he thought about three lives changed forever in an instant, an instant documented in a few words. Jake knew about that. He had written about similar cases during his career. Then his thoughts turned to the ancient computer in the office, the new cell phone

Avery had sent him, and the hours he would have to spend sitting at a desk if he wrote a book.

He found the TV remote under the newspapers he had dropped on the floor and flipped through the channels, settling on the CBC news. As he pushed his recliner back and put his feet up, his eyes drifted shut. The news anchor droned on about tension around the world, and Jake soon joined Oliver in a deep sleep.

CHAPTER SIX

J AKE SPENT THE next two days researching everything he could find online about writing and publishing a book. The internet was full of free information and many sites offering to help at a "new low, low price." The speed of his computer slowed his research. He watched the spinning graphic that he described to Avery as a "thingy" in the middle of the screen until a site would pop up. This was the first time Jake had used the computer for much since his retirement, and the tepid response surprised him. He decided he needed to upgrade if he was ever going to take his friends' advice about writing a book.

The book idea was beginning to appeal to him. The research aspect of it intrigued him, and he felt renewed energy. He leaned back in his chair with his fingers knitted together behind his head, contemplating his experience that might be relevant. He spent his entire career as a newspaper reporter. It started by writing for a local newspaper in the suburbs of Ottawa. He was one of a handful of reporters who covered everything that happened in the neighborhood, from church bake sales to disappearances.

His life changed when he scored a job with the *Ottawa Citizen*. It was a time when print media was the primary source of news and people relied on their newspaper. He started writing about sports for the 175-year-old paper and eventually secured a transfer to the news department. He received awards for covering street gangs and interviewing their members. Then the perfect storm of events hit that led to his early retirement. Technology was taking over, and readers demanded different platforms for their news. Opinion pieces overshadowed the hard news. The declining readership forced layoffs, his wife died and frankly, Jake just wasn't as interested or productive anymore.

Now he agreed with his friends that he needed something to do, and there might be some parallels between reporting and writing a book. Researching and writing were his forte. Some of his contacts would presumably still talk to him. As he pondered the possibilities, Oliver wandered into the office and gazed up quizzically at him. Jake bent down to pet him.

"What do you think, Oliver? Do I have it in me to write a book?"

Oliver meowed once, and a smile creased Jake's face.

"I'll take that as a 'yes' and you know, I always follow your advice." He glanced at the clock, surprised to see it was evening. He said, "I think I've wasted enough time today. I better get the mail."

Jake dialed Tony's Pizzeria down the street to order a medium with pepperoni. It was another ritual and the owner, Tony, wrote it down before Jake had the words out of his mouth. He pulled on his coat and boots and made sure he had his mask in his pocket. He glanced at the mirror and his image stared back. His wife had always commented on his deep blue eyes. His hair seemed grayer and much longer than the last time he checked, but some original blond curled over his ears. He knew the back was thinning because his barber showed him in the mirror every damned time he had his hair cut. Jake believed in the adage of what you can't see won't hurt you.

There were more wrinkles around his eyes now, too. As he absorbed that fact, he continued his critical assessment. At five feet ten inches tall, he considered himself average, but his posture, or lack thereof, made him appear shorter. The winter coat seemed to shrink in the closet over the summer. Nothing that the gym membership he had been promising himself since his retirement wouldn't fix. At least he shaved this morning, not something he did every day since he retired. He shrugged, and the person he barely recognized in the mirror duplicated the gesture as he tugged his gray toque down over his ears. He retrieved his lined leather gloves from the shelf in the closet, put them on, and he was ready.

As he strode out into the clear, crisp night, he was greeted by the close-to-full moon shining through the branches of a huge, barren tree on the opposite side of the street. His boots crunched in the snow as he walked, and a vapor cloud surrounded his face with each breath. At least it wasn't windy.

Jake hurried down the street and clambered over a snowbank to reach the mailbox, leaving deep footprints in the snow. Inside was a rectangular-shaped box from Avery. Jake remembered the smartphone and appreciated that she always looked out for the old man. He pulled out the box, a pile of flyers, and an envelope offering another chance to win a million dollars by buying a lottery ticket for some charity.

He picked up the pizza from the boisterous restaurant owner, a former Special Forces member, whose booming voice echoed through the room. Tony was a large, muscular Italian with dark curly hair who wore a body-hugging white short-sleeved t-shirt and tan shorts under a food-stained apron. Perspiration dotted the foreheads of the youthful workers toiling behind the counter, but none wore shorts in the winter like Tony.

Jake acknowledged Tony with a wave and paid the young woman at the cash for his pizza. He hurried home and took off the winter garb. That's what he disliked the most about winter. It wasn't the shoveling or the snow or even the cold. It was putting on and taking off the damn winter clothes.

He removed two slices of pizza from the box and put them on a plate, wrapped the rest in saran wrap, and shoved it in the fridge, ready for tomorrow's lunch. He picked up the box Avery sent from the table where he had set it and carried it and the pizza into his office.

Oliver eyed his owner as Jake picked at the pizza and scanned the instruction book for setting up the new phone. To his surprise, it was not that difficult, and the person representing the provider helped activate it. He would call to thank Avery for sending the phone and to remind her the old man was sound of mind, if not body. He would also ask what apps he needed. Then he would call Daniela.

CHAPTER SEVEN

JAKE WOKE EARLY the next morning, refreshed and looking forward to the day. It wasn't something that happened often in recent months. Even Oliver seemed to sense a renewal in the house as he wound himself through his owner's legs in a morning greeting. He followed in Jake's footsteps to the kitchen where his master poured the food and milk. Jake thought the cat's world revolved around nourishment and sleep. Oliver used Jake for the first so he could enjoy the second. Jake still took whatever affection the cat offered these days.

After he showered and shaved, Jake dressed for another winter day in an ancient gold-colored sweater and black jeans. He shoved the curtain aside to check the weather as the kettle boiled and bread browned in the toaster. The previous night's cloudless sky carried over to the day as the sun's rays glistened off the snowbank on the front yard. The car next door spewed vapor clouds in the air as it idled in the driveway. Jake shut the curtain and shuddered as he proclaimed the day clear and cold.

The blast of arctic air that greeted him and followed him inside when he stepped onto the doorstep to pick up the paper, confirmed his suspicions. He carried the paper, his coffee, and buttered toast into the sunroom and sat in his favorite chair. Once he finished his toast, he took out his new phone and tapped the icon to make a call. While still feeling his way, a lot of it was intuitive. He tapped the keyboard icon, dialed, and Avery answered right away. Her voice was chipper.

"Hey, Dad. Still using the flip phone, I take it."

"Good morning to you. No, I'll have you know this is the new phone, and thank you very much for your thoughtfulness."

"Uh, okay. Who set it up for you?"

Jake laughed as he said, "I set it up. It's not that difficult, honey, and I'm quite capable of reading the instructions. Tell me what apps I need, though, and how I get them."

Avery spent the next few minutes telling her dad how to download apps he might need for browsing, video calls, sports scores, weather, social media, and music. He dutifully jotted everything down and promised to call her on the video app one day. Then he said, "Okay, honey, thanks again for everything. I appreciate you trying to drag me out of the stone age."

"We'll take baby steps first, Dad. Who knows what you'll do next? Maybe throw your VCR in the garbage? Any plans for the rest of the day? You're eager to do something."

Avery was so perceptive.

"Not really, honey. I think I'll give Daniela a call. She wanted me to talk to her if I thought writing a book might interest me. I've given it some thought, and I might try writing something just to see how it goes."

"Great, Dad! That's awesome news. Daniela, eh? Has she written a book, or does she just want to get together with my handsome father? I'm going to have to watch you."

"Thanks for the compliment, but I think my handsomeness may be a few years and pounds behind me. I don't know exactly why she wants to talk. She said she had information about a murder a few years ago. It won't hurt to see what she has on her mind."

Avery's voice took on a teasing tone. "Oh yeah, okay, Dad. Good idea to see what she's thinking."

They chatted a few minutes longer about Avery's day before saying their goodbyes. As soon as he hung up, he dialed Daniela, who picked up on the second ring. Her voice sounded sleepy.

"Hi Jake, this is a surprise. Is everything okay?"

The question took Jake aback, but then he realized he had never called her before.

"Good morning, Daniela. Everything's fine, thanks. I hope I didn't wake you."

"No, I'm just lounging this morning. I've had zero days off lately, so I thought I would just relax and enjoy it. I got up late and I'm just sitting here in my PJs having a coffee and contemplating life. What's up?"

Jake hesitated, wondering about the style of pajamas she wore. *Wait, where did that come from? She's just an acquaintance, for God's sake.* He gathered himself and said, "Listen, I don't want to bother you if you're taking it easy. I've been thinking about this whole book thing, and I might like to try writing something. You said I should talk to you before I start. We can do it another time, though. There's no hurry."

Daniela's voice became more animated, sounding as pleased as Avery had. Jake wondered if his friends all thought he was going to drop dead from boredom, and then he remembered Daniela had brought up that very point. He realized she was asking him a question.

He lied. "I'm sorry, Daniela, Oliver just jumped on my lap. Startled me. Could you please repeat that?"

"Ah yes, Oliver, the wonder cat, and brilliant conversationalist. I asked if you had figured out what you're going to write about."

Jake chuckled. "I don't have a clue. I could write about the thrills of working in a newspaper office." He laughed and was pleased to hear Daniela snicker on the other end.

She responded with, "Well, I have something I want to run past you. I need to talk to someone about it and I consider you a friend. It could be a subject you can write about. Do you have time for lunch? My treat?"

Jake smiled at the thought of having lunch with her—alone—but he gallantly asked, "Are you sure you want to do this today? I can wait. You should just enjoy your day."

"Nonsense. Give me an hour. I'll pick you up at your place."

As Jake hung up, Oliver jumped into his lap again, convincing him he hadn't completely lied to Daniela. One thing was certain, the day was turning out even better than expected.

CHAPTER EIGHT

JAKE WATCHED THROUGH the kitchen window as Daniela wheeled into the driveway in a white Hyundai Tucson SUV at the precise minute that she said she would. The exhaust cloud that had been trailing behind swamped her car when she parked.

Westboro, where Jake's house was situated, was a diverse neighborhood of tree-lined streets, trendy one-of-a-kind shops, and a lively street scene when not shuttered by a worldwide pandemic. The Ottawa River established its northern border. It was one of many neighborhoods in Ottawa, a city of close to one and a half million people, including Gatineau across the river. Jake appreciated the large city with a small-town feel, even if it was the seventh coldest capital city on the planet.

He said goodbye to Oliver as he locked the door, hustled to Daniela's car, and said hello to her as he jumped in and buckled up. She wore a welcoming smile and a yellow winter coat with a contrasting scarf over blue jeans. Jake thought she was gorgeous with her hair down and much more relaxed than she was the last time he saw her at the restaurant.

Daniela raced the car backward out of the driveway. The wheels spun on the icy street as she pulled away, but he admired how much more controlled her driving was than the kid's the other morning. The street signs sailed past in a blur.

Jake said, "Thanks for picking me up, Daniela. It's nice not to walk in this weather, but I hate to pull you away from your relaxation day. I'm sure you need every available day off with your job. If it had been easier, we could have met at Brew and Buns." He wondered if it sounded like he was babbling.

"Good morning to you. It's no problem, really. I prefer to be somewhere other than Brew and Buns this morning. By the way, you can call me Dani. All my friends do."

"Well, okay, Dani. I don't think I've ever heard you use the shortened version in all the time we've been meeting at the restaurant. It's pretty. I like it."

Dani sped down the snow-covered streets and drifted around the corners. Apparently, the speed limits were only a suggestion.

"Thank you. No, I like to keep it kind of formal at the breakfasts. You guys were great for asking me to join you at the table and I enjoy the get-togethers, but the others can call me Daniela." She glanced at Jake, a grin brightening her face.

Dani surprised him at a stop sign when she tapped the brake to pause the car for a microsecond before continuing. She slowed at an orange traffic light and wheeled around the corner onto Bank Street. He marveled that they didn't land hood first in a snowbank. The thought flashed through his mind that Mario Andretti would also be a suitable name for her, but he said. "Well, my name is Jake Scott, but you can call me Jake." He bit his lip, thinking it was a stupid thing to say, as she concentrated on maneuvering into a tight spot between two cars in front of a Second Cup restaurant. Dani shut the car off and rewarded him with a laugh.

They went inside, ordered sandwiches and coffee, and found a seat in the back.

As usual, the shop required its patrons to wear masks when not eating or drinking, and the enlarged spaces between tables offered plenty of room for private conversations. Jake and Dani removed the masks as the sandwiches and coffee arrived and chatted about the weather. Jake enjoyed watching Dani as she talked. He knew she was attractive but seeing her in a form-fitting sweater and jeans that hugged her hips took it to a whole new level.

Finally, Dani said, "I'm going to tell you something in the strictest confidence, Jake. It isn't something I have shared with anyone, but it has bothered me for a long time and Gary Thomas's sentencing brought it to the forefront again. I don't know if it's a book or not, but I need to talk to someone. Promise me you will treat it with the utmost confidence."

Jake leaned forward in his chair, intrigued by what he was hearing. He gazed into her dark, sincere eyes. He almost felt like an insect being enticed into a spider's web, but he was enjoying it and didn't want it to stop. It thrilled him to think this woman respected him enough to confide in him. He didn't want to appear like a puppy dancing around eager to please, but he was dying to know what she was going to tell him. He said, "Of course, I'll keep it quiet. What is it?"

"I don't think Gary Thomas is guilty."

Jake jerked upright. He felt his face tighten, forcing his eyebrows toward each other. "Gary Thomas? You mean the guy sentenced to prison a few days ago? I read about it in the newspaper after Ryan mentioned it. Wasn't the evidence overwhelming?" His voice came out a little louder than he intended.

Dani looked over her shoulder to confirm no one was within earshot.

"That's the one. I was one of the officers investigating the case. My partner, who retired a few weeks ago, convinced himself Gary was guilty or just wanted the case to be over. I'm not sure which. Quick and clean is my guess. A passerby saw the murder weapon in some nearby bushes and called it in. It had Gary's fingerprints all over it. Gary was a gun collector and did some range shooting, so the fingerprints were explainable. But the fingerprints, the timelines giving Gary enough time to commit the murder and return to a gathering with his friends and his statements in front of witnesses about wanting his wife and her lover dead were enough to convince the jury."

Jake realized he had been squeezing his cup and relaxed his grip. "The evidence sounds overwhelming to me. My newspaper career taught me that the most obvious person is often not the guilty one, though. There's more to the story, obviously."

Dani motioned to the server for a refill. "There is, Jake. I hope you don't get angry with me. It wasn't a complete accident that I joined you at the table for coffee that first morning. Ryan Cambridge is a senior partner at the law firm where one of the victims, Mathew Pawsloski, worked. I saw you guys in Brew and Buns one Saturday morning when I was off duty and sitting at the back with a friend. None of you saw me. By your conversation with Jason Pruitt, I gathered you met there every Saturday." She paused as the server approached, coffee pot in hand.

After their cups were refilled, Jake found his voice.

"You mean capturing that guy in the doorway was a setup?"

"No, that wasn't a setup. It was a lucky turn of events. When I realized where we were and what time it was, I used it as an opportunity. I wanted to join you so I could observe Cambridge."

The connection Dani drew between Ryan Cambridge and one of the murder victims, Matt Pawsloski, dropped into place in Jake's mind with the impact of a stone hitting a windshield.

"Jesus, Dani, do you think the murder involves Ryan somehow?"

Dani's shoulders rose in a shrug. "I don't know if he has any involvement. I just wanted to learn more about Pawsloski's job and anything that might have contributed to his murder. My boss considers the case closed, so I'm not supposed to be working on it. Any investigating I do on this case is in my spare time. I hoped Ryan would talk about it at the breakfasts, but he hasn't until now. Last Saturday was the first time he mentioned anything to my knowledge."

"Did you interview him at the time?"

"No, because his name never came up. Pawsloski seemed to have a future at the firm, but we thought he had little to do with the partners. I guess I'm just looking for another motive for the killing besides a revenge-seeking husband. Gary just doesn't seem like the type."

Jake noticed Dani's erect posture as he straightened his slouch.

"I still don't understand. I admire that you're trying to stick up for someone you think is innocent, but there must be more than gut instinct involved here. My God, this could eat you alive if you let it." He searched Dani's dark eyes as she clutched her coffee cup with both hands. He wondered if she was asking herself if she had gone too far. She remained silent.

He continued, "Why are you telling me this, Dani? I was a reporter reporting on the news. That doesn't mean I have any criminal investigation skills. I'm happy to listen, but I don't know if I can help. Why don't you just ask Ryan what he knows about Pawsloski?"

"I would rather keep it on the down-low for now. I'm looking into some things I would prefer to keep to myself. One thing I've learned is that evidence doesn't lie, but sometimes it doesn't tell the entire story. Like I said, I needed someone to talk to and when the subject of the book came up, it started me thinking that maybe I could talk to you. I also feel horrible about tricking you guys into letting me join you. It occurred to me I might feel better if I at least came clean to you. I'm sorry if it will make things awkward between you and Ryan."

Jake held Dani's eyes with his. He said, "Let me think about all this. I'm thrilled that you took me into your confidence. For sure it's not what I anticipated, but I don't know what I was expecting. I don't see a problem with Ryan. Maybe I could listen more closely if he talks about the case. He seemed preoccupied with it Saturday. It would be less obvious coming from me than you. Is that what you were hoping for?"

Dani stared at the coffee in her half-empty cup as if she hoped to find answers there. She said, "I guess. Yes. I don't know. I don't want to harm our friendship. Maybe I thought I would feel better after talking to you, but I'm not sure I do. I like you, Jake, so if you don't want to do anything, that's fine too."

"I'll do what I can, Dani. No promises. Between Avery and the breakfast group, it's all I have right now."

CHAPTER NINE

AN UNCOMFORTABLE SILENCE hung thickly in the SUV as they drove back to Jake's house. Dani frowned and said in a low voice as Jake exited the car, "I don't know if this was a good idea. Just forget everything I said, and we'll go back to having coffee and talking about music and sports and weather. I'll understand."

Jake knew that would not happen.

"Nonsense, Dani. I enjoyed our conversation and I hope it helped. I'll call you."

Dani nodded as he closed the door. He waved as he watched her back out of the driveway into a sliding stop and race away.

As he sat in his recliner, his feet up and his head back, he thought about everything Dani had told him. Something niggled at the back of his brain, and it was the same inkling that had accounted for his silence on the way home. Was it something Dani said or hadn't said that bothered him? He thought pretty much everything she had said bothered him, but maybe there was something she hadn't said that made it worse.

He gazed at the picture on the wall. His wife Mia looked so relaxed in her wide-brimmed hat and bathing suit. Sunglasses hid her blue eyes, but the Caribbean sun seemed to make her larger than life. Jake loved the picture as it was a reminder of the fun that they had on their last trip together. He said into the silence, "I wish you were here to talk to, Mia. As usual, I need your advice. I love you."

Whatever bothered him scratched at the back of his brain, refusing to reveal itself. His mind wandered. So many questions. Was Dani using him to get to Ryan? But why talk to him at all? She's part of the breakfast group. She could do her own investigating. Why hadn't she brought it up at breakfast before, if she thought Ryan might have some information? Why not interrogate him at the station if she was convinced that he had something to do with the murders? He didn't remember her ever asking Ryan about the case in all the times they had met, but maybe he just hadn't noticed. She's a homicide detective, after all, so her questions would be subtle. What did she suspect Ryan of doing? She talked about something she didn't want to divulge.

Was she dangling a carrot in front of him to get him to do something? Maybe she thought this would get him off his butt. Jake wasn't sure, and all this speculation was getting him nowhere.

His mind continued churning. Could their friendship develop into more? He realized there was an attraction, and she said she liked him, but could it ever be more than that? He glanced back at the picture, knowing Mia would not have wanted him to be alone. Would he just be using the investigation to spend more time with Dani if he agreed to research the murder?

All the questions and the warmth from the fireplace he had turned on earlier caused his eyelids to droop. He yawned noisily. His mind stopped swirling as he drifted into the early stages of a nap. Suddenly, he bolted upright, slamming the footrest down with a bang as the elusive thought sprang into his consciousness. He tossed it around in his mind to recall if Dani had mentioned it. She might have. He couldn't remember it coming up, though. He dug his new cell phone out of his pocket and dialed. Dani answered right away.

Jake jumped right in.

"Hi, I'm sorry to bother you again, but I have a question."

Dani's voice sounded relieved. "Jake, I was wondering if I scared you off. After what I told you, I worried you wouldn't want to talk to me. I want to apologize again, and I wouldn't blame you if you kicked me out of the breakfast group. I shouldn't have . . ."

Jake interrupted. "It's okay, Dani, really. I have more questions. Why would Gary just toss the gun into the bushes if he had just murdered someone? Wouldn't he take it home and destroy it or throw it in the canal, or—I don't know, do any of a million things to get rid of it? Why leave it where someone would find it? Did he *want* to get caught?"

"I've asked myself the same question over and over, Jake. The defense lawyer tried to use that argument, but the prosecution countered that he panicked. A teenager said he and his friends were hanging out in the park when they heard shots, so it's possible they spooked him, and he got rid of the murder weapon as quickly as possible. But, if you buy the theory that Thomas planned the murders, he would have had an idea for ditching the gun as well. It makes no sense to me."

Jake mused, "It doesn't to me either. I had another thought, too. Did Gary ever report the gun missing? If someone stole the gun, wouldn't he do that?"

"Your investigative skills are on high alert, I see. You're right. Gary said he didn't know it was missing. He had bought a new gun that he was using at the range. He said he was planning to sell the one that ended up being used in the murders. Forensics did a fingerprint sweep of the house and they accounted for all the prints. No sign of unusual activity. There were just so many things in Gary's favor left unproven, and the evidence against him was enough to convict him. You should have seen him when the judge handed down the verdict. His face went chalk white, and I thought he was going to be sick. I think he was still in love with Melissa despite her cheating on him. He seemed to hope they could get back together."

One question led to another. Jake said, "Who reported finding the gun?"

"The person never gave his name. He said he spotted a reflection off a metal object and when he investigated, he found out it was a gun. He just gave us the location and hung up."

"Huh! Could have been the murderer who called it in. Gary didn't notice the gun was missing? It should have been locked up. And the fact it just disappeared tells me that either someone he knew stole it or someone broke in without leaving a trace of any kind. That would imply a professional. I'm sure you've thought of all this."

"I've rolled it all around in my head. Countless sleepless nights. I don't know why this case is bothering me so much. I just don't think Gary Thomas is guilty of murder. He may be guilty of a lot, but he isn't guilty of murder. I've met some nasty people in my years with the police force. Gary doesn't seem nasty, but something happened between him and his wife. I'm still sure we have the wrong man for the murder rap."

"What do you mean about 'guilty of a lot'?"

Dani took a deep breath. "My colleagues visited the Thomas house for a domestic disturbance. The neighbors heard fighting coming from the house. Gary didn't have a job, and it erupted into an ugly fight about money, but Melissa claimed at the time he never hit her. It was a verbal argument that got carried away. A few dishes were broken, and it got loud, but that's about it. Gary said he was responsible because he didn't have a job, but it was Melissa that did most of the yelling and throwing things."

"And you *still* want to protect him? Melissa's dead. The arguments could have led to her murder."

"Arguing with your spouse doesn't carry a life sentence. Every married person would serve time. If he's innocent of murder, he shouldn't be in prison. Period."

"Ok, I'm convinced that you're convinced. I doubt I can help, but I'm happy to be a sounding board."

"I know, and I appreciate the opportunity to talk to you. Thanks for calling. Take good care and hopefully, I'll see you at the next breakfast."

"Are you working Friday night?"

"No, my daughter will be with me on the weekend."

Jake hesitated. Then, "Your daughter!? You're full of surprises, Dani Perez. You never talk about your daughter."

"No, as I said, I prefer to keep my personal life private. I don't mind telling you though. Her name is Emilie, and she's sixteen. It was a drunken evening when it happened but she's the best thing my husband and I did together. If you do the math, you'll figure out we weren't that young when we had her. But she's a handful. She doesn't get any discipline when she's with him and I can't spend all my time doing it or she would hate me. She doesn't seem to like me much now. It's complicated, but we're getting through it. Maybe you can meet her one day but prepare yourself." Dani chuckled mirthlessly.

"I'm sure you take excellent care of her, and I would love to meet her."

They continued chatting for a few minutes. It felt to Jake like they could talk all day, but they eventually hung up. When Jake disconnected, he thought about the breakfast a couple of days away. Would he be able to look Ryan Cambridge in the eye? He sensed that although Dani didn't say it, she hoped he would raise the subject of the murders to get Ryan talking. He felt invigorated and excited for the next breakfast. Life had become infinitely more interesting.

CHAPTER TEN

JAKE PECKED AT the numbers on the screen and listened as the phone rang on the other end. He pushed his recliner back and waited until the familiar voice answered. It was the private number for Janice Richardson, a woman he had mentored, and whose name now appeared in the byline at the head of the article about the double homicide at Hog's Back Park. A rush of guilt raced through his conscience as he hadn't called her since his retirement, and now here he was calling when he wanted something. It was a common human trait he knew, but not one of which he could be proud.

She had come to the *Citizen* straight out of the journalism program at Algonquin College. Her attitude and skill impressed Jake. She was a talented writer and soaked up all the knowledge she could from the veterans. A quick search online told Jake she had written about the trial from the beginning.

"Janice, how are you doing? It's Jake Scott."

"Jake, I'd recognize that voice anywhere, even though you dropped out of sight when you retired. I'm doing well, although this job sometimes drives me nuts. How are you?"

"Great and enjoying life." Well, Jake thought, at least recently. "Yeah, sorry, I haven't called. I've been kind of busy. I thought you loved your job. What's going on?"

"I still love reporting the hard news, but things are changing. Ever since world leaders, and I use the term loosely, have been screaming about fake news and the media being the enemy of the people, it's difficult to get genuine news out effectively. Readers don't believe us when we quote 'reliable sources' anymore. They want to know who said what, and you know there are many reasons people don't want their names in the news. Plus, readers love opinions now as opposed to facts, as long as they match their own. Anyway, you didn't call to hear me rant. You must have caught me at the wrong time. I still love my job and it's a great place to work. Did I ever thank you for everything you did for me?"

Jake chuckled. "Many times, Janice. I understand your frustration, but I have to tell you there's still something about picking the paper up off the front porch every morning. I love the smell of it and the broadsheet format is still my favorite. It always will be. Sitting in my chair with a coffee and the newspaper is always special. We need people like you and don't you forget it. Anyway, I know you're probably on a deadline, so I don't want to keep you. I have a question about some articles you've written.

"Oh, okay. I thought you were calling because you missed me and wanted to take me out to dinner," she teased.

"I would, but I think your husband and three daughters might object." Jake hoped she was still married. A sense of relief washed over him when she said, "He wouldn't notice I was gone, and the kids are old enough now to be out on their own dates." She laughed. "What can I do for you? Are you going to give me advice on how I should have written one of my columns? I miss those days."

"Your columns are great, Janice. You don't need any advice from me. No, I just read your article about Gary Thomas's trial and I went back to refresh my memory by reading the others you wrote about the case." He shuddered at the thought of spending so much time watching the spinning thingy as it sought relevant sites. "I'm just wondering what you thought of Thomas or if you had any concerns about the trial."

"That's a strange question out of the blue. Why do you ask?"

Jake was forthright with his former colleague. "I have a friend in Ottawa Police Services who doesn't think Gary Thomas is guilty. I can't divulge the name, but she's convinced the wrong man is in prison. The subject piqued my interest and I have some time on my hands, so I thought I might investigate a bit. No better place to start than with you."

"A Police Services officer, eh? You know I could probably track down the name, but I won't. I followed the police investigation and sat through the trial. The evidence was overwhelming. Gary Thomas seemed like a nice enough guy, but he had a temper when he got angry. I've covered many nice guys who fly into a rage when something happens, and they become the Incredible Hulk. Dated one, too. What makes her think Thomas isn't guilty?"

"She thinks they rushed to judgment. That the lead investigator wanted one last case resolved before he retired. She thinks there are others with motive. From what I know about the case, there's one big question still to be answered to my satisfaction."

"What's that?"

"Why would Gary Thomas throw the gun where someone would find it? Why wouldn't he destroy it? If he's guilty, he must have planned the killing. Wouldn't he have a plan to get rid of the gun?"

Janice hesitated. "That bothered me a bit, and it came up at the trial. The prosecutor argued he got spooked by something and panicked. Kids hang out in the park all the time, and apparently, some teenagers were there that night. Whatever happened, the prosecution's argument was enough to convince the jury."

"Yes, that's what I understand. It just seems off."

"His fingerprints were all over the gun, Jake. No one else."

"Yeah, I know. How did they handle the fact the person who reported finding the gun didn't stick around?"

"The prosecution did a good job. They convinced the jury the person was a good Samaritan who didn't want his or her name in the paper. His, I guess. They said it was a male voice that reported it. Kind of like the reliable sources we were talking about earlier."

"Okay, thanks for your help, Janice. I appreciate it. I won't keep you any longer."

"Before you go, Jake, I have two questions. Well, a demand and a question. Don't take so long to call next time. Let's go for lunch. I'd love to catch up with everything that's going on in your life. The question I have for you is, will I get the story when you prove everyone was wrong about Gary Thomas?"

"I promise I'll call you for a lunch date, Janice, no matter what happens, and as for Gary Thomas, you'll be the first to know if he's innocent."

CHAPTER ELEVEN

JAKE ROSE EARLY Saturday morning and called Avery to pick her brain about computers. She put Nick on the phone so he could walk Jake through some choices. It was a slow and comical process as Nick patiently instructed Jake on where and how to open the browser on his phone and search for various brands. While Jake was familiar with the process, doing it on his new phone was another matter altogether. With Nick's guidance, Jake chose a laptop and printer that would do the job and placed the order, reluctantly entering his credit card information on the phone.

The computer discussion with Nick and feeding Oliver made him late, and he was sure he would hear about it from his buddies. The day turned out to be bitter as Jake hustled to Brew and Buns with his hands buried deep in his pockets. A slight breeze made it feel just that much colder, and the forecast warned that a cold air mass had moved in and would hang over the city for a few days. Jake thought weather reporters in southern states would call the forecast ominous. In Ottawa, everyone called it normal.

Another brave soul on the street walked by with his chin buried deep in his coat and a high-stepping dog on a leash who seemed quite unimpressed with the weather. Jake arrived at the restaurant fifteen minutes late and peeked through the window to see the regular group already there, minus Dani. Even Pierre Chevrier sat at the table. Jake frowned under his mask as he opened the door.

The room's décor had always fascinated him. The building had been a warehouse, and the high black ceilings featured large fans and exposed plumbing pipes and heating ducts. Long thin light fixtures hung on chains from the ceiling. Modern art adorned the vivid yellow drywall that ended about halfway up. A built-in linear electric fireplace near their table provided an amazing amount of heat. The blended industrial and contemporary décor appealed to the regular patrons. The aroma of brewing coffee and baking cinnamon rolls that greeted visitors didn't hurt either.

Jake removed his toque as he strode to the table and greeted the group.

"Did I miss the email about the early start?"

Eric Jacobson peered over his coffee cup. "Um, I think you're late again, Jake."

Ryan Cambridge nodded a greeting and Pierre Chevrier said, "Comment ça va, Gloomy Gus?" Chevrier was in his early fifties, short and stout. He wasn't as bald as Eric, but he combed his thinning hair forward, attempting to hide the barren spots on his round head. He wore his glasses pushed as high up as they would go, so he had to look down his nose to find the sweet spot to look through. While his English was excellent, he frequently resorted back to his first language when he couldn't grasp the precise word he was looking for. Jake had little to do with him and was never sure how he became part of the group. He drove a city bus and if

Jake recalled correctly, Eric was a regular rider on Chevrier's route when the two had struck up a friendship.

Jake glanced at Chevrier and said, "Do you really enjoy these hebdomadal get-togethers, Pierre, or do you just like to come to torment me?"

Chevrier blustered some nonsense about coming out to meet with "Mes amis." Jake chuckled to himself at the new word he had stumbled across referring to "weekly." Clearly, the word perplexed Chevrier, who was now silent. Everyone else around the table ignored it.

Jason Pruitt brought Jake's coffee and a cinnamon roll. Jake glanced at the owner and said, "You know what, Jason? I'm going to forego the roll today." He patted his stomach. "I need to lose a few pounds and weaning myself off cinnamon rolls would be a good starting point. Thanks anyway."

The others gaped at Jake in stunned silence. Ryan finally spoke. "Are you okay, Jake? I don't remember you turning down a cinnamon roll in all the times we've been coming here. Hell is about to freeze over, guys."

Jake smiled and sipped his black coffee before he replied. "It's cold enough hell might freeze over, but no, I'm turning over a new leaf, guys. I want to live to see my grandchildren if I have any."

That started a discussion about how great grandkids are and the only two grandparents in the group, Eric and Pierre, swapped stories about theirs. Of course, each swore their grandchildren were the smartest in the world. When the conversation lulled, Jake swished his remaining coffee in his cup and said, "So, I read that article about Gary Thomas. What a shame. Three lives ruined like that." He turned to Ryan.

"You knew the Pawsloski kid, Ryan?"

Ryan nodded and said, "Yeah, he wasn't a kid. He was in his thirties, but he had a future at the firm. Intelligent. Hard working. He sat in the bullpen with the other staff, but he would stay late at night sometimes and I'd chat with him a bit. He was working on his law degree."

Jake thought there was a little condescension in Ryan's voice, the implication being that the law partners rarely stooped to speaking with the rabble. He wanted the conversation to continue, so he said, "Did you know about the affair Matt was having?"

Ryan seemed to relish being the center of attention.

"I knew. I heard yelling in the bullpen around five o'clock one day. When I ran out to check, this guy was yelling about Matt. Fortunately, Matt left early for a dental appointment that day. I didn't know who the guy was, but the staff told me afterward he was Gary Thomas. I didn't hear him, but others overheard him say he would kill Matt and Melissa if they didn't stop seeing each other. Thomas stormed out of the office and when I spoke to Matt later, it looked like he would pass out. He denied everything. He said he and Melissa were friends and she used him as a sounding board about Gary. It was obviously more than that."

Jake said, "It seemed obvious Gary was guilty with his prints on the gun and everything."

Ryan's eyes narrowed. He stared at Jake and replied, "Yes, it was. Why the sudden interest? Are you writing that book we talked about?"

Jason was back to offer refills and overheard. "Write a good crime novel, Jake. Read the classics to pick up some ideas." He left, coffee pot in hand.

Jake regarded the group, saying, "I thought about your suggestion to write a book, Eric. I might try it. It would give me an activity to occupy my time. As for Thomas, it's not like we have a lot of murders in Ottawa, other than the gang bangers killing each other, so when you mentioned your connection, Ryan, it piqued my interest. You never know, I might just write about the Thomas murders."

He watched Ryan for a reaction and noticed an eyebrow raise, but that was about it.

Pierre chuckled; his pudgy fingers wrapped around his cup. He said, "Mon Dieu Jake, maybe I won't be able to call you Gloomy anymore if you find something to do, eh? I'll have to find a new name for you. What was that guy's name who lived in the Florida Keys? The writer? The guide talked about him when we were on a tour."

Eric frowned. "You mean Ernest Hemingway?"

Pierre snapped his fingers. "Yeah, that's it. Ernest. We'll have to call you, Ernest."

Eric shrugged his shoulders. "Or we could just call him Jake. By the way, guys. My band is playing at the Rainbow Thursday night. They have limited seating because of distancing, but it's a weeknight in the middle of winter, so there won't be that many there. You should come out."

None of them used cash as they settled their bills with Pruitt. As Pierre tapped his card, he said, "Not me, I have to drive my route early the next day."

Eric bent over and retied one of his boot laces. "We play from nine to twelve. You don't have to stay for the whole thing. There's no cover charge."

Ryan exclaimed, "Nine to twelve! I'm in bed by ten. Talk to young Jake here. He's the night owl."

Jake wondered if Dani would be busy that night. Maybe he could ask her if she wanted to go. "No promises, Eric, but I might show up. It's an opportunity to get out of the house. Remind me where the Rainbow is again."

Eric straightened. "Oh my God, how long have you lived in this town? It's in the Market at the corner of Murray and Parent. You can't miss it."

Jake nodded. "You might see me there. I'll see if Dani wants to go too." He expected someone would say something and of course, Pierre didn't disappoint.

"Ah, that sounds like a date." He shook his sausage-like finger at Jake. "You naughty boy, you."

The thought occurred to Jake to grab the finger that was inches from his face and break it. He just smiled grimly and ignored his tormentor.

The four said their goodbyes to Pruitt and continued their separate ways. Jake thought as he walked home that he had accomplished little with Ryan Cambridge. He would talk to Dani and see if he should have done something differently.

When he unlocked the door, Oliver opened one eye to a slit from his perch by the front window. Satisfied that Jake belonged there, he twitched his tail, closed his eye again, and went back to sleep.

Jake just settled into his chair to read a book when the doorbell rang. As he strode to the door, he thought it must be someone selling something, maybe a kid selling chocolate bars. He opened the door, and it was a kid alright, standing behind her mom, almost hiding.

Dani stepped aside, so the girl was visible in the porch light and said, "Jake, this is my daughter, Emilie."

CHAPTER TWELVE

FACIALLY, EMILIE WAS the mirror image of her mother. Dark eyes and hair highlighted a round face with an olive tinge. She was virtually the same height as her mom, but the resemblance stopped there. She wore tight jeans with ragged holes in the legs, a light winter jacket undone to reveal a tee shirt with a band name Jake didn't recognize, running shoes, and no hat. Jake noticed she tried hard not to shiver on the frigid doorstep.

Jake glanced over his shoulder, relieved that most of the dishes were in the dishwasher. The counter was relatively bare. He offered his elbow as a greeting, and Emilie bumped it with her own. When Jake told Emilie that he was pleased to meet her, she said, "Hi," without making eye contact.

He invited them in, but as they removed their boots and entered the kitchen, Dani said they couldn't stay. "I'm sorry to barge in like this, Jake, but I'm hoping you can do me a favor. The boss called me to a case, and I don't know how long I'll be. Emilie will be fine at home, but I wanted someone nearby that she would feel comfortable calling if she needed something. I thought of you. I hope you don't mind."

"Of course not. Emilie is welcome to stay here if she wants." He glanced at the girl who leaned her shoulder against the refrigerator, her fingers tapping furiously on her phone.

Dani turned to Emilie and said, "What do you think, Em?"

Emilie continued tapping without looking up, saying, "Sure, whatever."

Dani regarded Jake and shrugged her shoulders. "That's a ringing endorsement for you, Jake. Sorry, but I must run. Send her home when you tire of her."

Jake walked Dani to the door and said as she put on her boots, "If you're not doing anything Thursday night, Eric's band is playing at the Rainbow. I'd like to go to support him, and I wondered if you would like to join me if you're not busy. I can fill you in on this morning's breakfast."

Dani made a show of taking out her phone and glancing at it for two seconds before replying.

"Huh, you're in luck. I'm not doing anything. Unless this recent case takes longer than expected or I get called to something else. What time? I can pick you up to save you coming over to my place."

"Great, they start at nine, so how about 8:45?"

They agreed on the time and Dani turned at the door and said in a low voice, "She's hard to talk to, Jake. She's at that age and the divorce has hit her hard. If you tire of her, send her home." Then she raised her voice to a more normal level. "Bye, Emilie." There was no response from the kitchen.

Jake shook his head. "Don't worry about it, Dani. She'll be fine."

He shut the door and returned to the kitchen, wondering how he was going to deal with a teenage girl. It had been years since Avery was a teenager, and he had to admit his wife handled the hard stuff. He found the girl in the sunroom petting Oliver. The cat arched his back to direct her fingers for maximum pleasure, enjoying it as if Jake never paid attention to him. He could hear the cat's motor running as he sat in his chair and said, "Your mom told me about you, Emilie. It's certainly nice to meet you."

Emilie kept petting the cat and said nothing.

Jake thought swing and a miss. Strike one.

Jake tried anew. "His name's Oliver, and he really seems to enjoy that. You have the magic touch."

She rewarded him with a nod of her head and a slight smile.

Undeterred, Jake said, "How is school going?"

This time she spoke. It was one word. "Fine."

Just missed the corner of the plate. Ball one.

"What game were you playing on your phone?"

"Among Us."

Jake thought he had made a breakthrough, but it sounded ominous that she didn't want anyone else to know the title of the game. He said with a smile, "Sure, we can keep it *between* us."

Emilie glanced up, a huge eye roll accompanying the disdain on her face. "That's the name of the game." The unspoken word "dummy" hung in the air like a flashing neon sign.

Strike two. Not even close.

Jake laughed this time. "Oh, okay, I'm not up on these things. You'll have to teach me more about video games." Time to change tactics. "Are you hungry? Can I get you something to eat?"

"Sure."

"Well, just so you know, I make the best toasted tomato and cheese sandwiches in the country. How does that sound?"

"Sure."

Jake smiled grimly as he wandered to the kitchen, leaving Emilie and Oliver to themselves. He prepared the sandwiches and delivered them to the sunroom. Apparently, Oliver grew tired of the attention and left the room. Emilie had her head buried in the screen of her phone again. He placed her sandwich in front of her and ate his silently while watching her play the game. Finally, unable to take it any longer, he said, "Your sandwich is getting cold."

She mumbled her thanks, balanced the phone on her leg, and began devouring the sandwich. She stopped chewing long enough to say, "Are you dating my mom?"

It sounded like an accusation.

"No, we're not dating. We're friends and she's part of a coffee group I belong to. I'm thinking of writing a book and she's giving me some tips."

"I heard you ask her to see some band. Sounds like a date to me. Besides, what does *she* know about writing? All she does is work. That's why my dad left."

Jake tried not to be defensive. "Sorry, Emilie. I didn't make myself clear. She's not giving me *writing* tips. I'm thinking about writing about one of her cases, so she's advising me on that. Your mom has an especially important job, and it takes a lot of her time. I'm sorry that your dad left, but sometimes couples just can't stay together. I don't know your dad, but I think your mom is a wonderful person."

Emilie said nothing, preferring to finish her sandwich. Eventually, she asked, "Do you think they'll ever get back together?"

Jake responded with, "I can't say. I don't know what happened. They might, but sometimes couples become better friends when they're apart."

"Well, they never will if she likes you too much. I have to go."

Emilie shoved her phone in her back pocket and got up to leave. She pulled on her coat and running shoes at the front door, stuffing the untied laces in the sides.

Jake followed her to the door, thinking that now he knew the reason for her agreeing to stay, but he reminded her she could call if she needed anything. Halfway out the door, she mumbled, "Thanks for the sandwich." With that, she left.

He watched her sliding down the sidewalk in her untied running shoes like a drunken curler on a sheet of ice and returned to his chair with Emilie's words echoing in his head.

Strike three. You're out!

CHAPTER THIRTEEN

THE NEXT FEW days flew by. Jake's new computer and printer arrived and after a few hours and phone calls to Nick, he was up and running. The speed at which the computer navigated the internet pleased him. He read every bit of information he could about the murders in Hog's Back Park, including all the articles he could find by Janice Richardson. She certainly was a talented writer. Based on everything he read, he concluded Gary Thomas seemed to be where he needed to be.

He considered Dani's suspicions about Ryan Cambridge. Could he call them suspicions, or was it a fishing expedition? She mentioned there was something she hadn't told him.

He hadn't heard from Dani and he took that as good news as he waited, watching through the kitchen window. He glanced at the clock on the wall and as it ticked over to 8:45, the blue Hyundai raced down the street, slowing just enough to navigate the turn into his driveway. Jake smiled at her punctuality but had misgivings about her driving.

Oliver was missing in action again, so Jake locked up and hustled to the car. Warmer air had chased the cold air mass away. Jake climbed into Dani's car and buckled up. As she wheeled out of the driveway and drove along Wellington through Chinatown toward the downtown core, she asked how it went with Emilie. "Before you answer, I'll tell you her interpretation. She said it was 'fine.' That's pretty enthusiastic coming from her."

Jake had prepared himself for the question. He said, "I think it was fine too. She didn't stick around long, nor say much. She's concerned about you, though."

"Oh, really? I don't have that impression when we're together."

"I think she's more concerned than you think. She's worried that if you and I become too friendly, you and your husband will never get back together."

Dani sighed deeply before responding. "I've tried to explain to her that us getting back together will never happen. He has a new love in his life that he's never told Emilie about, and I've moved on. I told her I might meet someone someday, and she freaked out. We'll get through it." The ride had taken minutes at the speed Dani liked to drive, and they arrived at a parking lot on Dalhousie Street. She said, "Is this okay? It's a short walk to the Rainbow, and it's a pleasant night."

Jake replied that he looked forward to the walk, and he paid at the machine for overnight parking. They sauntered awkwardly down Dalhousie, each trying to maintain distance while being close. They turned onto Murray Street to the brick building housing the Rainbow Bistro. Smoke greeted them as they arrived, and two young hippie-looking men were soon to add to the growing pile of cigarette butts guarding the door. Band posters hung on the walls at the entrance, and thumping recorded music drew them up the stairway to the main floor. The carpet on the way up was threadbare in the middle, a victim of years of traffic. A tattooed doorman the size of a redwood tree greeted them at the top, his voice like sandpaper on metal.

"Welcome to the Rainbow."

Eric bustled about on the raised stage, plugging in cables and setting up microphones, while his bandmates assembled the drum kit and tuned their guitars. An imposing stone wall featuring a fireplace stood on the left. Giant wooden supports broke up the space and large overhead windows on the right side made patrons feel like they were sitting outside.

Jake glanced at his watch. Apparently, the nine o'clock start time was only a suggestion.

As they approached the stage, Dani pulled off her coat to reveal hip-hugging designer jeans and a white blouse. She looked trim, athletic, and, yes, gorgeous. Jake felt like a slob beside her with his old baggy khaki pants and an oversized sweater. He felt old beside her too, even though the age difference wasn't great. He shook it off when she leaned into him, close enough that he caught a whiff of her perfume. It was a wonderful contrast to the smell of stale beer and sweat of the well-established blues bar. She put her mouth to his ear so he could hear above the recorded music and said, "Let's go upstairs. There's a better view from there."

Jake caught Eric's attention as they passed the stage and waved. Eric acknowledged the wave and when he saw Dani, his lips opened in a wide grin as he gave Jake a thumbs up. His gaze never left Dani as she climbed the stairs.

Once upstairs, they sat along the side perpendicular to the end of the stage. They each ordered a beer and considered the stage and dance area below. Dani was right about the view. There were only about twenty people on the main floor so far, but Jake guessed it was early for the bar crowd. Since pandemic restrictions were just opening, occupancy remained limited. They tried to talk, but the noise made it difficult, so they gave up and stayed quiet, watching the people, and waiting for the band to start. Eric and his bandmates began playing around 9:30.

The band was well-rehearsed and played their parts professionally, sounding tight. The soundman did an outstanding job on the mix, and Jake thoroughly enjoyed the first set. Eric's vocals were perfect for the blues songs they covered.

Even though they couldn't verbally communicate without yelling, Jake enjoyed Dani's company. The pair laughed easily when Eric made a humorous comment into the microphone. Jake hadn't felt so alive in years, and an electric shock ran through his body when their knees touched. The 45-minute set sailed by, and before the recorded music began blaring again, Dani said, "I hate to do this, but I should head home. I have to work tomorrow, unlike some lucky people. I've truly enjoyed this, Jake, even if we couldn't hear each other."

Jake patted her hand and said, "Pardon?" He chuckled and said, "I'm glad you agreed to join me, Dani." He noticed the crowd had increased significantly. "At least Eric won't be alone when we leave. Maybe we can do this again sometime."

Eric arrived at the top of the stairs with his bandmates as Jake and Dani put on their coats. They all appeared to be around Eric's age, but they certainly hadn't lost their love of music or ability to play. Eric said, "Thanks for coming guys. I appreciate it." He introduced his bandmates, who looked pleased when Jake asked what they were drinking and bought a round. As he and Dani walked to the head of the stairs, he turned to see Eric nodding, his face stretched by a huge grin, and his arms facing forward with both thumbs pointing at the ceiling. Jake shuffled behind Dani so she couldn't see the gesture.

Jake and Dani discussed the band as they walked to the car. He scraped the frost off the windshield while Dani started it. While they waited for the car to warm up, Jake told her about the breakfast and Ryan's reaction to his questions.

She nodded, saying nothing at first. Finally, she said, "My boss really doesn't want me to look into this any further, but he's a reasonable guy. I know I can change his mind if I can find some proof that Gary isn't guilty. We're short-staffed and there's always a lot going on, so I get it. We can't waste time chasing our tails. I could be completely out to lunch, but I need closure. I won't be able to sleep until I have it."

As they pulled away from the parking lot, Jake said he understood and reconfirmed he would help any way he could. They drove down Bank Street and Dani stopped at an orange light, surprising Jake. He opened his mouth to tell her how amazing she looked when a black Audi Q5 whizzed by, just making it through the intersection before the light turned red. Jake said, "Wow, he's not wasting any time."

Dani stared at the taillights of the Audi. Without turning her head, she said, "You know who that is?"

Jake replied with a frown. "No idea. Idiots who think they own the road, I'm guessing."

"Not just any idiot. I'm sure that's Ryan Cambridge. I just caught a glimpse in my mirror as he roared past."

"Are you sure, Dani? He said he couldn't make it tonight because he goes to bed early. There must be 500 similar Audis in the city. I see them every day. It would be weird if it *is* him. He's in an awful hurry, whoever it is."

"Only one way to find out."

The light blinked green. Dani shut off the signal light indicating her intention to turn onto Somerset Street, and, with a glance at the side mirror, veered into the left lane. A horn blared behind as she stomped on the accelerator, speeding up to gain ground on the Audi.

Jake gripped the armrest with one hand and braced himself with the other on the dash. His body slammed back in the seat as Dani sped up. She was in full police mode now.

The Audi continued down Bank Street and sailed past Lansdowne Park. The football stadium loomed in the dark, quiet as it had been since the pandemic canceled the season. They cruised through orange and borderline red lights. Dani kept her distance but made sure the Audi was always in sight. Her driving skills impressed Jake more by the mile. Even though both vehicles drove too fast for the icy conditions, Jake never felt concerned for his safety. In fact, he felt exhilarated.

He regarded the foreboding surroundings. Snow-covered fields ending in darkness flashed past in a moving panorama.

He said, "We seem to be in the middle of nowhere. Why would Ryan be out here?" He tried to make a joke. "Even if it isn't him, it's a pleasant night for a drive."

Dani's eyes never left the vehicle ahead, saying, "It's him, and we're almost there. It ties in with some information I have."

The Audi eventually reached Albion Road and turned into a driveway. A large sign identified the property as the Rideau Carleton Casino.

CHAPTER FOURTEEN

DANI CIRCLED THROUGH the parking lot far enough from the Audi that she and Jake could confirm without being seen that the driver was Ryan Cambridge.

"Are we going to go in?" asked Jake.

"No, I've seen enough. We know what everyone does in there. They gamble. Some win, most lose. I've followed Ryan here before. He seems to be in the latter category."

The implication shocked Jake. Was Dani saying Ryan spent a lot of time playing here and a lot of time losing? *Gambling? Ryan?* He stared at her as she pulled the car back onto Albion Road.

"What do you mean?"

While there was hesitation in Dani's voice, there was none in her actions as she mashed the accelerator down. She glanced at Jake whose eyes stared straight ahead at the lane markings flashing by in the glare of the headlights. He thought if a deer popped up from the ditch, they would all be dead, including the animal.

"Okay, Jake, you deserve to hear the complete story. I told you my boss doesn't want me to pursue this since the case is closed. He thinks it's a waste of resources and that I should focus my efforts on other cases. I've done that during working hours, but I've been looking into this case in my spare time. The more I dig, the more I think Gary Thomas is innocent, but also the more frustrating it becomes.

"When we interviewed some staff at Matthew Pawsloski's office, one of them told us Matt was suspicious about something that was going on. A young lady who works there said he was looking into some illegalities in the firm.

"She said Matt worked late at night, but he was poking around the office looking for something and she thought he might have gained access to the firm's financial records. He told her he found something, but he didn't know who to talk to. He told her he didn't trust anyone in the office."

Jake listened attentively as Dani wheeled the car back the way they had come onto Bank Street.

Dani continued with her story, saying, "It seemed to be pure speculation on her part. She had no proof of anything. She seemed to crave attention, and as they say, she wasn't a reliable witness. We still thought it could be a motive for someone to get rid of Matt, but then the gun showed up with Gary's fingerprints all over it and the focus shifted to him. Gary's alibi didn't hold up well and witnesses overheard him threatening to kill his wife and Matt. Everything pointed to Gary, and we thought we might have our man. As I mentioned before, my partner was absolutely convinced Gary was guilty. I can't blame him completely. I have to admit, I shifted my focus along with everyone else."

Dani fell quiet as her motivation for pursuing the case began to dawn on Jake. If there was one thing he had discovered about Dani in the time he had known her, it was that she was conscientious about her work; thinking she had made a mistake could cause her sleepless nights. He also knew she wouldn't be able to leave it alone until she was satisfied.

They neared Jake's house and Dani said. "I told you there was information I couldn't share with you, but I want you to understand my interest in Ryan. Just before I figured out the way to join you guys at breakfast, I did some digging into Cambridge and Tremblay, Ryan's firm, where Matt worked. They specialize in real estate, and there are two senior partners. I investigated Ryan's personal finances and found out he's in hock up to his ears. He earns a good income from the firm, but it's not enough to pay back the debt load he's carrying. His credit line and cards are maxed out. I knew where he was going tonight because I've followed him before, and this isn't the first time he's gone to the casino. Matthew seemed to think something illegal was going on at the firm. I wondered if Ryan could have stolen money, and he's trying to recover by gambling. It could be pure speculation, but I wanted you to see firsthand why I'm interested in him. I have no proof, but if Ryan found out Matthew knew he was abusing the trust funds, that could have been a motive for murder."

As they pulled to the curb in front of Jake's house, he sat with his mind spinning, trying to absorb everything Dani had told him. Finally, he said, "I honestly don't know Ryan that well, other than meeting for coffee and having a few laughs. I like him, and I would be shocked if he murdered someone. Murderers are rarely typical people, based on the interviews I've done during my career. Although there are some you wouldn't suspect. I suppose he could have hired someone. I see where you're going with this, Dani, I do, but you're right, it's all speculation. There might be a white-collar crime to investigate. But are you sure you aren't torturing yourself for nothing about the murders?"

"Maybe I am, Jake, but I couldn't live with myself if I find out somehow that Gary's life is being wasted in prison for no reason and I had a part in putting him there."

Jake decided the night had taken an unexpected turn from the first date type of evening he had expected. He unbuckled his seat belt and opened the door to get out. Then he came to a conclusion. He shut the door again and contemplated the woman who had just taken him completely into her confidence. A woman he trusted. A woman he liked.

"Okay, I get it, Dani. I don't know if I can be of any help to you or not. I was a reporter, not a police officer. What's Gary Thomas like? You've talked to him. You obviously think he's innocent, but what is he *like*?"

Dani sat thoughtfully for a minute before saying, "I could give you my impression of the man, but that is something I think you should decide for yourself. If you're interested in meeting him, I'll set it up." A smile lit up her face. "We'll call it research for your new book."

CHAPTER FIFTEEN

D ANI EXPLAINED TO Jake that officials had moved Gary Thomas from the Ottawa-Carleton Detention Centre to the Millhaven Institution in Bath, Ontario, about ninety minutes from Ottawa. She also informed him about the forms required for a visit. As soon as he shed his winter clothes in the house, Jake used his new computer to call up the paperwork and printed it off. He completed the clearance form necessary to determine his overall suitability to visit a prison and to absolve Correctional Services of any responsibility should any harm come to him while there. He learned that a Visit Review Board would review his application.

The second form took longer. The visitor application allowed the Millhaven Institution to approve or reject his visit to the jail. He mulled over one question that required him to explain the extenuating circumstances for his visit. With Dani's helpful suggestions, he explained he was writing a book about the case and that an interview with the prisoner was vital to his story. He attached the required photos and identification and mailed the information.

Dani told Jake to prepare for a phone call from Correctional Services. Other than that, Jake heard little from her during the days that followed. She told him her case load kept her busy, and she mentioned in one of their brief conversations that Emilie visited at least once during that time. The days flew by for Jake without surprises. He was grateful as recent events had rocked his world. It seemed like he was in a race car speeding around a track with no one steering. He passed the time documenting his notes and working on his story while he waited for word from Correctional Services.

Now he sat in his office chair contemplating the words on the screen in front of him. Somehow, during the last few days, he had typed close to 100 pages. He scrolled to the beginning and scanned the pages on the screen. The early part of his story documented his loneliness after losing his wife. As he read, he recalled how cathartic it was just to let his feelings pour out through his fingers as he tapped the keys. After typing the opening section, he slept like he hadn't in months and woke up refreshed. The next day, he typed the story of his retirement and its impact on his life. Would anyone ever read this stuff? Who cares? It felt good to be doing something. He planned to put everything down in a mind dump and edit it later but, as he reread it, other than a few typos, the words satisfied him.

Then he tackled recent developments. The first half of his document covered years; the last half spanned the last few days. It just seemed like years. He described the headline that attracted his attention and Ryan mentioning Gary Thomas's sentencing at the breakfast. The discussion about writing a book followed. All innocent enough, but it became kindling for the fire. Things heated when Dani brought him into her confidence by talking about Thomas and her suspicion of the convicted murderer's innocence. The revelation that Ryan was severely in debt and perhaps stealing from his law firm was like pouring lighter fluid on the blaze. His last sentence read, *Looking back, it is possible boring is not so awful.*

He mentioned nothing about his growing attraction to Dani. He didn't know if she felt the same, and until he did, it would remain untyped.

Jake pulled himself away from the keyboard long enough to attend the Saturday morning breakfast. Besides Jake, only Eric and Pierre showed up. Even Jason Pruitt was missing. His personable young server, Amanda, revealed that Pruitt had come down with a cold. Jake discussed the Thursday night show with Eric and tolerated Pierre's usual barbs. Pierre would have had more fodder if he had learned that Dani accompanied Jake to the Rainbow Bistro. Thankfully, he didn't.

He hadn't been home from breakfast long when the expected phone call came from Correctional Services. Jake replied to the questions about why he wanted to meet Gary Thomas. He assured the caller he had no intention of writing about the inner workings of the jail, other than for backstory, and his approval arrived a few days later.

Now, as he prepared to leave for the trip to the Millhaven Institution to speak to a convicted murderer, Jake reached for the ceiling in a deep stretch. He was happy that drafting the book brought normalcy back to his life. He just had time to browse relevant sites to refresh his memory about the storage of handguns in Canada. The theft of Gary Thomas's gun still bothered him. He glanced at his watch, surprised yet again at how absorbed he became in his research. It was almost time to go.

At the recommendation of the Corrections' employee, he called the jail to ensure it was not on lockdown or that Covid-19 had not somehow snuck into the facility despite the vaccines. The Institution cleared him, so he spent a few minutes with Oliver before dressing in blue dress slacks and a plaid shirt. He made certain his mask was in his pocket before leaving the house. Although the provincial government had relaxed the mask rules, he didn't know what the expectations were at the jail.

He hadn't started his 2015 Subaru Outback in a week, and even before that, he only drove short distances to run errands. Jake thought if it could, the poor vehicle would have developed an inferiority complex by now.

The new battery Jake had purchased in the fall started the vehicle in the wintry weather without difficulty. The cold tires could have belonged on Fred Flintstone's car as he backed out, as they always seemed square in the winter until they warmed up.

Jake wound his way through the streets of Ottawa until he reached the country. If any positives resulted from the pandemic, one had to be fewer cars on the road. Many business operators and government officials discovered that working from home was practical and continued to do so. The increased vacancy rate in office buildings reflected the downside.

It was a clear, crisp day, and the sun glistened off the dazzling, untouched snowbanks along the Veteran's Memorial Highway, forcing Jake to put on his sunglasses. It was a magnificent day for driving, and the scenery was worthy of a Hallmark postcard. Wintry beauty surrounded him as tree branches sagged under the weight of icicles, and the ditches brimmed with snow. Expanses of virgin snow-carpeted fields, spoiled occasionally by snowmobile tracks, sparkled to a tree-guarded horizon. A snowy owl perched on top of a hydro pole, his keen eyes scanning the fields for a wayward rodent.

Jake amused himself by listening to an all-news radio station until the signal faded, after which he switched to a classic rock station. Once he swung onto Highway 401, mud and slushy snow tossed from the salted road by passing vehicles, splattered his windshield. Large smoke-spewing semis roared past; their drivers oblivious to the road condition as they tried to meet some deadline. He stopped at a Tim Hortons service center for coffee, a bathroom break, and gas. After helping two embarrassed twenty-something-year-old women find the latch to open the gas cap on their rental car, he continued his journey.

A short time later, Jake saw a large sign announcing the Millhaven Institution in English and French and he turned the corner into the driveway. Correctional Services Canada established the prison in 1971 east of Bath, Ontario, a town of about 2000 people. Two trees framed the sign, but in case there was any doubt, a guard tower loomed in the background. Anyone looking from the air would see a spiderweb of low buildings connected by a series of corridors with observation towers at the corners. Jake learned from his research that a double-layer 30-foot high razor fence surrounded the perimeter and guards armed with rifles patrolled the area. Motion sensors and closed-circuit TV cameras monitored the grounds.

Jake drove along the snow-covered road leading to the jail. He checked in with the security guard at the gated fence where he pulled down his mask and showed his identification. The guard asked him to step out of the car for a cursory examination of the vehicle's interior. When the guard completed the search, he pointed to a parking lot close to a building separate from the others. Jake pulled into an unused spot and nudged the car up against a snowbank guarding the building like the sentries in the towers.

Jake passed through a metal gate and once inside he faced a solid wooden desk between a bench on one wall and a counter on the other. He completed a Register for Official Visitors form and once again produced his two pieces of government I.D. The guard compared the photos to his face after Jake pulled down his mask, took his keys and wallet, and gave him a visitor's pass on a chain. Jake draped the pass around his neck and walked through a metal detector that scanned for weapons and an ION scanner that would detect drugs. A brief non-invasive frisk search followed, after which a female guard materialized to escort him to the visitors area.

She said, "You're here to see Gary Thomas?" When Jake confirmed he was, she said, "I'm glad. He doesn't have many visitors. He's one of the nicest here. Stays to himself pretty much. Your meeting with Gary isn't considered a security risk, so you're welcome to visit in the common area."

Jake said, "What's the alternative?"

"If considered a risk, you would meet in a room with a glass partition separating you, and your conversation would be by phone."

Jake said, "I'm happy to meet in the common area."

They entered a spacious area, not unlike a cafeteria. The room featured several small round tables, each supported by a single metal leg. Joined to the leg were four metal tentacles, each supporting a basic chair. In the middle of each table was a round pod that Jake assumed held microphones for monitoring the conversation.

His escort guided Jake to a table in a quiet corner of the room and said, "The warden or another senior official would have to approve any interception of conversations. I can assure you your conversation will be private. Please keep your mask on as a precaution against spreading the virus. Enjoy your visit."

She left and Jake observed visitors chatting with inmates in orange coveralls at a few tables as soft murmuring drifted throughout the room. Brilliant sunshine brightened the area from windows on one side, but his reflection bounced back from a glassed-in room on the other where he assumed guards monitored the activity.

Then he waited. His heart rate climbed in anticipation. He had interviewed members of local street gangs before at the Ottawa-Carleton Detention Centre, but the stakes seemed higher this time. He wanted Gary to be innocent for Dani's sake, but he needed to satisfy himself. This was his opportunity to assess the man and draw his own conclusion. He laid his phone on the table and sat back in his chair.

Minutes later, a door opened at the end of the room and a lanky man accompanied by a guard strolled through. The man was dressed head to toe in orange coveralls.

Jake sucked in a breath, bracing to meet Gary Thomas.

CHAPTER SIXTEEN

THOMAS SAT AT the table on the opposite side of Jake. Cool, pale blue eyes, as penetrating as an X-ray machine, peered earnestly over the mask that hugged a well-defined jawline. His skin was pasty white above the mask, and he combed his brown hair straight back. He observed Jake, waiting for him to speak.

Jake started by thanking him for the meeting. He got to the point, explaining the reason for his visit. He left out Dani's role for now.

"Mr. Thomas, my name is Jake Scott and I'm a former reporter with the *Ottawa Citizen*. My job at the paper was to write about crime in the city. I've been at loose ends since I retired, so I researched your story. Some things about your case interested me, and I wanted to talk to you about them. Depending on this conversation and how the rest of my research goes, I'm looking into writing a book about your case. Some material I read makes little sense. I'd like to have your take on it and if you don't mind, I'll record our conversation." This brought back memories of interviews he conducted in the past, and it felt good. He tried to gain Gary's trust with a smile and a joke. "My memory is excellent, but it's really short."

Jake couldn't tell through the mask if Gary smiled or not and the convict's eyes betrayed nothing. Thomas sat erect with his hands clasped in front of him, listening attentively to what Jake was saying. Not a word until now. When he spoke, the softness of his voice surprised Jake.

"Can I trust you, Mr. Scott? If I can, you can record. Will your story describe how the system jailed an innocent man for a crime he didn't commit or will it be sensationalized, so I look like a monster?"

Jake said, "I'll write objectively and justly. One angle I'm hoping to pursue is whether you committed the murder. It all depends on this meeting. Are you *really* innocent? I'm sure everyone in here says the same thing."

He took Thomas's statement as approval and reached forward to turn on the phone's recorder app.

Thomas nodded. He said, "They do, but I *am* innocent. The bigger question is why *you* think I might be innocent. You wouldn't be here otherwise. There would be nothing to write about. Just another murder."

Jake noted the conviction in Thomas's tone. "I understand. I get it that the gun had your fingerprints on it, and the timelines and everything. The evidence appeared to be overwhelming, but there are still things I don't understand."

He wished he could see Thomas's face. Over the years he had interviewed enough guilty gang members with a propensity for lying that he considered himself adept at watching for telltale signs.

Jake pushed Thomas for a reaction. "Why did you throw the gun in the bushes after killing the couple? Why not throw it the canal or someplace where no one would find it?"

Thomas spoke in an even tone. "Perhaps you didn't hear me, Mr. Scott, but I didn't *throw* the gun anywhere. Someone stole it from my house. I'm sure you realize I've had lots of time to think about my situation. I think someone framed me."

There was a certain serenity about Gary Thomas. It wasn't passiveness, but more like resignation. That was telling.

"Who would try to frame you? Do you have enemies? Is there someone so upset with you they want to see you behind bars?"

Thomas sighed. "If I had enemies, it would help me make sense of everything."

Jake pressed further. "I understand a handgun is a restricted weapon that must be inoperable or locked up in Canada. Did you have your gun locked up? Did you follow the rules, Gary?"

"I had a safe for my guns. I remember taking the gun out and taking pictures of it, which I planned to use when I put it up for sale. Never put it back, I guess. Careless."

"Okay, who stole your gun? You must have some ideas. According to the police, there was no evidence of breaking and entering at your house. It must have been someone you know."

Thomas nodded. Then he said, "No-one had been to the house to my knowledge in the weeks leading up to the murder. Unless Melissa took Pawsloski there. I stopped using the gun when I bought the new one, but I just hadn't got around to selling it. There's a lot of paperwork involved, and I just hadn't done it. It had been a few weeks since I used the gun, so I don't know when it disappeared. That's my problem, I can't prove anything. It's so frustrating, Mr. Scott. I need help. The one person who might have stolen it is Melissa."

Jake sat back in his chair. *Melissa*? His *wife*? "Why, Gary? Why would she take the gun?"

"I don't know, I'm grasping at straws. As you said, the police didn't discover any signs of breaking and entering like nicks on the door or window frames, even though someone removed the gun. She had the opportunity, but I don't know why she would do it. Apparently, I didn't know her. She and Pawsloski had an affair after all."

The premise made no sense to Jake. What would she do with the gun? Give it to someone so they could sneak up and kill her and her boyfriend?

He said, "Were you and Melissa having difficulties before the affair?"

Gary's pale blue eyes penetrated Jake's. He responded with, "I didn't think so. Not more than other couples do. We had loud fights, and the police showed up at the house once just before the murders. That didn't help my case. It upset Melissa that I wasn't working, and she didn't think I was trying hard enough to find a job. She often got mad about that, and one time she blew up. It was ugly, but I didn't love her any less."

"What was your career? Why weren't you working?"

"I'm a chef. The owner of the restaurant laid me off before they went under. No one was hiring. I considered taking courses at Algonquin College before Melissa's death. Training in another field seemed like my only course of action."

Jake nodded as he checked his notes.

"I understand you threatened to kill Melissa and Matt in front of witnesses."

"Yes, it's the stupidest thing I've ever done. I had just found out they were having an affair and lost my mind. I sat in a bar and had a few drinks before I went to the office, but when I got there,

Pawsloski wasn't around. Yes, I threatened to kill them, and people witnessed it, but I would never murder anyone. I shoot at targets at a gun range. That doesn't make me homicidal. It's a hobby." His voice trailed off, and he added softly, "I could never shoot a person or even an animal."

Jake felt himself wanting to believe this soft-spoken man, but more questions needed answers.

"Where did you go the night of the murders?"

"To pick up beer, but I drove back to my house to see if Melissa and her lover were there. I wanted to confront them. My buddies vouched for the fact I picked up beer and there was a camera at the store that verified I was there. No one could verify the side trip. My buddies asked where I had been, and I told them. I didn't tell them why I went to the house. It was none of their business. They vouched for my character at least. That's why I'm *only* here for fifteen years." The last sentence hung bitterly in the air.

Jake glanced at his phone to ensure it was still recording. He asked sharply, "Do you know Ryan Cambridge?"

A frown formed on the forehead above the mask. "Cambridge. Cambridge. It sounds familiar. Should I know him?"

Jake shook his head. "Not necessarily. I was just curious. I have one more question, Gary. Did you hire someone to kill Matt and Melissa?"

Thomas drew his head back and said, "No, I did not. I wouldn't know where to start."

Jake closed his notepad. "Okay, I don't know the process for making phone calls, but please call me if you can think of anything else. They have my number, but I'll make sure it's okay to give it to you. You can all me collect."

Gary nodded, sadness reflecting in his eyes.

Jake had no more questions, so he thanked Thomas and waved to the guard for an escort from the building. He retrieved his belongings at the front desk, asked them to give Thomas his phone number, and walked to his car. He reached for his sunglasses on the dash and thought about the conversation. Gary Thomas was either telling the truth, was an Academy Award-worthy actor, or had two personalities. If it were the latter, the meeting convinced Jake that the one he just met was not capable of murder.

As he approached the 401, he thought of turning west towards Toronto. He could reach the city to visit his daughter and her boyfriend in two and half hours and forget this whole thing. Instead, he turned east. He had things to tell Dani.

CHAPTER SEVENTEEN

J AKE SAT IN front of his computer, summarizing his conversation with Gary Thomas. He decided once again that he had learned little that was new but at least he heard it directly from the horse's mouth. Gary's suspicion that Melissa may have taken the gun was interesting, but not very plausible. He checked his watch, and it occurred to him that Dani might be home, so he dialed her number.

"Lo?" answered the uninterested voice of sixteen-year-old Emilie.

"Oh, hi Emilie. It's Jake Scott. I meant to dial your mom's cell phone, but I guess I called the house phone."

Emilie mumbled, "It's Mom's phone. She's in the bathroom."

Jake thought that might be too much information, but said, "Okay, can you have her call me back, please? She knows the number."

Emilie managed, "I'll bet she does," before the phone went dead in Jake's hand.

Phew, Jake thought as he shook his head, there's some work to do to please her. He put Emilie's attitude out of his mind to focus on something he had put aside for months. He looked up the number for a local gym and, with some trepidation, arranged a meeting with a personal trainer the next morning. His phone rang before he put it down. Dani's name appeared on the screen.

Her bubbly voice brightened Jake's day.

"I've been thinking about you, Jake. How did it go with Gary Thomas?"

"I was kind of hoping we might have coffee and talk about it. Are you free sometime soon?"

Dani hesitated for a few seconds before she said, "I have Emilie here. I'm taking her back to her dad's in a couple of hours and then I have to work. Why don't the three of us meet at Brew and Buns in half an hour? You can tell me what happened, and it'll give you and Em a chance to get to know each other a little better."

It was Jake's turn to hesitate. "Uh, okay, if you think that's a good idea. She doesn't seem to like me much and I would like to talk about the case."

Dani laughed before admitting, "She doesn't like *anybody* much right now. Well, except for a few friends and a new boy she's met. And as for talking about the case, I'm slowly introducing her to what I do. It'll be fine. We'll have a blast." Her voice became distant. "Right, Em?"

Jake sensed the same eye roll she gave him about the iPhone game she had been playing a few days earlier. He could almost hear it through the phone. He agreed to meet them in half an hour.

Oliver benefited from Jake's attention, allowing himself to tolerate it until he hissed and batted Jake's hand away. When it was time to go, Jake glanced in the bedroom full-length mirror. He shuddered at the image. All his clothes should have retired when he did. His eyes zeroed in on a pull at the shoulder in the knit sweater he wore, a scar from too much wear. His pants, although tight around the middle, were baggy at the seat and legs. It looked the same as the outfit he wore to the Rainbow Bistro, and it must have embarrassed Dani to be seen with him. If he had to put a label on his ensemble, he thought humorlessly, he would call it retro frumpy chic. He added shopping for clothes to his mental list of things to do.

He bundled up and headed out into the Ottawa winter, following the familiar route to the restaurant. Dani and Emilie were already sitting at a table when he arrived. The detective greeted him with a dazzling smile while Emilie ignored him, as she slouched over the table concentrating on her phone.

Dani wore her usual bright colors. Her vibrant red sweater made it hard to visualize her as a hardened homicide detective.

Emilie wore a rainbow watch cap. The sun shining through the window emphasized blueish highlights in the naturally curly hair that hung beneath the cap to Emilie's shoulders. Jake noticed for the first time a few freckles dotting her nose and a hint of dimples in her cheeks. Looking beyond the slouching and attitude, she was a cute young lady with untapped potential. Her tee-shirt bore the name of another boy band Jake failed to recognize.

Jake greeted them and received a cheery "good morning" from Dani and nothing from Emilie as he slid into his seat. He mouthed a "good morning" to Jason Pruitt and gestured for coffee. Jake said, "So, how are you two doing?"

Dani said, "We're doing great. Emilie signed up for some online art classes. We must show you her art sometime. Won't we, Em?"

Emilie responded with an almost imperceptible nod, a noticeable grimace, and a prominent shrug.

Just as Jason arrived to pour the coffee, Jake glanced at Emilie.

"I would love to see it. I always admire people who have artistic abilities. What kind of art do you do, Emilie?"

Her voice was barely above a whisper. "People, monsters, animals—shi—uh, stuff like that."

Was this a breakthrough? Even a minor one? Jake jumped at the opening. "Good for you. I love to write. I suppose you could consider that an art or an ability. It would be great to see your work."

A deafening silence followed, so Jake asked Dani, "Are you sure you want to talk about my visit to Millhaven?"

"Yes, Jake. Emilie and I talked about it. Fill me in."

As they drank their coffee, Jake detailed his meeting with Gary Thomas. Emilie played with her phone and sipped her hot chocolate. Dani sat thoughtfully when he finished before asking, "What's your overall impression?" Before Jake could answer, her phone vibrated noisily on the table. She flipped it over and glanced at the screen. She shrugged and said, "It's my boss. I need to take it."

The person on the other end did all the talking, but Jake gleaned from the few words Dani interjected that the conversation focused on his trip to Millhaven. Jake could hear enough through the phone's speaker to know the person was male and not happy. He concentrated on Dani's portion of the conversation.

"He's writing a book, Sir. Yes, I spoke to the warden at Millhaven to clear the way. I'm not spending any of my working hours on the case, Sir. As I mentioned to you, I have doubts that Gary Thomas is guilty."

Dani sat silently for a few minutes as a red blush crept from her collar to her hairline. "I'm not giving him evidence that isn't in the public domain, Sir. I'm just answering his questions to help him with his research."

"Okay, Sir, thank you."

Dani smacked the screen twice with her finger as if to make sure the call ended. The red in her face subsided.

"That was my boss. His name's Bill Sharpe and as you probably guessed, he's not too happy with me. He's under a lot of stress with everything that's going on in the policing world these days. The Thomas case is officially closed, and he wants me to move on. I guess the warden from Millhaven called him to find out more about the book you're writing." She laughed mirthlessly before adding, "There's always a concern that writers will reflect badly on the prison system. They like to prepare themselves for any fallout from a story. It's a government-run organization." She added the last as if that explained everything.

Jake said, "It's completely understandable."

The tightness in Dani's features told him everything he needed to know about the heat smoldering beneath the surface.

Finally, Dani said, "I guess I should let it go. I'm not getting help from the office and I feel like I'm beating my head against a brick wall. If I could just gather enough evidence, I might get the case reopened."

Emilie concentrated on her phone, but she said in a low voice, "Don't give up, Mom. Eyes on the prize. Isn't that what you always say?"

She surprised Jake since she seemed oblivious to the conversation. It was good to hear her take part, and he agreed with her 100 percent.

"Emilie's right. You asked for my overall impression before your boss called. Either Gary is an amazing liar or he's incapable of committing murder. There isn't any in-between. I want to continue working on this story. You've told me enough and after talking to Gary, I'm convinced it's worth pursuing. There's something I'm curious about, though. Ryan says he didn't know Matt well, even though they worked in the same office. I looked up their firm on the internet, and it's not that big. Ryan's a personable guy. Unless he's different in the office, it seems impossible that he didn't know him well."

Jake didn't see Jason Pruitt's lanky frame hovering over him as he spoke. Pruitt's deep voice made Jake jump. As he stood over Jake with the debit card machine ready to accept their payment, he said, "Are you talking about Ryan Cambridge and that Pawsloski guy that was murdered? He had coffee with Ryan at that very table a few days before the murder. I recognized Pawsloski from his picture in the paper."

CHAPTER EIGHTEEN

JAKE AND DANI stared at Jason. Ryan and Matt met outside the office? This was news.

Finally, Dani managed, "Are you sure it was Matt Pawsloski?"

Jason handed the machine to Jake so he could tap his card to pay the bill as he replied to Dani. "I can't be 100%, but I'm reasonably sure. They sat right over there." The table he gestured to was at the back of the room, close to Pruitt's work surface. "I was standing behind the counter, so I heard bits and pieces of their conversation. It got pretty heated. I didn't understand the whole thing, but they seemed to discuss financial problems at the office. It sounded like the guy that looked like Pawsloski was accusing Ryan of something, but as I said, I couldn't hear the whole thing." He took the machine back from Jake.

Dani said, "Is there more you can add, Jason? This is important."

Jason pulled the receipt from the whirring machine and handed it to Jake. "When I got to the table to drop off their bill, Ryan didn't see me coming. I hear bits of conversations all the time. I wasn't eavesdropping. I heard part of your conversation too, so that made me think of it."

Jake thought it interesting that Jason considered it necessary to justify overhearing conversations.

Jason said, "Ryan told the other guy to keep *it* quiet. Whatever 'it' is. The other guy, Pawsloski, said something like, 'I don't know if I can do that.' Then they saw me and didn't say another word. When they got outside, I saw them talking again through the window. Ryan got in the other guy's face, like nose to nose. It looked like he was yelling, but that's all I can tell you."

Jake stared at Dani, watching Jason walk back toward the counter. He said, "What do you think?"

Dani's lips pursed in frustration.

"The boss says they had a solid conviction and to leave it alone. He said the evidence was overwhelming and I have to agree. But if Ryan used the firm's trust funds as his personal ATM and Matt found out about it, that's a motive for murder. This is so frustrating."

Jake reached out to touch Dani's hand before glancing aside at Emilie and withdrawing it.

He said, "Maybe you can't investigate, Dani, but I'm going to continue looking into it. This case has me in its claws now, so I need to find out what's going on."

Concern swept across Dani's face.

"What are you going to do, Jake? I'm regretting getting you involved. If Ryan murdered Matt and Melissa, or even if he hired someone to do it, it's serious enough that two people were killed over it. If they'll do it once, they'll have no problem doing it again."

"No need to concern yourself, Dani. You mentioned a woman Matt talked to at the office. I would like to talk to her. Gary's friends, too. Maybe even the defense attorney. I'm curious to know why Ryan talked to Matt Pawsloski before the murder. He said he didn't know Matt well." Jake glanced out the window. "It would be nice to be able to confirm it was Matt talking to Ryan. These stores must have security cameras, but it was so long ago. No one would keep footage from that far back. I think hotels keep the footage for about 90 days. Even banks rarely keep it beyond six months." He noticed Emilie now sat with her hands between her knees, leaning forward and absorbing every word. He continued, "This is completely on me. If I find out anything important, I promise I'll let you know."

Dani squinted. Her dark eyes burned like embers smoldering in their sockets.

"Like hell you will, Jake Scott. You will keep me posted every step of the way."

It was exactly the reaction Jake expected. He laughed and held up his hands, palms outward.

"Okay, okay. I surrender. I'll keep you posted."

Dani softened her tone. "I can't do anything to help with an audit of Ryan's firm's finances. We would bring in a forensics team to go through the books if there was a formal investigation, but I can't do much. All I can do is give you a couple of names of people you could talk to. The paralegal's name is Sarah Brown, and Gary's friend who testified at the trial is Damon Brooks."

Jake retrieved a pen from his jacket pocket and jotted the two names on a napkin. He folded the napkin and put it and the pen back in his pocket.

As they got up to leave, another thought totally unrelated to the case occurred to Jake. It was a stab in the dark, but worth a shot. He asked as they walked towards the door, "Would you two be interested in helping a guy pick out some new clothes. It's been a long time for me and I'm kind of out of the loop. I might end up picking the same thing I'm wearing if I do it alone. I need a woman's perspective. Maybe we could do it next time you're visiting your mom, Emilie. What do you think?"

Emilie cast a sideways glance at her mom. Jake noticed her dimples deepen for the briefest of moments as Dani said, "Sure, that would be fun." He caught a wink exchanged between the two and wondered if they had been discussing his attire at some point.

As Jake pushed the door open and stepped aside to allow Dani and Emilie to pass, he noticed the skin of the girl's leg just below her right butt cheek through the rip in her jeans. He asked himself what he'd done. Somehow, he just couldn't picture himself walking around with his bum hanging out of a pair of ripped jeans.

CHAPTER NINETEEN

JAKE GROANED INVOLUNTARILY as he rolled out of bed. He couldn't remember his muscles aching so much in his life. On the way to the bathroom, he recalled with a grimace the meeting with the personal trainer that was followed soon after by an introductory session.

Rows of treadmills, ellipticals, stationary bikes, and weightlifting machines filled a spacious room on the gym's first floor. The second floor had separate rooms for floor exercises and benches for free weights. His trainer turned out to be a tall and enthusiastic redheaded woman in her early twenties wearing a tight-fitting jacket emblazoned with the gym logo and white leggings that showed off her muscle definition. Despite Jake's age and lack of fitness, she expected him to do everything she could. At least, that was his impression.

She tested his blood pressure and ticked "high" on the chart she carried. His body mass index earned him another "high." When she measured his strength, she ticked "low." Same for endurance. Jake found it discouraging, but she beamed and advised him a lot of clients are the same at the beginning, and over time he would see drastic changes. He realized he should feel reassured. The discussion of his diet that followed elicited an occasional, virtually imperceptible, head shake from the young woman. He did as many sit-ups and push-ups as he could muster while she counted off with her fingers. She required only a few fingers to tally the totals. Then she introduced him to the machines. Oh, the machines. Each tortured a muscle group in a distinct part of the body and, Jake convinced himself, elicited as much discomfort as the human body could endure. As he mopped his brow with a towel, she cheerfully assured him she could improve his overall conditioning with diet and exercise. She neglected to estimate how many sessions that would take.

As he brushed his teeth, he couldn't imagine what it would be like when he really exercised. Oliver wandered in and cocked his head and Jake could have sworn the cat's morning meow ended in a question mark.

Muscles loosened as Jake wandered around the kitchen, making breakfast, and feeding the cat. He showered and declared himself fit to make it through the day, albeit with more aches and pains than usual.

He retrieved the morning paper, which he set on the table beside his recliner, took out his cell phone, and Googled the number for Ryan's firm. The wrinkled napkin with the two names he had jotted down lay under his newspaper. When he found the number, he double-checked the first name, dialed, and asked for Sarah Brown. A soft voice came on the phone.

Jake introduced himself and got right to the point.

"Sarah, my name's Jake Scott. I'm a former journalist and I'm writing a book about the murder of Matt Pawsloski and Melissa Thomas. I understand you knew Mr. Pawsloski, and I was hoping we could meet so I could learn more about your association with him and your overall impression."

A sharp intake of breath was followed by a long pause. Jake wondered if she had hung up. He removed the phone from his ear to ensure the call was still active. Confirming it was, he put the phone back to his ear.

Finally, Sarah said, "I knew him, but it was a long time ago. I have nothing to tell you. I'm sorry, but I can't help you."

Jake didn't want to lose her.

"My sources told me you and Matt knew each other well, and he confided in you about something illegal in the office. Is that true?"

More indecision on the other end of the phone, followed by another deep sigh and a voice so low Jake pressed the phone harder to his ear. Then, "Matt and I talked, and he told me about some things. I'm afraid to talk about it. If that's why someone murdered Matt, I don't want any part of it. Besides. I want to keep my job."

Jake tried anew, "Sarah, there's a possibility that the man serving time for the murders, Gary Thomas, is innocent. If he didn't commit the murders, someone else did. An innocent man could spend fifteen years in prison. That's not fair to him, and it means guilty people are free and running around in public. Can you help me, Sarah?"

The line went dead. This time she hung up.

Jake stared at the silent phone in his hand with his lips pursed. That didn't go well. Not the response he expected, although he had to admit he didn't know what to expect. He needed another way to get Sarah Brown to talk. In the meantime, he flattened the napkin with his hand and verified the second name, Damon Brooks.

A 411-search produced Damon's number and Jake dialed. The phone rang five times before going to voice mail. Jake left a message and set the phone on the side table. He picked up the paper and was about to read when the phone vibrated.

He answered without checking the screen, assuming it would be Brooks. It wasn't. Sarah Brown's soft voice came over the phone. He wondered how she had his number, but he suddenly remembered it would have shown up on her screen. Jake could hear traffic noise in the background and Sarah confirmed she was standing on the sidewalk.

She said, "I'm sorry I had to hang up. Someone was nearby. Can you promise me you will keep my name out of anything you write?"

Jake said, "I promise I won't mention your name. I understand your firm is rather small, so I can't assure someone won't figure out who you are. I can tell you this, though. If there's nothing to this story, it will go nowhere. No book and nothing to worry about. If something can be proven, police will arrest the guilty person and you may have to testify at some point. Either way, you'll be fine."

Sarah whispered, "Okay, but I can't meet you downtown because someone could see me. Can you meet me at the Bridgehead Coffee shop on Preston at five o'clock?"

Jake barely heard above the traffic noise, but after confirming the location and time, he agreed to meet. One thing was certain. Something that happened years ago scared Sarah Brown, and he hoped to find out what it was.

CHAPTER TWENTY

THE CLOCK SEEMED to stop for Jake. He decided he didn't hurt so much as his muscles felt tight, like elastic bands wound around something one too many times. He still groaned every time he moved. Gary Thomas occupied his mind, but the routine everyday sounds of an empty house seemed amplified as if he had tried on hearing aids after years of near deafness. He noticed the phenomena more and more lately as the furnace roared into life, the refrigerator hummed, and the ticking clock grated on his nerves like a dripping tap at night. He tried to speed up the day by working on his manuscript, tightening the wording, and moving paragraphs around.

Oliver checked in periodically but mostly did his own thing.

There was absolute silence from Damon Brooks.

The time finally arrived to leave, so Jake grabbed his winter attire and mask, put them on, and headed out into the cold. He started the Subaru and drove down Wellington Street to Preston for his meeting with Sarah Brown.

The coffee shop was at the corner of Anderson and Preston, and it was practically empty. Jake ordered a cappuccino and an apple cranberry muffin and found a table at the rear. He regarded the cappuccino and muffin on the table, and his personal trainer popped into his head. He supposed he would have to report his dalliance next time he saw her. She would not approve.

Time for Jake suddenly sped up. Compared to earlier in the day, it passed at warp speed. He glanced at his watch frequently as the front door opened and closed with people arriving and departing. The minutes ticked by. 5:15. *Where was she?* The door finally swung wide as a woman rushed in. Jake knew immediately it had to be Sarah Brown.

The woman scanned the area, her anxious eyes resting on each customer one by one. Eventually, she spied Jake, the only one occupying a table by himself in the room. A purse hung over one shoulder and a heavy-looking laptop case dangled from her other hand. She wore glasses and her straight dirty blonde hair hung to her shoulders. Jake doubted her stylish knee-length woolen coat would keep anyone warm this time of year. Although plain, she carried herself professionally in a manner that many would find attractive.

She hastened to Jake's table and sat opposite him, appearing jumpy and glancing over her shoulder as the door opened and closed. She removed her mask and her eyes sought Jake's briefly before turning away. The woman had not said a word nor changed her expression. She rose again and shrugged off her coat, draping it over the back of the chair.

Jake heard her order a brewed coffee with room for cream at the counter.

When she returned after topping up her coffee with sugar and cream, Jake smiled, held out his hand, and introduced himself.

Sarah took his hand as Jake said, "Thank you for agreeing to meet Sarah, but I'm curious. You assumed it was me when you came in. I understand I'm the only one sitting alone, but I thought you would want to confirm it before sitting down."

Sarah flashed a brief smile that lasted less than a second.

"I Googled you before I came. I confirmed everything you said about being a reporter and your picture is online. It confirmed everything except the part about the book."

Jake nodded and said, "Yes, the book is a new idea. I have a friend close to the case, and she's convinced Gary Thomas is innocent. I've done enough investigation to have my own suspicions. My research led me to you."

Sarah contemplated Jake as she stirred her coffee over and over.

"Who's your friend?"

Jake smiled inwardly. Sarah may be a paralegal, but her inquisitive mind and suspicious nature qualified her to be a lawyer. He said, "I'm not at liberty to tell you that right now."

Sarah hesitated for a moment as she picked up her cup, blew on the coffee, and sipped. She cast another scan over her shoulder before she asked, "What do you want to know?"

Jake leaned forward to bring Sarah into his confidence.

"I know it was approximately three years ago when all this happened, but I understand the police interviewed you and other members of the staff and you divulged that something in the office concerned Matt. I understand the police found the gun around that time and didn't pursue the conversation."

Sarah nodded. "Yes, it scared me. I was happy the police never asked me more about it. I just let it drop. Whatever concerned Matt wasn't really my business. I had my first job as a paralegal, I liked the firm and the people, and I wanted to keep working there. It surprised me that the police didn't ask more questions, but I was so relieved. Then, when I read during the trial about the gun with Mr. Thomas's fingerprints, I thought it was over. Now you're saying it's not."

"I don't know for certain." Jake urged her to continue. "Tell me what Matt told you. It will help with my research. I'll take notes if you don't mind." He pulled his notepad and pen from his jacket pocket.

Sarah's chest rose and fell as she took a deep breath and exhaled slowly. A frown creased her forehead.

"I know I'm going to regret this, but I suppose I should tell someone. Matt told me he stumbled across some unusual activity in one of the trust funds. He found a discrepancy in a client's fund. Transactions in and out of the fund without substantiating documentation. Matt brought it to Mr. Cambridge's attention, and he said they invested the money. But Matt said the wording of the fund specifically prohibited investment at the request of the client. The client was nervous about financial markets and wanted his money left in the account."

Jake listened calmly as Sarah continued.

"Matt said he reminded Mr. Cambridge about the terms of the fund, and Ryan said it had to be an administrative error, that he would look after it. Matt became obsessed, and he said he and Mr. Cambridge had words about it. He didn't believe it could have been an administrative error, and he didn't see any evidence anyone corrected the error if that's what it was. I told him to leave it alone, but he wouldn't let it go. He started staying late after everyone left. He said he found more discrepancies." Sarah sniffed and retrieved her handbag from the seat beside her. She rummaged around inside until she found a tissue and dabbed her eyes.

Jake studied her as she composed herself. She was visibly distraught at telling her story. He waited for her to continue.

Sarah pushed the coffee cup forward and folded her hands together on the table with the tissue clasped tightly between her fingers. She glanced around again before uttering, "I did nothing. I should have gone to the police. Or tried harder to convince Matt to stop what he was doing, but he was so determined to find something wrong. When he said that Mr. Cambridge called it an administrative error, if it had been me, I would have accepted that and moved on. But Matt didn't. I feel so guilty that I didn't do more. The murders happened a few days later."

Jake said, "Sarah, do you know if Matt confronted Ryan Cambridge about it more than once?"

Sarah nodded, dabbing at her eyes repeatedly. "I think so, just before the murders."

Jake jotted notes on his pad. He said, "I understand that Gary Thomas came to the office one day. Were you there?"

Sarah nodded again, her red eyes downcast and her mouth quivering. "Yes, it was horrible. I heard Mr. Thomas yelling, but I couldn't make out everything he said. I was in the coffee room, so I didn't hear the whole thing, but others in the bullpen said he was beside himself. They said he looked like he would have killed Matt. His eyes were bulging, and his veins were popping. They could smell alcohol. He was yelling about Matt trying to steal his wife and that he would kill them both if he ever caught them together. Some of my colleagues had to testify at the trial. When the police found out I heard nothing directly, they didn't ask me any more questions."

Sarah looked spent. Telling the story exhausted her. It certainly appeared that Ryan Cambridge might be hiding something, and Dani's assertions about the visits to the casino cast more suspicion on his activities. Jake closed his notepad and shoved it back in his pocket. He patted Sarah's hand and asked if she was okay.

She nodded and looked up, saying, "I'm sorry, Mr. Scott. It's hard reliving everything that happened. I've tried to put everything behind me, but I'm not great at doing that."

Jake thanked her for her time and attempted to make her feel better. "It sounds like you couldn't bring yourself to get more involved. I've just had that discussion with myself recently and it's a hard decision. If you feel you made a mistake a few years ago, I think you can be proud of yourself for telling your story now. If we can satisfy ourselves once and for all of Gary Thomas's guilt or innocence, we can all put it behind us and rest easier. The prints on the gun certainly point to his guilt. Thank you very much for your time, Sarah. I appreciate it."

He watched the young woman gather her things. When she stood and strode to the door, she didn't appear to be the nervous person who walked in. Her posture was erect, her stride confident, as she stepped through the door into the night. Jake sensed he didn't yet know the woman he just met.

He ordered another coffee at the counter and sat at the table, flipping through his notes. He had questions about Sarah Brown. A side note he scratched on the page during the conversation shouted back at him. "Crush??"

He added lines to his notes.

Is Sarah Brown hiding something?

Was she in love with Matt Pawsloski while he was having an affair with Melissa Thomas?

Was Ryan Cambridge stealing from the trust funds?

Did Melissa have enemies?

Could Sarah have killed Melissa and Matthew? Or hired someone to do it?

Jake didn't have answers to any of the questions. One thing was certain, though. Gary Thomas may not have been the only one with a motive for murdering Matthew Pawsloski.

CHAPTER TWENTY-ONE

THE WIND BUFFETED the freshly falling snow as Jake drove home, and it danced through the beam cast by the car's headlights. While his lights tried valiantly to pierce the white blanket, the distance he could see was rapidly diminishing. When he left the restaurant, the outside temperature was just warm enough to melt the snowflakes when they landed. Now, it was borderline freezing rain. As he slowly navigated the slippery street, a glance at the car's thermometer convinced Jake the outside temperature had plummeted five degrees. The snow turning to tapioca-like pellets confirmed it. He was happy to be going home.

He weighed his conversation with Sarah, tossing around possible next moves in his head. Sarah's apparent feelings for Matt were intriguing. He wanted to speak with others at Sarah's workplace to confirm his suspicions, but how to do that without raising Ryan's suspicions? He wanted to pursue the trust fund angle, too. Ideally, accountants should investigate it, but even Dani couldn't request a forensic audit. And why hadn't Gary's friend Damon Brooks called back?

Cars slithered to a stop at the red light ahead as the weather deteriorated. Jake thanked the winter tires he put on each year as his car slowed well back of the vehicle ahead. As he stopped, he decided to check Ryan's firm's website again when he got home. He planned to identify other people at the firm and contact them. If Ryan found out, Jake decided he would confront him, but he hoped it didn't come to that. Not yet.

The row of cars started again, and as he approached a park near his home, he noticed a startling sight through the barren trees. His headlights reflected on something as he turned the corner. Any faster and he would have missed the lone figure hunched over on a bench. For a moment Jake thought the individual was a drifter and concern swept over him, leaving a dull ache in his stomach. Nobody should be sitting outside as the temperature plunged, and the snow accumulated. But the troubled feeling turned the ache to churning in the pit of his stomach. The small person on the bench in a snow-covered toque had an unsettling familiarity.

Jake slowed his car and stared at the figure to confirm his fears. A horn blared, and a car swept around him, too fast for the conditions. The angry driver's mouth moved rapidly as he shot a single finger into the air. Jake barely noticed.

No, it can't be. But it was. The person on the bench was Dani's daughter, Emilie. Jake was sure of it. *Why would she be sitting on a bench in the middle of winter?* He had seen the way she dressed. She probably wore scarcely enough clothing to keep her warm on a summer evening. He pulled onto a side street and located a parking spot between two cars. He didn't bother buying a ticket to allow him to park there; this was too serious. He held his arms out like airplane wings for balance as he slipped and slid on the snow-covered icy sidewalk, rounded the corner, and peered through the white curtain to see that the figure hadn't moved. Ice pellets battered his face and bit his skin like a swarm of black flies at a picnic as he rushed to the park.

She's going to freeze out here with what she's wearing! I hope she's okay.

He dug deep for breath when he reached her. Blood rushed in his ears and his heart hammered against his chest from the exertion. Any doubt left his mind as he approached the girl. It was Emilie. Thankfully, she was wearing a heavier coat and toque, not the same light jacket she wore when he saw her last, but she had only running shoes and no gloves. Bare pink skin peeked through the rips in her jeans. Leaning to see her face and gulping for breath, he touched her shoulder. He could see tracks of ice crystals where tears had dripped on her cheeks. Her body quivered in the cold.

"Emilie, it's Jake, are you okay?"

The girl said nothing, but after a few seconds, a barely perceptible nod.

Still bending over, Jake pointed to a space beside her. He said, "Mind if I sit?" He thought he had to before he collapsed.

Silence again, but Emilie slowly shifted her body slightly and Jake took it as consent.

As he brushed snow off the empty spot and sat, Jake said, "I don't know about you, but I'm getting a little chilly. I'm pretty sure Oliver and I have some hot chocolate and marshmallows at the house we would willingly share. If someone doesn't help me drink it, it could last a lifetime. Interested in helping me with this problem?" He draped his arm around the girl, drawing her close to share his body heat.

Emilie bit her lip. The cold bench vibrated as her entire body trembled. She sat on her bare hands. She said, "Go. Away."

Jake tried again. "C'mon, Em. You can't sit here in the cold. You'll freeze stiff in less than an hour. Let's go, sweetheart."

Maybe she hadn't heard.

Distressing seconds passed until her trembling lips moved. Jake had to lean closer to understand. He asked her to repeat it. The rapidly dropping temperature chilled him to the bone, and as she spoke louder, her deliberate words alarmed him even more.

"I. don't. care. Go away."

Jake removed his coat and draped it over Emilie's trembling shoulders. He felt his tight muscles instantly stiffen even more at the frigid temperatures.

"Well, at least we can freeze to death together."

He pulled her close again and heard no objection. The wet, hard snow, heavier now, continued to fall, covering them in a thin white veneer.

His gesture of giving up the coat and his offer to stay seemed to have an immediate effect on the teenager. She hesitated for a moment until a frown furrowed her forehead and she turned her head to face Jake. He could hear the clicking of her teeth as she pulled the coat tightly around her shaking body. Snow and ice crystals clung to her toque, shoulders, and thin eyebrows. She clenched her teeth so hard Jake thought they might shatter. The frozen tears glistened on her face.

Relief washed over Jake as he heard her mumble through quavering blue lips, "Okay."

Jake exhaled slowly through his own clenched teeth as the wind picked up and seemed to sail right through him like he was vapor. Large jewel-studded snowflakes replaced the ice pellets, but the cold bit into him. *What was going on with Emilie?* Obviously, she was troubled, and he needed to help. Any thoughts of Gary Thomas vanished, at least for now.

Jake stood and held out his hand to pull Emilie to her feet. She withdrew her shaking hands from beneath her legs and accepted his. Her hands felt like death. She rose stiffly, and Jake wrapped his arm around her shoulder again as he led the way to his car. Emilie walked deliberately, her movements slowed by sitting in the cold for who knows how long. A car slowed, the driver staring at the pair walking sluggishly across the park.

Jake wondered what could have prompted her to be there. What would have happened if he hadn't come along? Would she be a statistic in the morning's news? Was the girl taking drugs? And where was Dani? She must be frantic.

When the pair arrived at the car, Jake started it and cranked the heat to high. Emilie had said nothing more, and he left her in the car with the heat running while he scraped the ice and snow off the windows. He scraped a hole barely large enough to peer through, even though he often complained at the breakfast gatherings about drivers who didn't clean their windows properly.

Time was of the essence. For both of them.

It took Jake ten minutes to drive to his house and park the car. He noticed Emilie staring at the radio as classic rock blared from the station that he tuned it to on the drive to visit Gary Thomas. From her expression, he guessed the music was utterly foreign to her, so he turned the radio down. His speed would have rivaled Dani's driving if it hadn't been for the icy conditions and slow traffic and, yes, his lack of driving skills compared to hers. Emilie sat shivering beside him, but at least her teeth had stopped chattering. Warm air finally blasted from the heater, and that helped to slow Jake's own trembling. And return feeling to his numb feet.

As if he had a sixth sense, Oliver greeted them promptly when they entered the house. Emilie shrugged off the oversize coat, handed it to Jake, and bent to pet the cat. Jake removed his boots and the remaining winter gear and hastened to the sunroom to turn on the gas fireplace. He suggested to Emilie that she should take a hot shower, but she declined, choosing instead to sit on the floor in front of the fire with Oliver folded in her arms.

Emilie complained her nose was on fire and upon closer examination, Jake realized from the whiteness of the surrounding skin she had mild frostbite. He hustled to the kitchen where he warmed a cloth with water from the tap. He wrung out the cloth and hurried back to the sunroom where he told Emilie to hold it on her nose. Jake pulled a blanket with the Ottawa Senators' logo on it from his recliner and draped it around Emilie's shoulders. Then he strode back to the kitchen where he filled the kettle and turned it on. As he did so, he marveled that Oliver allowed Emilie to pick him up. He usually dictated the terms. Jake thought the cat sensed something was wrong as he had nestled as close to Emilie as he could, sharing his body heat with her.

Jake peered around the corner to see Emilie with the cloth over her nose. She and Oliver stared at the flames dancing in the fireplace as if of one thought, comfortable in each other's presence. He thought he must have found her soon after she sat on the bench, as she didn't seem to be suffering from hyperthermia and was warming quickly. Maybe he should try to encourage Emilie to talk before calling her mom. He recalled when his daughter had teenage problems, it was usually mom to the rescue. It had been so long since Avery was a teenager, Jake wasn't sure he could deal with this.

Oliver seemed to handle it just fine.

Jake found an old cardigan in the closet and pulled it on. He poured extra marshmallows into Emilie's hot chocolate and carried the two cups into the sunroom where she still cuddled with

Oliver. The cat's patience with her was incredible. Jake didn't think he had seen the cat so content since his wife died. He handed Emilie her cup, and she sat cross-legged on the floor with Oliver nestled on her lap. The cat's eyes closed.

Emilie dabbed at her marshmallows with one finger and Jake blew on his hot chocolate as he observed her over his cup. Finally, he said, "Are you feeling warmer? It was getting pretty cold out there."

Emilie nodded and said, "Yeah, thanks for the coat."

Jake wanted her to talk, to make sure she was okay, and he wondered if she might share her problems with him easier than with her mom, even though previous conversations had not gone well. His conscience wouldn't just let it go without at least trying. He knew he was diving into the deep end without a life jacket. Dammit, conscience!

"Uh, must be pretty serious for you to sit in the cold like that."

Emilie removed the cloth, insisting her nose felt better, and handed it to Jake. She put her head down again as she continued to poke at her marshmallows, watching them dance on the steaming liquid. She said, "I had a big fight with my dad. He introduced me to his girlfriend and told me they're engaged. I didn't even know he had a girlfriend and now they're getting married. I'm supposed to be happy for him. They ignored me the rest of the time I was there. She seemed to think I was the one who shouldn't be there. She as much as told me that. I asked my dad why he didn't tell me, and he said he wanted to be sure before saying anything. I told him I thought I was important to him and he gave me some bullshit about how I was important, but there was someone else in his life now who was also important. I told him he's an asshole and walked to my mom's place. Even if she's working, I know she cares. She calls all the time to find out what

I'm doing and asks about my day." Emilie sniffed. "At least I feel welcome there. How old does a kid have to be to choose which parent to live with, anyway?"

Oh boy, Jake thought, although he was relieved that she was talking. He knew there is no age limit in Ontario from a newspaper article he had written. It's whatever is in the best interest of the child, but he treated the question as rhetorical and said, "Does your mom know where you are?"

"I pressed the buzzer at her condo, but there was no answer. She's probably working. I sat in the lobby, but then I got another call. It was the guy I really like telling me about this amazing girl he met, and that he wanted to go out with her." Her voice rose. "Seems like all men are assholes. He said he's going with Alicia now."

Oliver woke up, stretched, and rubbed against Emilie, his tail brushing her face as she wailed, *"She was my best friend."* Through the sobs, Emilie said, "They're all. . ." Jake couldn't quite make out the distorted words, but he was sure they were an adjective and a noun that she shouldn't use in polite company and especially in front of her mother.

It had been a long time since he had dealt with teenage angst over a lost boyfriend. That hurricane of emotions, added to the revelation there was someone else competing for Emilie's attention with her dad, would not be easy to deal with. Only one solution came to mind.

It was time to turn this problem over to Dani.

CHAPTER TWENTY-TWO

BEFORE HE MADE the call, Jake pulled a chair closer to Emilie and rested a comforting hand on her shoulder. Oliver did his bit by continuing to rub against the girl's chest, demanding her attention. He purred dramatically to ensure she noticed.

In a low voice, as if a third person was in the house, Jake said, "I have to call your mother, Em. She needs to know where you are."

Emilie stared at the flames flickering in the fireplace. Then she noticed the picture of Jake and his wife. Her crying had subsided to a whimper and a few sniffles. Jake handed her another tissue from a box beside the chair as she said, "I know. Don't tell her everything, okay? Is that your wife?"

"Yes, we sailed on a Caribbean cruise not long before she died. We had a great time, and I'm really glad I have that memory."

"How long were you married?"

Jake wasn't sure if this newfound curiosity was a ploy to keep him from calling Dani or if she was really interested.

"29 wonderful years."

"Holy shit, that's a long time. How did you find someone like that? It sure didn't work for my mom and dad. It hasn't worked for most of my classmates' parents." Her voice lowered, and her bottom lip trembled. "Obviously, it hasn't worked for me."

"Well, sweetheart, sometimes people discover they just can't get along even when they're married. Marriage is work and nobody gets along all the time. Sometimes, people become better friends when they're apart than when they're together. My wife and I married when we were in our late twenties. Remember, you're 16 years old. You have plenty of time to meet the right man and believe me, he's out there somewhere. You should also remember that no one is perfect. We all have flaws; we all do stupid things sometimes. You'll know when the right guy comes along, and you can live with each other's imperfections. In the meantime, enjoy your life. I try to treat every day as a good one, even though occasionally, something makes me sad.

"There's one positive thing you can take from this. Your boyfriend had the courage to tell you; he didn't sneak around behind your back. Now, my dear, I have to call your mom." Jake thought he had done okay with his speech and left well enough alone. He fished in his pocket for his phone.

"You mean like my dad?"

Jake gulped, assuming she was referring to her dad's new girlfriend. He prepared to dial, pretending he hadn't heard.

Emilie shook her head as her fingers probed the bottom of her cup, searching out a remaining marshmallow.

"I saw him with another woman before he and my mom divorced. He told mom he left because she worked all the time, but my dad liked other women." She sighed and said, "I guess he's always been a shithead."

Jake pondered this latest revelation.

He said, "Have you ever talked to your mom about this? She feels guilty because she thinks it was her work that caused the breakup. It might help her if you told her there might have been another reason."

Emilie loudly sipped the last of her hot chocolate. She pulled the cup away, leaving a brown mustache on her upper lip that she licked off. She shrugged the blanket off her shoulders and asked, "Do you have more hot chocolate? And can you give mom the recipe? Oh, and Jake, please don't tell her where you found me. She'll have a shit fit."

Jake sighed as he rose from his chair and walked to the kitchen, out of Emilie's earshot. At least the girl was talking, although he probably would have shoved a bar of soap in his own daughter's mouth if she used the language that rolled off Em's tongue so easily. It was probably common language among her friends, but he just considered it laziness to fill in cracks in a vocabulary. Maybe he really was getting old. He hoped he handled the situation well, but he had no way of knowing. Besides, it wasn't his business. If Emilie needed someone to talk to and if he could help somehow, he would happily spend all the time she needed. Right now, the girl needed her mom.

He called Dani, who picked up on the first ring, cheerful as ever, and completely oblivious to everything that had happened.

"Hi Jake. I only have a minute. I'm at work, but it's nice to hear from you. What's up? How did it go with Sarah Brown?"

Jake ignored the question about Sarah. He eased into telling Dani about her daughter. "Dani, Emilie is here. I spotted her on my way back from meeting with Sarah. You weren't home when she buzzed up to your condo, so she agreed to come back to my place. We're having some hot chocolate, and Oliver is taking good care of her, but she's having a bit of a crisis."

Dani's voice registered some worry. "Okay. What kind of crisis?"

"The first thing is, the new guy she liked told her he's dumping her and going out with her best friend."

Dani snickered and said, "I can see how that could seem like a world-shattering event, but she'll recover. Something similar happened to me when I was her age, and I cried for a week. I ended up with better friends and a definite upgrade on the boyfriend. You had a daughter, so you know that teenagers, and especially girls, can be just a tad emotional. I'll talk to her when I'm done with my shift."

Jake plowed ahead. "There's something else you should know, Dani. Your ex introduced his girlfriend to Emilie and told her they are engaged. Emilie said she feels abandoned by her dad and it sounds like they ignored her after breaking the news. She said at least you pay attention to her."

Dead air hung in the phone's earpiece. Then, "Thanks for telling me. I tried to tell her about the girlfriend, but she wouldn't believe me. I'm going to get someone to cover for me and come home. Do you want me to pick her up or will I meet you at my place?"

"I don't mind driving her home. You two need some time alone." Jake hesitated before lowering his voice. A peek around the corner revealed Emilie lying on her back, her eyes closed. "There's something else I'm not supposed to tell you, but you need to know. I found Emilie on a bench in the park, dressed the way she usually is, and the wind was howling. Her teeth were chattering when I found her, and her nose is a little frostbitten. It took some coaxing to convince her to leave, so I'm glad I arrived when I did." Jake hesitated before adding, "I think she would have been in considerable difficulty if I hadn't shown up. It was pure luck that I saw her."

Dani gasped. "Oh my God. Are you serious? Is she okay now?"

"Yes, we've been chatting. She's more talkative than I've ever seen her, but I think she would like to see you. We'll meet you at your place in about half an hour."

CHAPTER TWENTY-THREE

JAKE THOUGHT DANI would have no interest in discussing the case when they arrived at her place. After she checked Emilie's frostbite, her exhausted daughter announced she was going to take a shower and go straight to bed. While they waited, Jake detailed the night's events, and when Emilie emerged from the shower, Dani asked him if he had more time. When he nodded, she followed her daughter into her bedroom.

She called out, "There's a bottle of wine in the fridge. Hope you like white. You wouldn't like to pour a couple of glasses, would you?"

Jake said, "Sure," and stood up from the kitchen stool. He splashed the wine into two glasses he found in the cupboard and sat at the counter again until he heard bare feet padding down the hall. Emilie popped her head around the corner, trying extremely hard to make sure Jake didn't see her pajamas as her weary eyes sought his. She mumbled, "Thanks again for the coat and hot chocolate," before her dimpled cheeks melted in an embarrassed grin and she turned on her heel to go back to her room. She was a great kid that some bad things happened to, Jake thought, but he was content in knowing a mother-daughter discussion was about to take place.

He wandered into the living room, where he set the glasses on a coffee table. The condo was a large two-bedroom facing north. He glanced through the window but saw only yellow-tinged streetlights through the swirling icy snow. The Ottawa River and Gatineau Hills were out there some place, and he thought as he ambled back to the sofa that the view must be spectacular in the daylight. A long bookcase along one wall captured his eye. Someone altered the shelves to hold vinyl, and they sagged under the weight of an impressive collection of blues and jazz recordings. A turntable sat on top.

Dani eventually emerged wearing pink cuffed hip-hugging sweatpants and an oversized white tee shirt. Her hair spilled to her shoulders, and her feet were bare. She slumped on the leather sofa close to where Jake sat, picked up her wine glass, and clinked his in a toast.

"I don't know what we're toasting, but let's choose something positive."

Jake thought she looked tired but amazing. He said, "Here's to the first drink of the day. How's Emilie?"

The tension drained from Dani's face as it stretched in a tired smile, her eyes sparkling.

"That works for me. She's out for the count. I'm so glad you came along when you did. She said she couldn't move from the bench. She wanted to, but she was so cold and stiff, she had trouble moving. I think you have a new fan. She couldn't stop talking about how you gave her your coat. She's pretty mad at her dad and ex-boyfriend or whatever he was. We'll have conversations about that over the coming days. She wants to move in here, but I'll talk to her dad. She's at an impressionable age and she needs him, even if he is a jerk sometimes. We'll work something out. Thanks for looking after her; I owe you for that."

"You're an exceptional mother, Dani. I'm happy to know you better, and I'm getting to know your daughter. What I did was nothing. Once we got to my place, Oliver, the emotional support cat, took over. He realized something was amiss and paid more attention to her than he's ever paid to me." Jake chuckled and said, "I'm glad he did because it took the load off me. It's been a long time since I've dealt with a teenage girl and, I admit, I sweated bullets for a while. She's welcome to come over any time you're stuck at work, though."

He sipped the wine, enjoying the smooth taste as it slithered down his throat.

Dani flashed her beautiful smile. She said, "Oh, I couldn't let you do that. You already did a lot more than you're letting on, Jake Scott, and I'll be forever grateful." She leaned to the side to reach a sketchbook from the coffee table. She lowered her voice to barely above a whisper. "Don't tell Emilie I showed you these but look. I'm biased, but I think the kid has talent."

Jake set his glass down so he could page through the large pad. It was full of drawings of elaborate monsters, lifelike young women, and incredibly detailed animals. The sketches were multi-dimensional with shadows drawn with different pencils. Jake became more impressed with each turn of the page.

"I'll say she has talent. I'm sure you're encouraging her." He stopped at a drawing of a male lion stalking off the page from the jungle. "Look at this!"

"I know, that's one of my favorites. Ask her to show you her sketches sometime and when she does, pretend you haven't seen them. I'm so proud of her. She's a good kid going through a rough time, but she'll be stronger in the end." Then Dani abruptly changed the subject. "Are you going to the breakfast tomorrow?"

"Tomorrow? Is tomorrow Saturday already? Man, the week flew by. Yes, I want to go. I'm planning to tell everyone about the book I'm writing and the progress, or lack thereof, so far. I want to see Ryan's reaction."

"Are you sure you should do that? If he's involved in this, you could put yourself at risk."

"Dani, it's the only way I can think of to move this forward. We can't get in to look at the firm's books. Damon Brooks hasn't called me. So far, it's like biting into cotton candy. You take a bite, and it vaporizes in your mouth. Maybe I can flush Ryan out a little by talking about it. By the way, I got the sense Sarah Brown had an interest in Matthew Pawsloski for more than his suspicions about the firm's trust fund accounting. She seemed extra distraught over his murder. I could be completely wrong, but I think she wanted a relationship with him that wasn't reciprocated."

Dani's dark eyes widened as she stared at Jake.

"Now that's interesting and something that wasn't considered. What else did Sarah say?"

Jake recounted his meeting with the paralegal, and they concluded they were taking baby steps in the case. Dani offered more wine, but Jake regretfully declined as the tapping on the window reminded him of the ice pellets still coming down. It was time to go.

As they rose from the couch, Dani followed Jake to the door. She watched him pull on his boots, coat, and scarf, and when he finished, she smiled and grabbed his hand. The hall light reflected in her dark eyes.

"Seriously, Jake, thank you so much for what you did for Emilie. I don't know what would have happened if you hadn't come along and handing over your coat in this weather just goes way beyond. Please promise me you'll be discreet with Ryan. I don't want to see anything happen to you."

The touch traveled Jake's body from his toes to the top of his head like an electric shock. Jake promised he would be careful and as he left, he wondered if something was happening between him and Dani. He hadn't felt such emotions since Mia. He was giddy as he scraped the snow and ice off his car in the guest parking spot. This had been quite the day. He had to admit life had suddenly become considerably less boring.

CHAPTER TWENTY-FOUR

SOON AFTER ARRIVING home from Dani's place after the treacherous drive on the icy streets, Jake poured a Scotch and documented his conversation with Sarah Brown. Oliver received a treat and extra attention for being Jake's backup with Emilie. Or, Jake considered as he scratched the cat's ears, he was Oliver's. The jury was still out on that one. He finished his drink and fell into a restful sleep.

The next morning, he woke invigorated, showered, dressed, and checked his email for the regular Saturday morning reminder. Eric, punctual as ever, made sure the usual attendees didn't forget and suggested they should be careful with the icy conditions. It occurred to Jake that everyone should be capable of reminding themselves of the weekly event. Even *he* had the technology now to set up a weekly reminder. He replied to everyone that he planned to be there.

Jake thought of calling Dani to inquire about Emilie, but he realized they might still be sleeping. He took his time on the way to the restaurant, half walking and half sliding on the slippery sidewalks, making sure not to lose his balance. A broken arm from a fall would seriously impede his book writing. The sun reflected off the diamond-like ice crystals wrapped around branches and dripping from shrubs, creating picture-perfect scenery. There was a certain beauty in the hazardous surroundings.

A glance through the window when he arrived told him everyone was there except Dani. They greeted him as he arrived at the table and removed his coat and mask. He waved at Jason, who motioned to a cinnamon roll with his chin and grinned. Jake twisted his face into an unpleasant expression and waved his hand to decline the tasty treat. Jason shrugged and poured steaming coffee into a mug.

Jake said, "How's it going, boys? Everyone happy with the freezing rain last night?" He played innocent. "Where's Dani? Uh, Danielle?" He inhaled at the slip-up.

Eric Jacobson replied, "No Danielle today. She's working. The freezing rain sucks. We all live here to enjoy the summer and survive the winter. Freezing rain is just Mother Nature's reminder that there's no such place as paradise, although it's close."

Ryan said, "Hey, I like winter. C'mom, guys. Embrace it. Get out and play hockey. Ski. Skate on the canal. Look how pretty it looks outside. Who could ask for more than that?"

The others nodded with varying degrees of enthusiasm. Pierre Chevrier grunted.

Jason brought Jake's coffee and Pierre said, "Don't you want a yogurt parfait or maybe a fruit bowl to go with the café, huh Jake? Tabernacle!" Chevrier grinned after using the popular French cuss word and glanced around the table, seeking support for his sarcasm. None was forthcoming.

The conversation carried on as the men ticked off their list of usual grievances, criticizing the mayor for the lack of snow removal, the provincial premier for the slow vaccine rollout, and the country's prime minister for everything else. The local hockey team took a beating, Pierre touted the week's win for the Montreal Canadiens, and they all agreed that professional athletes made too much money. Jake pointed out that no one at the table would turn down the contracts offered to players, and the blame should fall on the rich owners, the corporations buying advertising, TV stations paying to televise the games, and the fans willing to pay exorbitant prices. Viewpoints would remain unchanged, and the topic would rest near the top of the weekly discussion list until the end of time.

A lull in the conversation descended on the table until the question Jake had been waiting for came from Eric Jacobson.

"How's the book writing coming along, Jake?"

Pierre Chevrier jumped in before Jake responded. "What's the title, Jake? See Spot Run, *non*?"

Jake wondered again why someone invited this guy, but rewarded Chevrier with a chuckle and said, "I think somebody already used that title, Pierre. You should Google it."

Now was his chance to watch Ryan's reaction. He said, "I'm working at it. I interviewed Gary Thomas. He doesn't seem like the type who would commit a double homicide, but who really knows, right? He swears he's innocent. I'm doing more research."

Jake glanced at Ryan as Jason arrived, coffee pot in hand, for the refills everyone anxiously awaited. Jake leaned aside as Jason refilled his cup and said, "I also spoke with Sarah Brown from your office, Ryan. I got the impression she had a crush on Matt Pawsloski. It didn't seem like he had any interest, though. I got the sense the two of them talked often."

Jason completed filling the cups before drifting away, back behind his counter.

Ryan straightened in his chair at the news and redness rose from his sweater collar to where his hair met his forehead. His face grew deadly serious as he drew figure eights on his napkin with the handle of his spoon. He stared at his handiwork as he said, "I hadn't heard you were pursuing this, Jake. I guess I missed the last breakfast. You don't seem to be making much progress. Are you sure this is the book you want to write?"

Jake wondered if that was a thinly veiled threat or was his imagination playing tricks on him? He pushed a little further.

"I have nothing but time, Ryan. There are lots of avenues I want to flesh out and I'll switch to something else if it turns out I'm getting nowhere. I just think Gary Thomas is innocent, and somebody needs to help him."

The others watched silently as the drama unfolded. The circles on Ryan's napkin grew more rapid, ragged edges appearing in the fragile tissue. He said, "You mean you actually went to the prison to talk to Thomas?"

"Yup, that was quite the experience. Just getting clearance is a challenge. I've been to the Innes Road Detention Centre to interview gang members, but Millhaven is on another level. Gary Thomas is a very convincing soft-spoken man. Not enough for the jury, I guess, but it seems other evidence offset everything that could have helped him at the trial."

Ryan said, "Yeah, he's soft spoken until he gets angry and has a few drinks, apparently. From what I read about him, he has two personalities and the other one showed up that day he came into our office threatening to kill Matthew and his girlfriend. They found his fingerprints on the murder weapon. I think your book is going to be short, Jake. What about Danielle? I'm sure the police closed this file."

Now *who* was fishing? This was turning into a dance.

Jake nodded and said, "Yes, I spoke with her and that's what she said. Her boss considers the case closed, so she can't do anything. He's tied her hands."

Jason returned and stood behind Jake, waiting to hand him the machine to pay the bill. As Jake took the machine and tapped his card, he said, "As far as I know, I'm the only one who is pursuing the case. I could be out to lunch here, but there just seems to be something that everyone may have missed. As I said, I've got nothing but time on my hands and I'm kind of enjoying this. I plan to continue to see where it goes."

Eric rose to put on his coat.

He said, "Well gents, I'll see you next week. I have a rehearsal to go to. We're working on an original song if you can believe it. The new guitar player and I wrote it. It's sounding good if I say so myself."

Everyone congratulated Eric as they walked single file to the door. Pierre tried to make fun of the band, but no one listened. As they parted company outside, Ryan nudged Jake. He said, "You're wasting your time, Jake. That case was all about a love triangle, nothing more. And it was a triangle involving Gary, his wife, and Matthew, not Sarah Brown. Find another subject to write about." He shoved his hands deep in his pockets, yanked his toque down over his ears, and stomped down the street, leaving Jake more determined than ever to sort this out.

CHAPTER TWENTY-FIVE

BUTTERFLIES LAUNCHED BY his impending gym visit flitted merrily in Jake's stomach as he chatted with Avery on the phone. As he drove to the gym after the call, the ice had melted in the warming sunshine, making the street navigation much smoother. His trainer greeted him with a full grin and immediately put him to work, confirming his concern was legitimate. He emitted embarrassing groans as she ensured he stretched every muscle beyond the limits imaginable. It was another reminder of the sad shape he was in. At the end, they discussed his weekly food and drink intake and she castigated him for the sweets but reminded him with a grin he could reward himself occasionally.

After recovering with his head between his knees in the change room for a few minutes, he dressed and returned to his house where he stood longer than usual in a hot shower. At least the trainer was gentle on his arthritic knee. As he emerged and toweled himself, he wondered if he would feel the pain in one, two, or three days. His trainer told him it works differently for people. Jake decided he was in no hurry to find out. He checked his body in the mirror. Nope, no difference yet, he thought with a sigh. Of course, he had only attended one full session. Improving his health would be a marathon, not a sprint.

He dressed and was pouring fresh litter into Oliver's box when the phone rang. Damon Brooks, maybe? No, Dani's name came up on the screen. He was still curious about what happened to Brooks as he answered. He reminded himself to call again when he finished speaking with Dani.

"Hi Dani. I thought you would still be working. It's great to hear from you."

"Hi yourself. I took leave this afternoon to spend some time with Emilie. You made it home okay last night?"

"It was a little treacherous coming home, but it was worth it. How's Emilie?"

"Oh, she's doing fine. We have some things to talk through but all in time. Besides, it gave you and I some time to get to know each other a little better."

Jake said, "I enjoyed our time together. You're so easy to talk to, Dani. I could have spent the night, uh, I mean talked all night." Jake fidgeted in his chair, and if he could have seen himself in the mirror, a crimson red face would have grimaced back. He heard Dani snicker at his clumsy turn of phrase as he sought to recover.

"I enjoyed breakfast as usual. Talked about the book, and Ryan seemed tense when I mentioned speaking with Sarah. He strongly suggested I consider writing about something else."

"Huh, that's interesting. Maybe we're on the right track, but that's not why I'm calling. Let's take a break from the case if you're up for it. You mentioned you wanted to shop for clothes. Emilie and I are going to Bayshore this afternoon for a little shopping therapy. Interested in joining us?"

Jake had that feeling of interrupting family time for Dani and Emilie. After last night's event, they needed it.

"That would be fun, although I have to warn you, I may be a little slow. I had a session with my trainer a while ago. She nearly killed me. I think I should sit this one out and lick my wounds."

Dani laughed and said, "I'm sure you'll live. We both want you to join us. We'll pick you up in half an hour."

That removed the decision from Jake's hands. He changed into his khaki pants and an old black cable-knit sweater his wife had given him for Christmas many years ago. He examined himself in the mirror and thought the sweater might soon celebrate its tenth birthday. It was like an old friend with whom he was comfortable. A new one would signal the death knell for his old pal. On some level, it would sadden him to see it go. A glance at his watch told him he had sufficient time to call Damon Brooks, which he did with, once again, no response.

He tugged on his coat and checked his pocket for a mask just as Dani and Emilie pulled into the driveway. Although masks were now just a recommendation in public spaces, Jake preferred to be cautious. Despite the vaccines, there was still concern about a pandemic resurgence.

Jake climbed into the back seat of Dani's car and greeted her and Emilie. He pulled on his seatbelt and tapped Emilie on the shoulder. Her dimples deepened with a smile. She seemed excited about the excursion. Dani wheeled the car to the shopping center in expert fashion and at breakneck speed. Jake thought he would offer to drive next time.

The shopping center was a multi-level structure in Ottawa's west end. Dani circled the parking lot a few times before finding a spot. Crowds had grown exponentially with people starved to do anything since the decline of the pandemic. Shopping wasn't

Jake's favorite thing, and massive crowds didn't enhance the experience for him. His wife had done most of the shopping. For Jake, shopping meant to get in, buy what you need, and leave. He sensed this trip might be more deliberate.

Once inside, Dani said. "How would it be if we meet in an hour? Emilie and I need to buy some things for her." She gestured to her right. "There's a menswear store and two women here willing to offer opinions. Right, Em?"

Emilie nodded with a wall-to-wall grin. "Oh yeah!" she said.

Dani pointed to the board displaying the list of shops in the mall. She said, "Let's see if there are other men's shops."

As they scrolled through the board, Emilie exclaimed. "Holy Geez. There's a shit ton of women's shops, but I don't see many men's places."

Jake was about to agree when Dani said firmly, "Emilie, language."

Emilie gulped and said, "Sorry, Mom."

Dani turned to Jake, saying, "I'm sorry, Jake. We're working on the swearing thing. Ready to go shopping?"

Jake feigned enthusiasm as he nodded and checked his watch. They settled on meeting in an hour and Jake decided his first stop would be for coffee in the food court. There was no way he could spend an hour shopping. He passed the time people-watching as all shapes, sizes, nationalities, and genders scurried about lugging bags. Pent-up demand and cash brought them out in droves.

When it was finally time to meet, he wandered back to the men's shop and poked around the clothing racks. The section with plain shirts hanging forlornly at reduced prices drew him in. As he casually shuffled through the shirts, paying little attention, he noticed Dani and Emilie both carrying bags from the corner of his eye. But there was something different. Emilie had abandoned the light winter jacket she had been wearing for a heavier brown coat that was long enough to cover her butt and with a fur-lined hood. She clumped along behind her mom in winter boots with a fur-lined collar. The shoelaces remained untied with the boot tops spread wide and the tongue sticking out like the iconic Rolling Stones' logo. Sill, it was a major improvement for winter. Jake decided only to nod his approval rather than make a big deal of it. Emilie rewarded him with a shy smile.

It was clear from the moment they arrived that the two women had other ideas for Jake's wardrobe than plain-colored shirts. Emilie brought two fancy paisley shirts Jake thought would look great on a much younger man in a disco and Dani had him try on snug designer jeans. Jake nearly fainted when he saw the price.

They settled on one brightly colored shirt with muted designs and another that was plain, a fitted navy blazer that Jake thought would look better when he lost a few pounds, the snug designer jeans, and another pair of wool dress pants. When he emerged from the dressing room wearing the jacket, the colored shirt with the two top buttons undone and the jeans, Emilie and Dani simultaneously flashed enthusiastic thumbs up. He thought the gesture looked choreographed, but it felt good. When he went to pay, comments about moths flying out of his wallet came from Dani. Emilie added an image of a spider web sealing it shut. He agreed his credit card hadn't seen such abuse for a long time.

They spent more time in the food court over coffees for Jake and Dani and a Coke for Emilie. The conversation inevitably drifted to the case and Jake asked, "Would you get in trouble if I interview your former partner? I think it's the next logical step."

There was some hesitation on Dani's part before she answered. "I don't know, Jake. I don't know how he'll react. If you talk to him, expect it to be unpleasant. He and I barely tolerated each other in the end. Prepare yourself for pushback. He probably won't speak highly of me either, but that's okay." Dani pulled a card from her purse and handed it to him. It was her partner's card. She said, "Let me know how it goes, okay?"

The conversation turned lighter with Jake asking Emilie about her art without mentioning he had seen her sketchbook. He reminded her he wanted to see it. As they strolled to the car, Jake noticed a piece of paper trapped under the windshield wiper on the passenger side, its edges flapping in the wind. Dani pressed the button on the fob as they drew closer and the doors clicked, signaling they were unlocked. Probably a flyer, Jake thought, but when he retrieved it, he realized it wasn't a professionally prepared poster. It was a note, and he could see typed wording in large black font through the folds. Even though it was on Dani's windshield, he was curious, so he opened it. The words staring at him sent shivers traversing the length of his spine. Emilie was already in the car, but Dani, sensing something amiss, leaned against the open door on the driver's side. He called out as he got in the car. "Look at this."

Concern creased Dani's brow as she slid into the driver's seat. Jake held the paper up and watched her read the threat.

STOP WHAT YOU'RE DOING! GARY THOMAS IS GUILTY! LEAVE IT ALONE!

Dani said, "Well, whoever wrote this obviously loves exclamation points. Do you mind if I hang onto it?"

Emilie's voice rose from the back with alarm. "What is it? Is something wrong?"

Neither immediately replied as Dani started the car, found the exit sign, and raced the vehicle from the parking lot. Jake and Dani contemplated the implications of the note, their thoughts melding into one as they regarded each other. They discussed their mutual conclusions on the drive. Dani went first. "You know what this means. We're on the right track. We've spooked someone."

Jake said, "Me, for one. I have to admit, I'm a little shaken by this because to me, it also means something else. Someone followed us to the shopping center. It's someone who knows us, Dani. Someone who knows I'm looking into the case. They put the note on the passenger side of your car. Could be a coincidence, but it's probably aimed at me. It's someone around that breakfast table. Someone who is convinced Thomas is guilty."

"Could be. Or as I said, it's someone trying to throw us off the scent. It could be someone around the table. Or it could also be Sarah Brown. Or someone else in the office she talked to. Did you leave a detailed message for Damon Brooks? Could be him. I'm not ruling out anybody. But it's time for you to back off, Jake. I'll show this note to the boss and I'm sure he'll let me reopen the investigation."

They still hadn't told Emilie what was going on, so she sat quietly in her seat listening to the conversation unfold.

Jake pulled himself together as they passed Dani's condo. He said, "As a journalist covering street gangs, I had my share of warnings. I heeded them and made sure I didn't take unnecessary risks, but it never once stopped me from pursuing the story. In fact, they gave me more resolve. I'm no hero, Dani, but I'm not stopping now. I won't take unnecessary risks, but I have a story to pursue."

Dani sat in silence the rest of the way. When they reached Jake's house, he thanked Dani and Emilie for the shopping trip and assured them he would wear his new clothes when his old ones wore out. That elicited the expected groans.

Dani grabbed his arm as he got up to leave the car, and her dark eyes zeroed in on his with laser focus. She said, "I'm serious, Jake. Leave it alone. This is a police force matter now."

He nodded without saying a word and carried his packages inside the house where he tossed them on the bed. He pulled the business card out of his pocket and glanced at the name. It would be an interesting discussion with retired Constable Enzo Leblanc. What could it hurt?

CHAPTER TWENTY-SIX

THE CONVERSATION WITH Leblanc did not go smoothly, just as Dani predicted. As soon as Jake mentioned to the former constable who he was and what he was doing, Leblanc hung up. Better people than Leblanc had hung up on Jake Scott during his working life as a reporter. It was merely the opening salvo. Jake found Leblanc's address on Canada 411, got in the car, and drove to his house.

The house was in a suburb of Ottawa called Barrhaven. It was an imposing two-story brick and vinyl siding building with a raised brick garden, a solar lamp, and a tall crab apple tree, all buried by snow to varying degrees on the front lawn. Jake rang the doorbell.

A tall, lean man in bare feet with steel gray hair and wearing blue jeans and a hockey jersey answered the door. Expression lines furrowed Leblanc's forehead and around his eyes, deepened by laughing, frowning, or smiling over the years. Jake suspected, mostly frowning. A scar, lighter than the rest of his complexion, separated the two sides of his chin, and a waxed handlebar mustache curled above his upper lip. He was in his sixties and said nothing; just glared at Jake, waiting for him to announce who he was and why he was standing on the doorstep.

Jake declared his name and said, "We spoke about half an hour ago, but unfortunately, we got disconnected somehow. I thought I would drop in so we could continue our chat."

As Jake suspected, the expression lines creasing Leblanc's face deepened. He said, "What do you want, Scott? I've read your articles in the paper and you're an excellent reporter, but if you're here to talk about Gary Thomas, you're wasting your time. The guy was guilty as hell. All the evidence pointed to him. He was the shooter. It was a clean case." The truncated sentences rolled off his tongue as if rehearsed. He growled, "Unless you want to tell the world how justice prevailed for once, choose another topic. You're just trying to create something out of nothing."

Jake shivered as darkness ushered in a chill. He said, "Thanks for the compliment. I'm retired, now, just like you, Mr. Leblanc. Mind if I come in for a minute? It's freezing out here."

Leblanc stepped back, which Jake took as encouragement to enter, but the former police officer was just giving himself enough clearance to close the door. Jake raised his voice through chattering teeth toward the rapidly narrowing gap in the doorway.

"Wait! Why would Thomas ditch the gun in the bushes? Why not dump it where no one could find it? It makes no sense."

Leblanc pulled the door open again and took a more conciliatory tone, saying, "You won't leave this alone, will you? Okay, come in. I'll answer your questions just so you'll see this is a waste of time. Don't bother taking off your coat. This won't take long. You can set your boots on the mat."

After Jake did as instructed, Leblanc led him into the kitchen and gestured with his thumb to a chair at the table. A lean, gray-haired woman in a white crew-neck sweater and light-colored blue jeans busied herself at the counter. She wore a cheery patterned apron over her clothes.

Leblanc mumbled to her that Jake was writing a book and had questions. She stopped what she was doing, smiled narrowly at Jake, and offered him coffee. When he declined, she handed him a plate of ginger snaps and said, "Take one of these at least. They're fresh out of the oven."

Jake took one and said, "My favorites. Thank you!"

He bit into the cookie and thanked her again as she scurried from the room.

Leblanc's eyes were flint-hard as he began speaking.

"I investigated the case with Constable Danielle Perez. Thomas's prints were all over the gun and only his. We suspect he heard something after the shooting, panicked, and tossed the weapon. Some teenagers were close to where the murders took place, so they might have spooked him."

He repeated slowly like talking to a child, "His fingerprints, and only his were on the gun."

Jake said, "Is it possible at all that someone set him up? I spoke with Matthew's colleague Sarah Brown and she seemed to have a crush on him. Was that angle ever investigated?"

"There was no need. We proved the timelines allowed Thomas the opportunity to commit the crime. He had time to travel from his friend's place, buy beer, commit the murders and return. He had the motivation because his wife was having an affair with Matt Pawsloski. And he had the means. The gun *with his fingerprints on it* placed him at the scene. There was no sign of a break-in at his house. No one else touched the gun. You're barking up the wrong tree, Scott."

"Did you know Matthew was looking into fraud at the firm where he worked? Couldn't that be another motive?"

Leblanc continued to stare at Jake, clearly convinced of the facts as he knew them, and not about to budge. He said, "We knew Pawsloski was concerned about something at the office, but it wasn't enough to pursue. It could have been discrepancies in the petty cash fund for all we knew. Besides, it would be up to the white-collar crime guys to investigate that. The evidence was so overwhelming against Thomas, I don't think anyone bothered looking at Pawsloski's concerns. It was nothing."

Jake looked at Leblanc evenly, saying, "So, the white-collar crime people didn't investigate?"

Leblanc reddened slightly when he answered. "No, I just said I don't believe they did. It was all speculation. No hard evidence that something was going on. Thomas is guilty. I was retiring, so we had to wrap the case up and we had solid evidence handed to us on a platter."

There it was. As Dani said, Leblanc was so worried about finishing his career on a high note, he didn't take the time to investigate other possibilities. Jake changed tack by saying, "What did you think of Gary Thomas when you talked to him? Was he cooperative? Aloof? Did he appear to be lying? Was he given a lie detector test?"

Leblanc inhaled deeply before expelling the air through his nostrils, obviously annoyed that the questions kept coming.

"He was sure of himself. Confident, I guess you could say. He stuck to his story throughout the proceedings. We couldn't shake him off his claim that he was innocent. Most criminals I've met in my 30-year career do the same thing. Nothing new there."

"Was he given a lie detector test?"

"No."

Jake asked a few more questions about the removal of the gun from Thomas's house to gain a feel for the man he was talking to. Former Constable Enzo Leblanc became more and more defensive. Jake wondered if that would have been the case earlier in his career. Did he take enough time to investigate all possibilities? He had an overbearing personality, so it was no surprise Dani followed his lead.

Jake rose from his chair to leave. "Okay, I appreciate your time. I hope you enjoy your retirement."

They walked to the door where Jake put on his boots. Leblanc's eyes narrowed and his jaw tightened. He said scarcely above a whisper, "I can't stop you from investigating this or writing a book about it or whatever you want to do. Thomas is where he should be. All the evidence pointed in his direction. My advice is to abandon this charade and write about something worthwhile."

Jake thanked Leblanc again and strode to his car. He reflected on how everything turned to Gary Thomas when forensics discovered his fingerprints on the gun. The investigation had ended for all intents and purposes when that happened. Yet there were others with motive and probably the opportunity. And it was the second time someone suggested he should write about something else. Ryan Cambridge was near the top of the list of suspects, and Sarah Brown might not be far behind. Now he wondered about Leblanc. Was it just his impending retirement that forced him to close the case without investigating fully? Could Leblanc have been desperate enough to plant evidence somehow? Jake shook his head, surprised that a thought like that would even enter his subconscious. He resolved to continue the investigation, no matter the consequences.

CHAPTER TWENTY-SEVEN

JAKE DOCUMENTED HIS discussion with Enzo Leblanc before spending an unsettled night in bed. The next morning, the phone rang as Jake finished feeding Oliver. He answered, tucking the phone between his ear and shoulder as he flipped the eggs in the frying pan. Two slices of the 12-grain bread he had purchased in deference to his personal trainer lay on top of the toaster. He peeked at his watch as he gripped the handle of the pan. It was now 7:15 in the morning.

Sarah Brown's soft voice came over the phone, saying, "I'm sorry to bother you, Mr. Scott, but I'm wondering if you have time for a quick conversation?"

Jake wandered to the cupboard to grab a plate for the eggs. The plates clattered as he pulled one from underneath a larger one sitting on top.

"Sure, Sarah. Please call me Jake. What is it?"

"Can we meet? I'm leaving for work in a few minutes, and I could meet you someplace—uh, if you have time now."

Jake glanced down at the plate, his robe and the eggs sizzling in the pan.

"Okay, there's a restaurant on Wellington called Brew and Buns. Finding a table shouldn't be a problem. People grab a coffee and leave in the morning. I could be there in twenty minutes if that works."

"Yes, thank you. It might take me a little longer, but I'll meet you there."

Jake sighed as he tossed the eggs in the garbage and contemplated shutting off the coffee machine that was building a head of steam. He left it. The coffee could wait until later, but he hated wasting the eggs. He tucked the bread back in the bag, hurriedly showered, dressed, and headed out the door. Jake grinned at the quizzical look on Oliver's face when he left. The cat must consider this peculiar behavior since Jake hadn't come and gone as repeatedly in four years. He thought Oliver probably enjoyed having the house to himself but would expect his human to be there promptly at mealtime.

Patrons occupied only two tables when he arrived at the restaurant, so he sauntered towards the back. He didn't expect to see Sarah yet, and a glance at the occupied tables confirmed she hadn't arrived. He sidestepped the takeout line snaking from the counter halfway to the door. Pruitt's server Amanda saw him and held up the coffee pot, a signal to which Jake nodded vigorously. She brought his coffee during a break in the line, looking harried. Her eyes shone, but the twinkle had given way to fatigue. Jake asked where Jason was.

"Oh, he's in the back baking cinnamon rolls. I hope he finishes soon. The coffee crowd is crazy this morning."

Jake said, "That must be a never-ending job. Yours *and* his. Nice to see people out, though." He retrieved his cell phone from his pocket and set it on the table in case Sarah called.

Jason emerged from the back, wiping his hands on his flour-dotted apron. He waved at Jake and hustled over. He dragged the vacant chair opposite Jake back from the table, the legs screeching on the floor. Amanda glanced back with a slight eye roll at her boss, who initially seemed oblivious to her workload. Then he said, "I'll be right there, Amanda." Turning to Jake, he said, "So, what brings you in today, my friend. This isn't Saturday."

"No, I'm meeting someone about the book I'm writing. Just trying to get some traction. It's slow going, but I'll chip away at it. How are you doing?"

"I'm doing good. Business has picked up since the vaccine, thank God. Good crowd today. Keeping Amanda busy. Takeout continues to be our savior, though. I'm hoping more people will start dining in when they feel more comfortable that the pandemic is slowing. Look at the people in line. Some are wearing masks; others aren't. No one knows what to do since the vaccine. I bake every day, so the rolls are fresh, and they sell well. It means getting up crazy early, but it sure beats the nine-to-five job I had before. I answer to myself and have no one to blame if things go wrong." He chuckled.

Jake sipped from the mug. He said, "Oh, I just assumed you've been doing this forever. What did you do before?"

"I was a computer geek. Worked in the high-tech sector until it went sour. I cashed in my shares and ran. The market was down, but the proceeds made a healthy down payment on the restaurant. At least my degree in computer science helps me do the books here." Wrinkles formed at the corners of his eyes as he chuckled again. "So, are you writing about that Thomas case Ryan was talking about?"

"Yes, I interviewed Gary Thomas. He doesn't seem like the type to commit a double murder. I'm investigating to see if others had the motivation to do it. Research is probably a better word than investigate."

"Have you come up with anything?"

"There are a couple of interesting leads I'm following. I don't know if it will go anywhere, but they're worth pursuing."

Jason nodded pensively. He said, "I thought the police would have investigated everything. That's what we taxpayers are paying for, isn't it?"

"You're right, but I wonder if they got sidetracked by a shiny object—the gun. It had Gary's fingerprints all over it, and they focused their attention on that."

"I would say that's pretty compelling. What does Danielle Perez think? Wasn't she one of the lead investigators?"

"She was, but she has questions in retrospect. We all consistently see after the fact with 20/20 vision. Her vision is still cloudy, but it's clearing as time goes on. She wonders if they should have been more thorough." Jake glanced at the entrance to see Sarah Brown slowly enter the restaurant, mask on, with her head bowed, as if she didn't want anyone to notice her.

Jake said, "Ah, I see my guest has arrived."

As Sarah glanced around the room, Jason rose from his seat and said, "Wow, I'll bet she's quite the looker under that mask." He nudged Jake and winked. "Good luck with the writing, Jake. Don't let Danielle catch you with this young lady."

He rushed away from the table as Sarah approached, leaving Jake to ponder if Jason knew more about Dani's feelings toward him than he did.

CHAPTER TWENTY-EIGHT

S ARAH SPOTTED HIM and edged past the lineup to join him at the table. She sat in the seat just vacated by Jason and removed her mask.

The proprietor brought coffee, his body turned so only Jake could see him raising and lowering his eyebrows with a smirk as he poured.

Sarah smiled nervously at Jake. Her hands shook as she leaned forward and picked through the plastic milk containers in a small bowl on the table until she found the low-fat version she wanted. It dropped from her hand as she tried to open it. She tried again, finally peeling back the top and pouring it into her coffee. She repeated the action until the color of the brew satisfied her. Her spoon rattled against the edges of the cup as she stirred the pale brown liquid. She said, "Thank you for meeting me, Mr. Scott—Jake. Sorry this is so last minute, but I want to explain what I've been doing at the office. It makes me nervous just thinking about it. I'm so scared of getting caught."

"You aren't taking unnecessary risks, are you Sarah? I don't want to see anyone else get hurt."

"That's what's scaring me. After talking to you, I decided I had to do more. Matthew deserved more." She scanned the room over her shoulder. "I worry that Mr. Cambridge, Ryan, was involved with the murders. If he had something to do with Matthew's death, I want him to pay."

"Were you in love with Matthew, Sarah?"

Sarah's face reddened.

"Am I that obvious? I don't know. He never saw me. It was like I was invisible, but he had such a presence. When he walked into the room, everyone noticed. I loved him from afar, I guess. He was nice to me. I could barely speak when he was around. It was like I was tongue-tied. I guess I hoped he would tire of Melissa Thomas or Gary would find out and stop their affair. When Gary stormed into the office that day, I was hopeful Matthew would stop seeing Melissa and look at me differently." She cast her sad eyes down and said, "But he never got the chance to stop the affair. Somebody killed him before he could."

"I'm sorry things didn't work out the way you wanted, Sarah. I know it sounds trite, but often, life just isn't fair. It seems like that's the way it has been for you."

Sarah's shoulders slumped as she clasped the tissue tightly between her fingers. He changed the subject, prompting her cautiously, "You said you are concerned that Ryan was involved."

Sarah leaned forward, her dark blue eyes staring at Jake, her voice barely above a whisper. "I have to admit, I wasn't sure I could trust you when I met you the first time. Your message that you wanted to see me shocked me. I just felt lost after the murders happened, so I pushed it out of my mind. I miss Matthew terribly, but I just let work take over. It occurred to me to leave Cambridge and Tremblay, but they treat me well there. Then you came along and started asking questions about the murder, and it brought everything to the surface again. It's always been in the back of my mind and it keeps me awake at night. I felt guilty for not doing more, and I'm glad you're looking into it. Really, I am. I have no one else to turn to."

She bent to retrieve her purse and pulled a folded and badly wrinkled piece of white paper from inside. She held it in her shaking hands, staring at it as she said. "Matthew gave me this to hold a couple of weeks before he died. He thought someone at the firm might discover what he was doing, and he didn't want to get caught with it. I teased him about being overly dramatic, but he insisted I take it. He said if he kept it at the office, someone might find it, and if he kept it at home, someone might break in and steal it. He convinced me it was important, but he wouldn't tell me what it was. I don't know why I kept it all this time. Since I met you, I've been doing some digging and I think I know what it is now."

She unfolded the paper and placed it on the table in front of Jake, flattening it so he could read it better.

It was a series of random letters and numbers.

ADX79437DFTBK44!

Jake didn't think he would have a clue what the numbers meant under different circumstances, but he sensed where this was headed. He let Sarah tell her story in her own time.

She said, "I stayed late one night, waiting for everyone to leave. I pretended I was completing one of our files. I had to stay until eight o'clock because a junior partner was still there. It took forever for him to leave. I was shaking like a leaf. Finally, he left, and I logged into the firm's accounting system. We have to enter our hours for billing, so that's not unusual. That system populates separate systems used for trust accounts and to bill the clients. The partners access it to monitor workloads, review employee performance, and that kind of thing."

She paused as Jason arrived at the table. He said, "Can I get you folks anything else?" He glanced at the paper before adding, "A cinnamon roll fresh out of the oven, perhaps?"

Jake watched as Sarah shook her head, but the rumbling in his stomach urged him to order one. He could hear his personal trainer's voice admonishing him.

When Jason left, Sarah continued.

"Ryan Cambridge controls the main accounting system, and the partners have access to it. They usually lock their doors, but when I tried Mr. Cambridge's it was unlocked. I guess he forgot to lock it. I left the light off, but the glow through the window from the area where I sit was bright enough that I could see what I was doing. It occurred to me the code could be a password to the main accounting system, so I tried it, but it didn't work. I thought maybe they changed the password when Matthew left."

Jake felt his shoulders sag when Sarah said she couldn't get into the system. He thought maybe they were getting somewhere when Sarah showed him the paper, but now it seemed that wasn't the case.

But Sarah had more to say. She waited until Jason delivered Jake's roll before picking up her story.

"There was another folder marked 'Personal' that I opened. I felt guilty about opening a personal folder. The app was password-protected, and when I tried the combination of letters and numbers on the paper, it opened. But just as I got into it, the main door to the office opened and the same partner came in. I shut off the computer and left Mr. Cambridge's office just in time. I rushed to my desk and gathered up my papers. The partner asked why I was working so late, and I told him I was just finishing a file. He told me to go home, which I did."

Jake sat on the edge of his seat with both hands gripping his cup.

"You're either foolhardy or very brave, Sarah. Did you see anything before you shut off the computer?"

Sarah glanced over her shoulder to ensure no one was listening before she said, "I think someone is stealing from the trust accounts. It looked like someone is maintaining a separate set of books."

Jake asked, "Were you able to take a picture or do you have any other proof?"

"No, it startled me when the door opened, so I shut everything down and left it the way it was. I left the office as soon as I could. I just about got caught." Sarah's eyes widened at the thought.

Many emotions swept through Jake as Sarah told her story. On some level, he wished she had discovered more, but it amazed him she found the courage to undertake what she did. He was afraid for her. Someone committed murder to hide a secret. Since they did it once, they could do it again. He recalled the note on Dani's car.

Lost in thought, Jake hadn't noticed Sarah shrugging her coat on and wrapping her scarf around her neck. He thanked her for talking to him and promised he would discuss it with his friend in the police department.

Sarah said, "Please let me gather more evidence before you go to the police." With that puzzling statement hanging like a leaden cloud, she was gone.

The crowd at the restaurant had quieted as Jake pondered the discussion, especially her last comment. He finished the cinnamon roll that was on hold while he listened, mesmerized by Sarah's tale, which raised more questions than answers. He pulled on his winter gear, left money on the table, and wandered out into the frigid air.

CHAPTER TWENTY-NINE

J AKE REALIZED AS he drove home that he hadn't contacted Avery for a few days, either by phone or text. He needed to rectify that situation as soon as he got home. The day was sunny, and the temperature hovered around minus twelve degrees Celsius, about ten degrees Fahrenheit in Jake's world.

He greeted Mr. Sharpe, his next-door neighbor who was cleaning the edges of his driveway with a shovel. The white-haired man must have been in his eighties by now and had lived in the house for as long as Jake could remember. Jake offered to help, but Mr. Sharpe declined as he gasped for air, saying it was the only exercise he got these days. Jake wondered if he would find him face down in the snow one day.

Once inside, Jake removed his winter attire and paid attention to Oliver before dialing Avery. She picked up on the second ring. After the usual "how are you?" and "how is work/retirement?" questions, Jake filled his daughter in on the latest regarding his research for the book. Avery had Jake on speaker and Nick listened in. As Jake finished his story, Nick said, "Are you backing all this up on an external drive, Jake? A USB or something?"

"I hadn't considered that Nick, but it's a good idea. What do you suggest?"

"I would put it on a USB and keep it in a safe location. It's not something you want to have to recreate if your computer crashes. Maybe give it to your sweetheart for safekeeping."

Jake could hear Avery stifle a laugh and himself getting defensive. He said, "If you mean Dani, she's not my sweetheart, but I'll take your idea under advisement, Nick, thanks."

They continued their conversation for another half hour. The time flew when Jake talked to his daughter and her boyfriend, and when she announced they had things to do, Jake reluctantly let them go.

His next call was to Dani. He knew continuing his investigation of the case would upset her. He braced for her reaction as he told her about his conversation with Sarah and the paralegal's suspicions that something illegal had been going on at Ryan's firm.

"Can you bring the police into the investigation now?" he asked.

Visions floated into Jake's head of Dani's countenance darkening and her eyes glowing like embers in their sockets as she absorbed the information.

She said, "I thought I told you to leave this alone." Her voice steadily rose. "You're putting yourself in danger. There still isn't enough to investigate. Sarah's suspicions about Ryan and a piece of paper with a password don't help us. She took an enormous risk. I showed the note to my boss. There's still no link to the murders, nor enough evidence of embezzlement from the trust fund to launch an official investigation." Her tone softened again. "I suppose you've spoken with Damon Brooks and you're too afraid to tell me."

"No, I still haven't. Maybe he's avoiding me. I think I'll pay him a visit to close the loop since I've already left messages. Then I promise I'll leave it alone." Jake tensed for the onslaught, but none was forthcoming. His mind wandered momentarily. *Should I ask Dani out on a date? No, she has enough on her mind with Emilie and this case.* His mind was in turmoil with mixed thoughts bouncing inside his brain. *She probably wouldn't go anyway now that I've gone against her wishes. Besides, am I ready? Yes, I think I am. No, I think I'll wait.*

Dani interrupted his thoughts. "Just be careful, Jake. I don't have to remind you again, do I? Just remember someone committed a double homicide. We're close to something. They might do it again, and you could put yourself in the crosshairs. Someone could come after you."

"I understand, Dani. I promise I'll be careful."

Jake agonized over his decision not to ask her out the minute they ended the conversation, but he convinced himself he had done the right thing. She certainly cared about his wellbeing, but, as a police officer, it was her job to worry about others. He gazed across the room at Mia's picture on the wall. Their marriage had been everything a marriage should be. Her death sunk him to the depths of despair where he had mostly remained for four years, but events lately were dragging him up from the bottom. Mia stared back from the picture frame and for a moment he thought he heard her voice.

"It's time to move on Jake. You've waited too long. I don't want you to be lonely forever. You need companionship. I will feel so much better if you find someone."

Was it his subconscious speaking to him? He shivered. He didn't believe in guardian angels, but her voice was as clear as if she had been standing right in front of him. And she was urging him to take control of his life. He shook his head. Was he losing it? Then he remembered he hadn't told Dani about his meeting with her former partner, Enzo Leblanc.

It was as good an excuse as any. He picked up the phone to call Dani again.

CHAPTER THIRTY

J AKE'S CONVERSATION WITH Leblanc slipped his mind when Dani excitedly accepted his dinner invitation. They agreed to go to an upscale restaurant on Wellington Street the next night. Jake spent an uneasy night tossing and turning. He woke in the morning with a sudden feeling of anxiety. *What had he done?* He stared at himself in the mirror as he brushed his teeth. His hair looked like a tornado had touched down, twisting it in countless directions. But that wasn't the worst part. Nor was the fact he had invited Dani for dinner. He was excited about that. No, the root cause of his uneasiness was that he had invited her for cocktails at the house first. The place was a disaster.

He dragged a comb through the knots in his hair, dressed, and sauntered into the kitchen to survey the damage. Clean dishes lay strewn across the counter, the frying pan from the previous day's aborted breakfast sat on the stove, and a stack of dirty dishes rose from the sink like the Leaning Tower of Pisa. Open cookbooks covered the rest of the counter and parts of the table. It occurred to him he hadn't seen the quartz countertop for some time since something invariably covered it. Boxes of pasta and other dry goods that belonged in the pantry occupied the remaining table space. Jake glanced at his watch. His appointment with his trainer was at two o'clock, giving him ample time to tidy up. If Dani saw the place like this, she might pity him, but her more obvious, and maybe smartest, choice would be to run.

Jake thought little about the case as he cleaned, dusted, scrubbed, and tossed things in the garbage until the interior of the house resembled the way Mia maintained it. Some dishes and cookbooks took up residence in the oven, but to Jake's eye, the place looked acceptable. He just had to remember to remove the items from the oven before turning it on next time.

Later, his trainer put him through his paces again, but at least he felt a little less like throwing up when he finished. He slipped into the new jacket, pants, and patterned shirt Dani and Emilie picked out for him and chanced one last look in the mirror. He and his image nodded their approval. His slicked-back graying hair still stretched over his ears, but the overall appearance was not bad for an old guy, he thought.

The doorbell rang at precisely the arranged time, and he nervously opened it. Dani stood in front of him in a long coat. Her eyes sparkled more than usual, enhanced by eye shadow. She wore a touch of lipstick he hadn't seen on her before. Her lively pitch-dark hair fell to her shoulders. He stepped aside to let her in and helped her remove her coat. She wore a red sheath dress that flattered her already stunning figure. A thin gold bracelet and tiny earrings complemented the ensemble. The overall look took Jake's breath away. All he could say was, "Wow, you don't look like a policewoman tonight. You look amazing." He grimaced inwardly at the awkward phrasing.

As they passed the kitchen, she playfully said, "You don't look so bad yourself, for an author. Nice wardrobe! Wow, the place is spotless." She batted her eyes and said, "Do you have a housekeeper?"

Jake remembered the paraphernalia in the oven, confirmed he didn't have a housekeeper and suggested they could sit in the living room or in the sunroom where they could enjoy the fire. Dani opted for the sunroom as she suggested there was a chill in the air outside so the fireplace seemed appropriate. They spent an hour chatting about inane subjects over glasses of white wine. Jake's nervousness gradually subsided, and he even told her about the rush to clean up the house.

Dani burst into laughter, her captivating dusky eyes crinkling around the edges and dancing in the fire's glow. She told him she could just imagine him scurrying around cleaning up. She said, "You didn't have to do that. It's kind of like putting out the Bible when the Minister is coming. But I appreciate the effort." She rewarded Jake with a smile that melted his heart.

When it was time to leave, Jake hung on wide-eyed as Dani raced to the restaurant, and when she found a parking spot, the walkway was just slippery enough for her to hold Jake's arm. They both realized that, despite the icy patches, she was in little danger of falling as she leaned into him. If anyone needed support, it was Jake.

Inside the dimly lit, elegant restaurant, the head server took their coats and ushered them to a back corner where the silverware gleamed in the glow of a candle glimmering on the tabletop. Dani's features glowed in the candlelight as she teased, "Oh, how romantic, Mr. Scott. You must bring all your lady friends here. The server seems to know your preferences."

"I've visited once or twice over the years, but they wouldn't consider me a regular. Mia and I used to come here sometimes." Jake chuckled and said, "It's the only restaurant I know, other than Brew and Buns, and I thought tonight we should set a higher standard."

A server arrived at the table to explain the menu and they ordered a liter of oaked Chardonnay after she clarified it had a buttery vanilla taste and was one of their best sellers. Jake and Dani toasted to better days ahead. They agreed with the server; the wine was an excellent choice.

They started with French Onion soup and both ordered beef tenderloin. They laughingly agreed that each had good taste in food. After they placed their order, Dani said, "I have to admit I snooped a bit and noticed the picture of you and Mia in your sunroom. She was a beautiful woman. Tell me what happened. It must have been devastating for you."

Jake told her about the aneurysm and how quickly everything occurred. He described how one minute she was there, as vibrant and healthy as ever, and the next minute she wasn't. He spoke of the depression and lethargy that followed, and how pleased he was to be pulling himself out. The part about hearing his wife's voice urging him to meet someone remained unspoken.

They talked about his afternoon session at the gym and laughed at the lecture he got about his diet and the nausea that followed each session. Dani assured him things would improve. He tried to identify which muscles hurt most, but gave up, saying, "All of them."

Their meals arrived and between bites, Dani talked about Emilie. She said, "I spoke to her dad. He expressed surprise that she felt neglected and said he would try harder. I'm not sure it's going to happen, but Emilie agreed to try again. She wants to make the split arrangement work, and she swore to me she would call either you or me if she was having a tough time about it. I hope you don't mind. Dani held Jake's eyes with hers as she reached for his hand.

"She trusts you, Jake, after what you did for her at the park."

Jake said again it was nothing and assured Dani he had no problem with Emilie calling him if she needed to talk.

As their food arrived, Dani shared the story of her failed marriage when the muffled sound of his ringing phone drifted from Jake's pocket. He ignored it until it stopped, but they had no sooner returned to their conversation when it rang again. He continued to ignore it, but the ringing persisted.

Dani finally said, "Maybe you should answer that. Someone seems desperate to reach you."

Jake groaned. "I suppose it could be Avery." He set down his fork and rummaged through his pocket while he griped, "This better be important. I'm sorry, Dani. I don't know who would want to reach me this badly. A handful of people have my number and one of them is right here."

Dani smiled and set down her fork to wait, watching Jake with concern.

He finally retrieved the phone, hit "recent calls," and glanced at the screen, thinking it was probably the unknown number of a telemarketer. But he knew the name on the screen, and it surprised him. It was the Queensway Carleton Hospital. He turned the phone around so Dani could see it.

He said, "Perhaps their annual fundraising drive. I usually donate. I don't remember it being this time of year though." Then he noticed the message indicator.

Dani nodded, and pursed her full lips before saying, "You'd better listen to the message. If it was a fundraising drive, they wouldn't leave a message. They would call you later, rather than redialling like that. Somebody wants to talk to you, badly."

Jake reluctantly set his fork on his plate and hit the message button. A chill ran along his spine when a nurse named Julie Appleton requested that he return the call right away and ask for her. He did as the message suggested, and the receptionist connected him with Ms. Appleton.

Dani stared as Jake listened.

The woman reintroduced herself with a hurried, yet professional voice.

"Mr. Scott, my name is Julie Appleton. I'm a nurse at the Queensway Carleton Hospital. Ms. Sarah Brown was admitted to the hospital this evening, and she insisted I call you. She'll be fine, but she's determined that I let you know she's here."

Jake sat back in his chair, stunned. Dani regarded him steadily, unsure of the conversation on the other end of the line but concerned by his reaction.

"Is she okay? What happened?"

The nurse said, "I have to inform you that my speaking with you is extremely unusual. She said she has no family in town. X-rays show she has a concussion. She has some bruises, and she's mildly sedated and resting now. We'll keep her overnight for observation. She refused to tell us what happened. She just said to call you."

"Okay, thank you very much for calling. I'll be there soon."

Jake hung up the phone and relayed the conversation to Dani. She said without intonation, "Let's eat quickly and get over there." He noticed that despite the makeup, gorgeous dress, excellent meal, and romantic ambiance, she instantly transformed into the trained policewoman. Like Clark Kent into Superman.

He expected no less from Dani. He felt bad for Sarah, but he was more than a little disappointed that their date had abruptly, unexpectedly, and, sadly, officially ended.

CHAPTER THIRTY-ONE

WHY CALL *HIM?* Jake couldn't shake the feeling that whatever happened to Sarah was connected to the case. Why else would she call him? Apparently, she had no relatives in the city, so maybe that explained it. But no friends either?

They retrieved Dani's car, and he thought about Sarah as she drove. It had snowed while they were in the restaurant, making the streets greasy for driving, but it made no difference to Dani as they flew past parked cars. Jake watched a man slip on the sidewalk, his arms helicoptering in the air. He turned to see the man's companion holding him upright and the couple throwing their heads back in laughter when he stabilized. Another man brushed the snow from his windshield. All Jake could do was hang on as Dani deftly fishtailed around another corner onto Baseline Road. He realized he had feelings for this woman, but he wished she would slow down.

To take his mind off her driving, he said, "Dani, there's something else I need to confess. I spoke with Enzo Leblanc."

Dani didn't react. It was as if she understood by now that Jake couldn't leave it alone, but her reply wasn't a ringing endorsement.

"Oh yeah, how did that go?"

"He was exactly as you said. Upset that I was writing a book about the case. Convinced he did everything perfectly. Satisfied Gary Thomas is where he should be. He said a couple of interesting things. The first was that he was determined to wrap up the case before he retired." Jake waited for a reaction, but since none was forthcoming, he added, "He also said I should write about something else."

"There seems to be a lot of that going around," Dani said, her lips scarcely moving.

They arrived at the hospital where surgeries postponed by the pandemic were now finally being done. Dani glided into a spot in the jam-packed parking lot like a baserunner sliding into home plate, stopping inches from a wooden barrier. Her reaction to Jake's admission he had spoken to Leblanc despite her warning to leave the case alone brought an unsettling coolness into the car. Jake's mood turned somber as he contemplated how quickly their date had gone south, thanks to the phone call and now this. He grumbled about the outrageous cost of hospital parking but brightened considerably when Dani held his arm again for support on the slick pavement.

The door slid open with a whoosh as they approached, and after Dani flashed her detective shield, the receptionist directed them to a room on the third floor. They took the stairs and walked down a hallway crammed with blue-clad nurses, some with stethoscopes slung around their necks. Some entered stats on computers and others bustled about carrying sheets and towels.

Jake and Dani found the room with four occupants at the end of the hall. An elderly woman slept on one side of the room while a younger woman across from her studied them as they passed. Sarah occupied a bed by the window. A few guests chatted with a middle-aged woman in the bed opposite.

Sarah sat propped up on her pillow. The drapes had been closed for the night, but a lamp revealed her ashen face. Her eyes drooped. A heavy bandage hid a wound on the side of her head.

"Are you okay, Sarah?" Jake asked.

Sarah took a deep breath, and her soft voice cracked when she said. "Thanks for coming. I... I didn't know who to call. The nurses said they would call the police, but I wanted to discuss everything with you first. They weren't happy about it, but one nurse finally agreed." A question crossed her face as she regarded Dani's dress and makeup, but she said nothing more.

Jake realized he hadn't introduced Dani and he let Sarah know she was his friend, a homicide detective who was working independently on the Gary Thomas case. He told Sarah she was free to talk in front of Dani.

Sarah frowned, but reluctantly continued, her voice barely above a whisper. "Someone attacked me. I was walking to my car in the underground garage, and a man ran up from behind and knocked me down. I hit my head on the car bumper as I fell, and it stunned me. There's a cut on my head and the nurse described the lump as a goose egg." Sarah sighed and added, "And I have a throbbing headache. I guess I have a concussion. It hurts to talk. I'm scared to death that if I go home, he might show up. My phone was in my purse, my driver's license, everything. He just has to look at my identification to know where I live. What should I do?"

A nurse hastened around the corner with her outstretched hand holding colorful pills. She smiled at Jake and Dani before offering the pills to Sarah and asking how she felt. Sarah swallowed the pills with water and repeated that it hurt to talk. The nurse nodded, told Sarah the pills would help with the headache, and advised Dani and Jake they had a few more minutes before she turned and bustled out of the room.

Dani said, "Is there anywhere else you can go, Sarah? A friend or relative?"

"I could ask one friend. We've kind of been on the outs lately over some stupid argument." Her shoulders fell as she said, "If she says no, I guess I'll have to go home. I'll have to go home to get a change of clothes at least."

Jake said, "I don't mind picking you up and taking you to your place when you're ready. I assume your car is still in the garage, anyway."

Sarah nodded and said sleepily, "It's there, but that's not why I needed to talk to you. I appreciate the offer of picking me up and I'll take you up on that." She battled to keep her heavy eyelids open as her words became slurred. "There's something you have to understand. The man stole my purse. I tried to hang on, but he was too strong, and I think I lost consciousness." Jake and Dani leaned closer to understand the mumbled words. "The password was in my purse. It was the only copy. It's too many numbers and letters for me to remember what it was." Her voice trailed off. "I can't investigate now. The man also said something. It wasn't clear through the mask and everything was hazy from bumping my head, but it was something to the effect of, 'Leave it alone.' His voice sounded gruff like he was trying to disguise it."

Dani rested her hand on Sarah's arm as the girl continued the fight to keep her eyes open. She said, "Just one question, Sarah. Do you know who called the ambulance?"

The words were barely perceptible. "Uh, yeah. I don't think anyone called the ambulance, but someone drove me to the hospital. He didn't stick around though—just dropped me off and left." The last words drifted into the ether as Sarah's head dropped to her chest. She woke with a start as Dani said, "So you don't know who it was that dropped you off?"

As Sarah's head bowed again, she said, "Yeah, uh yeah, I do. It was, uh, Mr. Cambridge. Ryan Cambridge."

CHAPTER THIRTY-TWO

JAKE AND DANI watched the slumbering Sarah for a few minutes. The bed covers rose and fell slowly with each breath. Dani took out a business card and placed it on the table beside Sarah's bed. Jake fished in his pockets for a piece of paper, but when Dani realized what he was doing, she suggested he add his phone number to her card. Jake leaned toward Dani so she could hear without waking Sarah. He said, "She has my number, but I want to make sure it's handy." He wrote it along with his name on Dani's card. "I think we might as well go."

When Dani nodded her agreement, they left and dodged nurses, doctors, and humming equipment as they walked down the bustling pale green corridor away from Sarah's room.

Jake said, "Do you think Ryan would drive her to the hospital if he knocked her down and stole her purse? It makes no sense to me."

As they arrived at the front door of the hospital, Dani said, "It does if he's trying to make sure the blame for the murders remains with Gary or divert it somewhere else. He didn't bother calling the police to report the incident. If he killed Melissa and Matthew and hid the gun with Gary's prints all over it, he would be smart enough to make the attack on Sarah look like a simple purse snatching. The password is conveniently gone now, too. What better way to keep the attention away from himself than to pretend to be the knight in shining armor riding up on his trusty steed to save the day?"

Jake nodded thoughtfully as they arrived at the car. Would Ryan really do that? Is the guy he'd been having breakfast with for months not who he claimed to be and worse yet, a *murderer*? Jake had met some hardened types over the years while he was reporting, but no one adept at being one person one day and so completely different the next if that's what this was.

The way Dani's mind worked astonished him. Her first thought kept Ryan on the suspect list, even though he drove Sarah to the hospital. Jake's mind veered in the opposite direction when Sarah mentioned Ryan's name. He was quick to give Ryan the benefit of the doubt; glad that the lawyer came along when he did to take care of the young woman.

When they arrived at the car, Dani started it and Jake brushed off the white fluffy snow accumulated on the windows. After he finished, he made sure he buckled up and hung on for the race back home. The streets were even slicker now, forcing Dani to ease up on the accelerator. At least a little. They sped into the driveway, sliding to a stop a few feet from the garage, and Jake invited her in, saying, "We didn't have time to finish our date. Would you like to come in for a nightcap?" He glanced toward the house as he said, "Not to put any pressure on you, but I spent all day cleaning."

Dani nodded as she unbuckled. "As long as you don't have to take clean drink glasses out of the oven."

She didn't seem mad at him for talking to her former partner, but Jake stopped getting out of the car in mid-air. Had he heard right? How could she know there were dishes in the oven? Or was it just a wild guess? He looked over the car roof at Dani, who was making her way to the walkway. The up and down motion of her shoulders convinced Jake she was chuckling to herself.

He didn't mention it again when they were in the kitchen, but he made a show of removing two glasses from the cupboard. He poured them each a glass of cinnamon whiskey on ice, which they carried to the sunroom. Jake clicked the remote to turn on the fireplace. The flames ignited with a pop and the rock wool embers glowed like a coal bed.

When they settled into their chairs, Oliver ambled in from his hiding spot and meowed a greeting. After glancing at Jake, he decided his preferred lap was the one belonging to Dani, and he jumped up. Jake told her to push him down, but Dani replied he was fine where he was. She said she wanted to know the brilliant conversationalist better. Oliver agreed and nestled in, purring softly.

Jake said, "So, does the attack on Sarah move the case forward?"

Dani smacked her lips and looked through the empty glass at Jake. "Is this ever tasty. I've never had it before. I could get used to it." She laughed and winked at Jake, saying, "Maybe too used to it." She watched Jake pour more mahogany brown liquid into her glass before answering his question. "I've been thinking about whether it moves the case forward. I think it does, so I'm going to discuss it again with my boss. He'll freak out when I raise it again, but after he yells for a few minutes, I should be able to get a few words in before he kicks me out of his office.

"Let's look at the facts. The deceased gave Sarah a code that turned out to be a password which she says worked on the accounting system. Not the main accounting system, but a second set of records. According to Sarah, it appears someone has been dipping into the trust funds." She took another sip. Actually, more than a sip. "Mmm, that's good," she said again. She set the glass down. "It's going down too easily. Good thing the coffee tabletop is clear, so there's room for me to dance later. Where did you hide all those magazines you were hoarding?" She laughed and continued outlining the case before Jake could say he would be interested in watching her dance on the table. He decided it was better left unsaid, anyway.

She said, "It's possible Matthew discovered the theft and was about to tell someone. Maybe the authorities? Melissa? Sarah? Either way, it's a motive for Matthew's murder. Ryan Cambridge seems to have or have had a gambling problem that could be a motive for him to steal money from the trust fund. Sarah was accessing the computer in the office when someone came in. She doesn't think they saw her, but maybe they did. Then someone attacked her and stole her purse, along with the password. According to her, she was also warned to back off the case by the attacker. Ryan Cambridge came along after the attack to save the day. Meanwhile, Gary Thomas still proclaims his innocence while the evidence against him is so far insurmountable. Have I left anything out?"

Oliver, apparently bored with Dani's dissertation, rose from her lap, stretched, and thumped to the floor as gracefully as he could considering his considerable weight. He gathered all the dignity he could muster and sauntered off with his head and tail held high in search of something more interesting, like any remaining food in his bowl.

Jake watched Oliver go and said, "There is also the unrequited love Sarah had for Matthew. And what about Melissa? Could she have been the target all along? Are we missing something? Do you think your boss will agree with you and open an investigation?"

Dani laughed as Jake glanced at her empty glass on the table. She slurred her words slightly. "He just might, but I think he put the 'cur' in curmudgeon. He's actually a great boss with the department's best interests at heart, and if I were in his shoes, I would act the same." Then she added, "You know Jake, I want to be mad at you for doing just the opposite of what I wanted you to do, but I can't. If Sarah hadn't called you, I think I'd be mad as hell. But you're connected to this case. I'm sorry I got you into it." She held his eyes with hers. "Just be careful, okay? Don't do anything stupid. Let us handle it now."

Jake said, "I hear you, Dani. I was a reporter, and I guess that part of me still draws me into a mystery. It's not an excuse, just a fact. I promise I'll be careful, and I'll keep you in the loop if I do anything more. Frankly, I don't know what more I could do. I still want to talk to Damon Brooks for backstory for the book, but that's it. I thought of talking to the staff at Ryan's office, but I'm sure you'll do that if you get the go-ahead."

Suddenly, Jake grew exhausted from talking about the case. He enjoyed it when their conversations veered to something else. He was glad the case brought them together, but he wanted to move on from it for now. Seeing her glass was empty again, he offered her another, but she mildly disappointed him when she declined. They chatted more about Emilie and their likes and dislikes, getting to know each other better. Finally, Dani rose from the sofa and announced she had to work in the morning and needed some sleep. She said the fact the whiskey went to her head as fast as it did was a clear sign of fatigue. Besides, she didn't need a colleague stopping her for a DUI on the way home.

Jake walked her to the door and helped her on with her coat. He couldn't resist. He said, "Did you really know there were dishes in the oven?"

She laughed loudly. She said, "I was only teasing. I thought it was a myth that bachelors put dishes in the oven. Guess not. By the way, that's a solid interrogation technique. Throw something out there and see if the perp will bite. Looks like you took the bait, my friend. Guilty as charged." She tugged at the inside of her cheek with her finger, emphasizing that Jake had fully and completely taken the hook in his mouth.

She stood on her toes and kissed him on the cheek. Then she wrapped her arms around him in a bear hug.

"You are a special person, Jake Scott. I look forward to getting to know you better."

With that she was out the door, leaving Jake with renewed feelings long suppressed. His heart thrummed like the wings of a hummingbird.

CHAPTER THIRTY-THREE

JAKE WASHED AND put away the drink glasses and even found space for the dishes stowed in the oven. He resolved he wouldn't do that again as he chuckled at Dani's skillful extraction of the information that he had stashed them there. He touched his cheek where she had kissed him. Sure, the way the romantic dinner ended was disappointing, but he enjoyed just spending time with her and he wanted more if she was willing.

The next morning, he dressed, fed the cat, and headed out the door. It was time to track down Gary Thomas's friend, Damon Brooks. He told himself Dani kind of gave him her tacit approval the night before by saying nothing when he said he was planning to talk to Brooks for background. He traveled east on the Queensway and after a few minutes swung left at a division in the highway known locally as "the split." Going right would put him on Highway 417 to Montreal. The left option on Highway 174 led to Orleans, a suburb of Ottawa.

Since the phone calls had proven fruitless, it was time for another surprise encounter, just like he had done with Dani's former partner. Traffic was light on his side of the highway as drivers drove in the opposite direction to their work in downtown Ottawa. Jake didn't know Damon's occupation or if he worked at home, so this could be an exercise in futility. He had no alternative plans, and he hadn't been to Orleans lately. He had already decided if Damon wasn't home, he would try to find out from Dani where he worked and track him down there.

In the typical crapshoot that had become Ottawa's winter weather the last few years, today offered overcast and cool conditions. The snow had stopped during the night and the roads were clear. Fortunately, traffic was unimpeded by construction crews building the modern light rail system at the roadside. He pulled off the highway and traveled north into an area named Convent Glen and found Damon's street and house number. The absence of a car on Damon's driveway was not a good sign in a city where most people used their garage for storage and beer fridges. Vehicles occupied driveways on the opposite side of the street.

Jake rang the doorbell and waited. No one came. He rapped solidly on the door until the muffled sound of footsteps thumped down the hall.

A tall, lean African American man in his late thirties opened the door. He wore a bathrobe, and his curly raven hair was damp, suggesting he just stepped out of the shower. He retrieved a pair of heavy framed glasses from a table at his side and put them on. A rich, full-bodied voice drifted from his lips.

"Can I help you?"

Jake's first impression was of a confidant, take-charge man. Even in his bathrobe, he had an aura about him, and the glasses added a nerdy hipster vibe. He stood at least six inches taller than

Jake with thick shoulders, which made him almost intimidating. Why had this man avoided his phone calls?

Jake said, "My name's Jake Scott. I've been trying to reach you. I'm writing a book about Gary Thomas and I just wanted to hear your version of what transpired the night of the murders and maybe learn your impressions about the man. It'll only take a few minutes of your time."

Brooks frowned but stepped aside, saying, "Okay, come in. You're a persistent man, Mr. Scott, I'll give you that. I've seen your messages. Take off your coat."

Jake did as Brooks instructed and handed over his coat, wondering again why this man had ignored his messages. Brooks hung the coat in a hall closet and led him to the sparse living room. He said he had to change, leaving Jake alone to examine the room. It featured eclectic taste. A tall bookshelf against one wall sagged under the weight of novels and DVDs of various genres. A large screen TV hung beside it with speakers on either side. African art sat on the coffee table and framed contemporary paintings hung on the other walls. Jake thought he could like Damon Brooks.

When Brooks returned in khaki slacks, navy sweater, and slippers, he apologized for not offering Jake something to drink. He spoke of a late night with his buddies and a slow start to the morning. But what he said next in that resonant voice was surprising and a little chilling.

"I've sort of been avoiding your phone calls for a reason. You might not appreciate what I have to say."

Jake declined the coffee. He said, "What you're saying sounds ominous, but I'm just trying to get to the truth. I've spoken to other people, including Gary Thomas, and some with motives are popping up. I want to know that an innocent man isn't sitting in prison. Can you tell me about that night? You were a friend of Gary's, right? His *best* friend, I understand?"

"Yes, we were good friends and I think Gary considered me his best friend." Jake noted the subtle difference between being best friends and Gary thinking Damon was his best friend. Damon carried on, saying, "That night was exactly as I described it to the police. We were playing cards, as we usually do. It was the same bunch of guys as last night, except Gary, obviously. The night of the murders we had some drinks, but I forgot to pick up more beer before everyone showed up. I had to work late, and it completely slipped my mind."

Jake had already noticed that the room and the visible portion of the rest of the house were spotless.

He said, "I take it you guys didn't play cards here last night. Either that, or you did an amazing job of cleaning up."

Brooks chuckled, saying, "No, we rotate. It was one of the other guys' turns last night. You wouldn't have been able to walk around the mess if we had met here."

Jake liked Damon Brooks even better. He said, "Sorry to interrupt. You said you ran out of beer."

"Yeah, it was stupid of me. I work for the feds and we had a deadline to produce a financial report, so I had to work late, and I was unprepared for the evening. It occurred to me to call off the gathering, but I grabbed some munchies on the way home. Forgot the beer though. The guys live for the get-together, but they consider forgetting beer to be a cardinal sin. The drinks are the most important part of the night." A sonorous good-natured laugh rumbled from the man's chest.

"Okay, so what happened?"

"Gary noticed there was only one beer left and said he'd put more in the refrigerator. It was then I remembered I didn't pick any up. You should have heard the howling. Gary volunteered to do a beer run before anyone else could say anything. He said it wasn't his night for cards anyway, so he didn't mind going. He didn't wait for an answer, he just left."

"Seems innocent enough. How long was he gone?"

"Too long. Everybody was complaining until he finally showed up. He was pale when he came back. When we dealt him in, he shook so bad the cards were trembling in his hand. When we asked what was wrong, he said he drove back to the house. That was it. No reason. We didn't press it, but everyone had this weird look on their face. Why would he be shaking so bad if he just stopped by his house? There had to be more, but we didn't know Melissa was having an affair. We found that out later."

"Do you think the affair would explain the way he acted when he returned?"

"I want to think that, but he didn't catch them at the house. How could he? They were at the park being murdered. I keep asking myself why a simple visit to the house would upset him like that." Damon's voice tailed off as he said, "I haven't found a reasonable answer."

Jake sympathized with Damon's concern about whether his friend committed the murders. After all, he had his own questions about *his* friend, Ryan Cambridge. One or both men could be very wrong about their friends.

Jake regarded Damon's troubled face. There was more. Something was eating at Damon that he preferred to keep to himself. He asked, "Is that the reason you thought I wouldn't like what you had to say?"

Hesitation. Damon shifted in his chair. He clasped and unclasped his hands as he stared at the beige carpet as if counting the threads. Jake waited patiently until finally, Damon said, "No, there's something I didn't tell the police. They didn't ask, and I didn't volunteer the information." More hesitation. "I've known Gary a long time. I even dated his wife Melissa before they got married. He's a great guy. But he's like the Incredible Hulk. He's fine until something makes him snap, and then he turns into someone else. It's worse when he drinks. I read the description of how he acted when he went to the office searching for Matthew Pawsloski. Yelling and cursing. That's what he's like. He's prone to violence when he's angry. You wouldn't know it normally. When you talk to him most of the time, his quiet demeanor impresses you the most. It's like he wouldn't hurt a fly. I was kind of jealous of him. He seemed perfect in every way unless he got angry. I had a hard time with that. I honestly liked the calm, rational Gary Thomas and wanted to be like him. Not the angry Gary Thomas."

Jake said, "Wait, you said you dated Melissa Thomas?"

"That was a long time ago and for a short time. It's water under the bridge as they say. She was always more interested in Gary."

Jake filed the information away for later. Damon was right, Jake didn't like the implication about Gary's anger issues. The quiet Gary Thomas was the one he had met. He leaned back in his chair, readying himself for more to come.

Damon glanced up. He said, "Gary and I were out one night tossing back a few drinks. It was a few years ago. We had rum and Cokes in the afternoon and continued drinking beer that night. Gary could barely see straight. Plastered. I suppose I was too, but not as bad. Some guy got into Gary's face about something. As I recall, it was nothing, but Gary flew into a rage. I had seen him lose his temper before, but this was on a whole new level. He slugged the guy with his bottle and when he was down and barely conscious, Gary jumped on him and started pummeling him. I don't mean just slapping him around. He was hitting the guy as hard as he could. The poor guy couldn't defend himself. I had to pull Gary off." Damon stared at Jake, his sad eyes moist at the recollection. "I think he wouldn't have stopped if I hadn't intervened. He was a mad man. Totally out of control. I think he would have killed the guy."

Jake sucked in a breath. He said, "Wouldn't the victim have reported the incident to the police? They should have a record of it. Wasn't it brought up at the trial?"

"We were drinking in the parking lot next to a grocery store in a strip mall in Barrhaven, and I don't think the guy ever reported it. I guess he walked through the lot on his way home from work. I don't know why he didn't report it. Maybe he already had a record."

"So, Damon, if I'm reading you correctly, you think Gary is capable of . . ."

Damon cut him off. "I can't stop thinking about it. I wish I could, but I lie awake at night with images of those two people being shot, and the guy Gary beat up comes to mind. He wasn't the first guy, either. I've seen him do that before. It's one example, and it's why I didn't want to talk to you. I think Gary likely killed that couple."

CHAPTER THIRTY-FOUR

WELL, THAT DIDN'T go as expected, Jake thought as he drove home. A heaviness settled over him as he rehashed the conversation. The more he thought, the darker his mood became at the possibilities. Gary Thomas had him convinced he was innocent, but if he believed Damon's story, the man sitting in jail was capable of murder. His cynical side reminded him that much of life is an illusion. Working in the news media all his life, he realized people are easily influenced. Most read news that agrees with and supports their beliefs. It's even worse now that social media giants guide people in certain directions by showing them the content that best suits and even bolsters their opinions.

This was no different. Gary Thomas had him convinced that he was innocent. But now Jake wondered if he could believe Thomas. Damon Brooks didn't think so. Thomas had a serenity about him that Jake assumed was acceptance of his situation. Did he misinterpret? Was it suppressed violence instead? And Brooks dated Melissa. That was news. Who could he believe? His mind delved even deeper. It shocked him when Dani raised the prospect of Ryan's possible involvement in a double homicide. He didn't want to accept that his friend could have been involved, but circumstantial evidence suggested he could have been. Was Sarah telling the truth about the double set of books? Why did Leblanc want to end the investigation so fast? Hell, was Dani leading him down a garden path for some unknown reason? What was true? Was he just believing what people wanted him to believe?

His mood didn't improve when something ahead ground progress on the highway to a halt. *What now?* Jake had no choice but to sit and contemplate the case. He shook his head, disgusted with himself. Of course, Dani was being honest. She was the one person he could trust in all this. Why would he think differently? She had given him no reason to think she was untrustworthy. Brooks had shaken Jake's trust in everyone, but he knew Dani well enough to know she was genuine.

As the traffic inched forward, he decided the negative thinking was getting him nowhere. He called Dani's cell phone. She picked up right away, but her voice was quiet. She explained she was in the office doing some paperwork and surrounded by colleagues. Jake asked if she could spare a few minutes for coffee, and she cheerfully agreed. Jake informed her at the rate the traffic was moving, it would take him at least thirty minutes to reach downtown, so he vowed to phone when he arrived at the agreed-upon restaurant on Elgin Street, close to the station.

He eventually drove past a fender bender on the highway and realized grumpily that the gawkers were causing the slowdown as the crumpled vehicles sat on the roadside. Once past the mangled cars, he reached downtown and found a parking spot to call Dani.

The restaurant was full of uniformed police officers and some in plain clothes whose stature and demeanor suggested that they too belonged to the fraternity. Dani strode through the door, nodded to some patrons, and located Jake. Her mood matched Jake's based on her unsmiling features, but her face brightened at the sight of the coffee prepared the way she liked it on her side of the table. She thanked him as he inquired if everything was alright.

She nodded but said she was helping the Sexual Assault and Child Abuse Unit with investigating the death of a four-year-old boy.

"The Homicide Unit helps them when we aren't busy, or the higher powers assign us to a case. It's a tough section and they need the help when we can provide it."

When she asked how his day had gone, Jake relayed his conversation with Damon Brooks. When he finished, Dani stared at him. She said, "I agree with you that his revelations aren't what I would have expected, and it adds another layer to the investigation. We knew this would not be easy. I talked with the Inspector in charge of special investigations. He's my boss. He was actually in a good mood." She paused as a uniformed officer greeted her as he passed by the table. "I told the Inspector about the note on the car, the attack on Sarah, and the potential link to something going on at Ryan's firm. I didn't dare link it to Gary Thomas's case, as I think that might have caused his head to explode. He knew anyway. Now, the fact Damon dated Melissa at one time is something else to consider. He didn't mention it when we talked to him or we would have investigated it.

"My boss said he would assign someone to it. I don't know how quickly it will happen, but it's progress. At least he didn't throw me out of his office. Now, my dear Jake, I must take my coffee and get back to work. It was nice seeing you."

Jake glanced over Dani's shoulder at the people surrounding them. Some cast glances their way, but most paid little attention as they chatted quietly, sipping their coffees. It was a bustling location as most bought their coffee and left.

He said, "Thanks for meeting me, Dani. I appreciate it. Damon's revelations about Gary's temper didn't put me in the best mood. Maybe I misjudged Gary. I'm glad your boss is going to look into it. It doesn't mean I'll stop working on the book, but I'm pleased to hear the news. How is your weekend looking?"

Dani put on her coat. "Emilie is scheduled to be with me this weekend, so breakfast is a stretch, but let's go skating on the canal early Saturday afternoon. You, Emilie, and me. What do you think?"

"Skating? I haven't done that in years." His mind flashed back to the nights he skated with his wife on the Rideau Canal before she died. They would skate hand-in-hand halfway along its length and stop for hot chocolate before turning back. They were some of his fondest memories. He glanced at Dani and realized she expected an answer.

"I'll rummage through some boxes in the basement to look for my skates. If I don't find them, maybe I can rent some. Let's touch base at the end of the week."

Agreeing they had a deal if the weather held, they got up to leave, but Dani stopped at the counter. "I'm just going to pick something up," she said. Jake waited while she chose a dozen pastries for her colleagues. As they walked towards the door, Jake said, "That'll make someone happy."

She chuckled and replied, "The path to a police officer's brain leads through their stomach."

They went in their separate directions, both in a better mood.

His phone rang on the way home. He swore under his breath and reminded himself to ask Avery or Nick how to connect it so he could talk hands-free. He pulled over on a side street but found a parking spot too late. The ringing stopped. A quick check of his recent calls list told him it was Sarah's number. When he called back, she told him she had been discharged. He had forgotten his promise to pick her up. He felt guilty that someone attacked her, even if she had investigated the firm's books on her own.

The drive was largely silent after he picked her up at the hospital entrance. She mentioned nothing about her ordeal. She said the doctors ordered her to stay away from work until the effects of her concussion subsided. Jake didn't think she should go anywhere near the place. He promised to help her pick up her car from the firm's parking garage if she needed it, and she told him she didn't want to bother him and that she thought she knew someone else who could help. She thanked him for the ride and Jake left her, wondering if she would ever be comfortable working at the firm of Cambridge and Tremblay again.

As he drove along the street to his house, local kids hurried to move their hockey nets aside so he could pass. He avoided the puck they left lying on the slick street. He remembered going to bed at night as a kid, hoping the street plow would leave a layer of ice so the game could continue the next day. The kids acknowledged his wave as he passed. As he pulled into his driveway, Jake had already decided he needed to speak with Gary Thomas again.

CHAPTER THIRTY-FIVE

THE NEXT MORNING Jake called Millhaven prison and requested to speak to the duty correctional manager. A pleasant-sounding woman answered, and Jake explained he wanted to talk to Gary Thomas.

She said, "Do you know if you are on Mr. Thomas's authorized call list?"

Jake replied he didn't know what that was, and she explained inmates can only call people whose names, addresses, and phone numbers they have submitted to Correctional Services Canada for approval. They can have a maximum of 40 names on their list.

"The lists are private, so I can't access his to check but I'll pass your message along. If your name is on Mr. Thomas's list, I'm sure he'll call. You said your name is Jake Scott? Can you tell me the purpose of your call?"

Jake heard keyboard keys tapping on the other end of the phone as he said, "I'm writing a book about his case and I have a few more questions for Mr. Thomas. Please tell him he can call collect." The keyboard went silent, so after the officer assured Jake again that she would pass the message along, he thanked her and hung up. With that completed, Jake worked on his book to pass the time, filling in background information about the judicial system and the process to visit prisoners. He couldn't just dryly retell the trial of Gary Thomas; it had to be interesting. The reader needed to empathize with a man who may have been incarcerated unfairly. He was careful to describe Ryan Cambridge's role because he didn't fully understand it.

As Jake worked, Oliver silently wandered into the room looking for attention. Jake didn't notice until he felt the cat pawing at his pant leg. When Oliver meowed, Jake bent down and scratched the white spot under the appreciative feline's chin as he stared at the words he had just typed.

"Is this leading anywhere, Oliver? Am I just wasting my time here?"

The cat purred softly at the attention until he didn't. Oliver decided after a few seconds he'd had enough, turned, and walked out.

"Pleasant chat," Jake called after Oliver's fleeting tail.

A few minutes later, the phone rang. It was Gary Thomas's soft voice.

Jake said, "Hello Gary. Thank you for calling me back. I hope they mentioned you could have called collect."

"They told me, Mr. Scott. I don't have many people on my call list, so it's nice to talk to someone. Most of my so-called friends abandoned me after the trial. Even my family gave up on me. We're granted a smart card that looks like a credit card, linking our Inmate Telephone System account to our allowed call list and bank account. It works well."

Jake shifted his phone to his other ear so he could write anything he heard. "I'm glad you called. I'm sorry to hear about your family and friends. There are a few more questions that are going to be pretty direct, but I want to hear your views on them. Are you okay with that? By the way, please call me Jake."

"Okay, Jake, go ahead."

"I met Damon Brooks yesterday. His story sheds a different light on you than the individual you seemed to be when I talked to you. I have to admit, what he said surprised me."

Gary stopped him there, by saying, "He told you about that guy I beat up a few years ago, didn't he? And that there were others. He said I had two personalities. He said I'm a different person when I'm angry and it's worse when I drink. Does that sound about right?" His voice became bitter. "He's one of the so-called friends I was talking about who abandoned me."

Jake said, "What do *you* have to say about it, Gary? It's essential that you're honest with me. Otherwise, it's a potential problem, no matter what we find."

"Everything he said is accurate. I have anger issues that I'm working to control. We were drinking heavily that day. This guy passed through the parking lot and made some smart comment about us trespassing on private property and that we should go somewhere else to drink. We had words and one thing led to another. I hit him with a bottle, but then I flew into a blind rage. I couldn't have stopped myself if I wanted to. I wanted to kill the guy. Good thing Damon was there or, frankly, I would have killed him.

"That's who I was back then. I wasn't a pleasant person when I lost my temper and especially when I had a few drinks. I was aware of the problem, but so were Damon and my other buddies. They never let me drink too much, and I appreciated that. When I was in a good mood, people liked me. Damon was even jealous of me because I had a lot of friends. He told me that. He even dated

Melissa for a while. My so-called friends disappeared when they saw the other side. Even my closest friends feared me when I lost my temper. I had one beer before it ran out the night of the murders."

Jake swung his chair back and forth as he listened.

He said, "But the alter ego you're describing went to see Matthew Pawsloski at the office, right? You had been drinking that day too."

Gary sounded contrite. "Yeah, when I found out about the affair, I alternated between mad and sad and that day I was mad. It was like I was a different person, as Damon said. The other me surfaced, and I had a few drinks, so it became worse."

Jake said, "It sounds like the man you're describing is capable of murder."

"Was, Jake, was. But I murdered no one. I admit I seriously injured people, but I killed no one. Since I've been here, I've taken anger management sessions and, of course, I haven't had a drink since I got here. I'm not proud of my past, Jake, but I'm a changed man. That night I drove to my house, thinking I might catch Melissa and Matthew. Maybe I'd be in prison for a legitimate reason if they had been there. They weren't at the house, and I didn't know where they were. I picked up the beer and went back to Damon's place. I promise you I did not murder them."

Jake started to believe Gary Thomas again, but he said, "Damon said you were pale and shaking when you arrived back at the house. Why, if you didn't find Melissa and Matthew at your place?"

"I spent the entire time driving back to the house wondering what I would have done if I had caught them. Especially if I caught them in bed. Think about how you would feel. I didn't know someone had already taken the gun. It scared me to think about what I might have done. The images rolled in my head like a movie reel. I decided on the way back to Damon's I was going to confront Melissa and ask for a divorce. That thought scared me too. I loved Melissa. I was so upset I had to stop and throw up on the way to Damon's house. The police said it was because I had just killed two people."

It all sounded plausible to Jake. He had one last question.

"Do you have any idea who could have killed Melissa and Matthew, Gary?"

"I've been wracking my brain. It had to be someone who either stole my gun or got it from Melissa and tried to pin it on me. It was a planned, deliberate misdirection to take the focus off whoever did it. Melissa knew my temper, so she might have taken the gun and given it to someone for safekeeping. But who? Wouldn't she sell it or hide it somewhere? I'm just guessing, but maybe she gave it to Matthew, and someone took it and used it on him. I don't know. It makes no sense to me."

Jake said, "What about Damon? He dated Melissa before you two got together. Could he have decided if he couldn't have her, no one could?"

"It was years ago that they dated. That just seems too far fetched."

Jake thanked Gary and hung up with the promise he would keep him posted on any developments. He leaned back in his chair and knit his fingers together behind his head. Something Gary said niggled at the edges of his brain. What if Gary was right? Did Melissa remove the gun from the house because she was afraid of him? What if she had given the gun to Matthew Pawsloski for safekeeping? What if Matthew kept the gun at the office because he didn't want it in his house? And what if Ryan Cambridge found it, used it on Matthew and Melissa, and framed Gary Thomas? But why were Gary's fingerprints the only ones on the gun?

Too many questions and not enough answers.

CHAPTER THIRTY-SIX

JAKE PREPARED FOR meeting the gang at breakfast, wondering what the day would bring. He watched the local news while waiting to leave. The forecast warned of a drastic drop in temperatures in a couple of weeks. Apparently, a warming event over the North Pole would be forcing cold air down to Canada and bringing with it not just freezing conditions, but face-numbingly glacial temperatures. The forecaster dramatically predicted overnight temperatures in the minus forties and a slight improvement throughout the day. He sensationally warned that frostbite occurs on exposed skin in fewer than ten minutes at those temperatures. Excellent information, but nothing new. Most winters brought a few days like that in Ottawa. Jake shut off the TV, thinking about the homeless and hoping they would find shelter before the polar vortex arrived. The rest of us will survive, he thought as he pulled on his winter gear.

When he arrived precisely at ten o'clock, it startled him to see everyone already there. His heart sank at the sight of the only vacant chair at the round table beside Pierre Chevrier, his least favorite member of the group. At least the chair was between Chevrier and Eric Jacobson, who sat beside Ryan Cambridge. His heart lifted when Dani greeted him with a smile. An extra member sat at the table between Dani and Chevrier. Emilie stared at the menu, but Jake suspected the teenager's cell phone would receive a workout while the adults chatted.

Jake removed his coat and draped it over the back of the chair. He stuffed his gloves and toque in the hood of his jacket. "How's everyone doing this morning? And who's this young lady?" He wished Dani had given him a heads-up. He wasn't certain how he should handle Emilie's attendance.

It sorted itself out when Emilie lifted her head from examining the menu and said, "Hi Jake," before returning to the task at hand.

Dani laughed and let Jake know she had already introduced Emilie to the group and explained he had met her daughter earlier.

Chevrier said with his French-Canadian accent, "We weren't aware Danielle even had a daughter. I guess you knew, eh Jake. It's nice to meet her."

Emilie ignored him.

Jason Pruitt brought coffee and Jake turned down a cinnamon roll, ordering whole-wheat toast instead. That brought head shakes and murmurs from the men, but Dani caught Jake's eye and winked. When Pruitt left, Jake wondered if the typical Canadian conversation starter of the weather had already run its course. The answer came quickly enough when Eric asked if anyone had seen the forecast of the impending minus 40-degree temperatures.

The conversation flowed smoothly as Pruitt served breakfast, but Ryan said little. Pierre talked about the mask policy still in effect on city buses and how difficult it was to police as a driver. He told them that fewer people complied since vaccines became available, but he had no plans to be punched in the face by someone ignoring the policy. He explained that if someone disregarded the policy, his job was to stop the bus and call the transit police so they could deal with it, but he described a couple of ugly confrontations. Jake felt a twinge of empathy for the man who spent most of his time at the breakfasts teasing him.

Eric, the former bureaucrat, said his old colleagues told him people were trickling back to the office after working at home for months. He chatted about his band and how live shows, the lifeblood of local performers, were slowly coming back, thanks to the vaccine. Of course, everyone shared their opinion on what "normal" would look like for the entertainment industry.

The conversation slowed as Jake glanced around the table. As he thought she would, Emilie polished off her meal and stared at her phone, her thumbs bouncing on the keypad. Attempts by the men to involve her with questions about school brought monosyllabic answers and wry smiles from Dani. The conversation clearly bored her, but Jake gave her credit for tolerating it until something better happened. Dani wouldn't have forced her, so she must have agreed to join.

A lull in the conversation afforded an opportunity for Jake.

"How are things going with you, Ryan?"

The whites of Ryan's eyes were a reddish color like he hadn't slept.

"Everything's good. No complaints. At least hockey is in full swing, unlike the music industry. Nobody can come out to watch us, but at least we can play. How's your writing, Jake?"

Jake couldn't help himself as his eyes darted to Dani and back to Ryan. He said, "I think I'm making progress. I spoke to Damon Brooks, a friend of Gary Thomas's. Gary attended a card game at Damon's place the night of the murders, but I guess the prosecution proved he still had time to kill Melissa and Matthew. Brooks told me Thomas has a temper, and he gave me some examples. I talked to Gary again. He admitted it but said he's getting help with his anger issues in prison. Gary certainly doesn't seem like a murderer to me."

Jason leaned over Jake's shoulder to refresh his coffee. Jake said, "I'm going to keep researching to see what more I can dig up. It's more about Gary Thomas now than it is about the book. If he's innocent, he doesn't deserve to be in prison." He noticed Dani's frown as he spoke.

Ryan's mouth opened to reply, but Pierre interrupted with a sharper tone than expected from a man who had little interest in Jake, other than to torment him. He said, "Why is this so important to you, Jake, eh? I know everyone talked about you writing a book but come on. It's like you're obsessed." He looked around the table for approval before turning his attention to Dani.

"Danielle, what do you think of this madness Jake is pursuing? Weren't you part of the investigation?"

Emilie, who appeared lost in her phone, glanced at her mom curiously, waiting for her response.

Dani handed her dishes to Pruitt, folded her arms on the table, and leaned forward to reply, obviously picking up on Jake's cue. She said, "I was part of the investigation and the evidence at the time pointed to a solid conviction. However, if Jake turns up something we may have missed, we'll reopen the investigation. Jake is a private citizen and as long as he doesn't cross any legal boundaries, he can do what he chooses. If it leads to freeing an innocent man, he should continue his research if he wants to."

Chevrier huffed, "Well, I think law enforcement and the legal system did its job and our friend Jake is wasting his time. What do you guys think?"

Eric said. "I agree with Danielle. It's a free country and if Jake wants to do some research and write a book, more power to him. He needs something to do. Since I retired, my wife makes sure I don't have that problem. She has a job jar for me." He laughed before saying, "I'll read the book when he's done."

Everyone's eyes swung to Ryan while he focused on the tablecloth in front of him. He mumbled, "I just hope you don't get hurt, Jake. Someone who committed murder could still be walking around in public. You could put yourself in danger."

Jake glanced at Dani again as the table fell silent. *Was that a threat?* He could certainly take it that way.

Dani almost imperceptibly shook her head.

Jake said, "I'm just working on a book. I don't think anyone is going to be coming after me."

He chose not to mention the threatening note on the windshield.

No one had anything more to add. The book discussion killed the conversation. They all paid their bills, and Jason hung around to say goodbye to his most loyal customers.

"So, what are you guys doing for the rest of the weekend?" he said.

There were a variety of answers. Chevrier said he had nothing planned. Eric said, "My wife will probably pull something out of the job jar." Ryan said he was leaving for a hockey tournament right after breakfast. Jake waited to hear what Dani was going to say. She surprised him when she spoke.

"Em and I are going skating on the canal. We're trying to convince Jake to come with us. He can add it to his new exercise routine. His trainer would be proud of him."

They all put on their coats and moved as a group toward the door.

Jake laughed along with the others. "I'm going to try it, but I have to find my skates and blow the dust off them. It sounds like fun. I have a training session again tomorrow morning, so I'll add a few more aches to the collection."

As they approached the door, Jason clapped Jake on the shoulder and said, "What time are you skating? I'd like to be there to video it. Could go viral. I can see the headline now." He drew a picture in the air. "Former reporter cracks head open on the ice."

Everyone laughed as they exited, but Jake stopped Dani halfway through the door. "It's a good question. What time are we going?"

They agreed to leave around one o'clock. Jake interpreted that to mean precisely one o'clock, and he said he would pick them up at the condo.

Dani told him about a girls' afternoon and evening she and Emilie had planned later in the day. As Jake walked with Dani and Emilie back towards their respective homes, Emilie said perceptively, "Boy, that French guy isn't very nice."

The wind whipped the chill through their coats, a portent of things to come. Dani pulled her scarf higher on her neck before responding. "I think he's just got a rough disposition, sweetie, but he seemed perturbed about the book."

Jake agreed. "I'll say. Do you know how or when Chevrier joined the group, Dani? If I remember correctly, he drove the bus route Eric used to take, and that's how they met."

They arrived at Jake's driveway. Dani said, "I honestly don't know. I came in after everyone else, remember?" As the wind gathered a swirl of snow and threw it in their faces, she said, "Are you sure you want to go skating this afternoon?"

Emilie peeked at her mom beneath her fur-lined hood and snapped. "Sure, if we want to freeze our asses off."

Dani frowned. "Language, Emilie. I wasn't talking to you, anyway. What do you say, Jake?"

Jake agreed with Emilie's sentiments, but he wanted to spend time with Dani. Besides, better this weekend than next weather-wise. But his mind was on Pierre Chevrier's overreaction to the book.

CHAPTER THIRTY-SEVEN

S KATING THAT AFTERNOON was everything Jake expected—cold, and his feet hurt. But the wind died down, the sun came out, and the laugh-filled afternoon ended with hot chocolate and the local delicacy, beavertails. Jake, Dani, and Emilie took full advantage of the Rideau Canal, which was built in 1832 and connected Ottawa to Lake Ontario. Originally constructed in case of war between Canada and the U.S., the canal now boasted two primary uses: boating in summer and skating in winter.

From the times he and his wife Mia had skated the canal, Jake knew the beauty of the ice surface with the snow along the sides and its inviting shacks could be spiteful, enticing skaters into forgetting about two things—its length and the wind. It was easy to become caught up in the moment and just keep skating on the nearly five-mile-long ice surface, forgetting you had to return. It was likewise easy to ignore the impact of the wind if it was in your back when you started. The canal worked its evil magic on the threesome, contributing to Jake's tender feet.

Still, it was worth it, as he enjoyed Dani's company. Emilie's disposition had improved dramatically since the night he found her in the park. A new boyfriend named Lucas had entered the scene, and any thoughts of the kid who broke up with her found their way into the dumpster of history. Things changed quickly in her life as they are wont to do for any teenager. Lucas enjoyed similar movies to Emilie, so according to her, they had "a lot in common." She had also reached what sounded to Jake like an uneasy truce with her father, although she clearly still much preferred being with her mom.

The cleared ice on the canal offered a smooth surface. Emilie was a natural, taking long smooth strides as her skates cut into the ice, the blades hissing on the frozen water. When Jake thought of his skating abilities, the image of a calf's splayed legs as it attempted to stand for the first time sprang to mind. It had been many years since he skated with Mia on his weak ankles.

Dani attributed Emilie's skating ability to playing competitive ringette, which she had done until the pandemic locked everything down. Jake had never seen a game, but he was curious. As they skated, Dani explained it was like hockey, but instead of a puck, they used a pneumatic ring, and instead of a blade the stick had a plastic tip. Dani said it was exciting to watch and had improved Emilie's skating skills tremendously.

As Jake watched Emilie sail past backward with her phone aimed at them, he replied, "Apparently."

At the end of their skate, as they crossed the rougher surface to reach the shack to change into their boots, Dani's blade caught in a crack, and down she went. She grabbed Jake's arm for support as she slipped. It didn't help. They landed in a tangle of arms and legs and gales of laughter. Passersby asked if they were okay, and they waved them off with thanks while untangling themselves and brushing snow from their clothing.

Emilie skated to them with her phone extended and said, "Check this out." She shaded the screen with her hand so they could see what she was showing them. The screen showed Jake landing on top of Dani with their arms and legs extended in an embarrassing video capture of their mishap.

Dani grabbed for the phone, but Emilie was too quick. She said to her grinning daughter, "Don't you dare post that on social media."

Emilie quickly shoved the phone in her pocket.

"Come on, Mom. That was sick. I'll just send it to my friends."

Dani whispered to Jake, "That means about 2,100 people on Instagram." Turning back to Emilie, she said, "Well, if you do, baby girl, I will confiscate your phone for a month. Sound reasonable?"

Emilie grumbled as she laughed and said, "Meanie."

Despite the cold temperatures, his achy feet, and the bruise on the knee that wasn't cushioned by Dani's soft but firm body when they fell, the afternoon disappeared too quickly for Jake. Dani reminded him on the way to the canal of the planned girl's afternoon and evening. They had appointments to have their hair and nails done, followed by dinner and a movie, and Jake understood he and Emilie's new boyfriend Lucas were not part of the plans. He hoped Lucas would approve of the movie choice for Emilie's sake, and he knew Dani and her daughter needed some time together.

After driving them home and urging them to enjoy their evening, Jake decided he needed groceries, so he pulled into the store near his place to stock up. He had a few more errands to run, and a stop at the beer store to replenish his supply followed. It was late afternoon by the time he finished shopping. The clouds obliterated the sun, darkening the afternoon. When he neared his house, the lights of the pizza restaurant attracted his attention. *Pizza and beer!* It would be another black mark with his zealous personal trainer, but she said he should reward himself occasionally. Tony, the large restaurant owner, greeted him in the usual boisterous manner and Jake soon had his pizza. He resolved to have his meal and then call Avery in Toronto.

Jake parked the car in the garage and pushed his key into the lock to enter the house. It met no resistance when he turned it. *What the hell!?* Evidently, he didn't lock the door before he left. He hesitated, thinking back. He *was* excited about meeting Dani and Emilie and going skating with them. It took some time to find his skates before he left, so he was almost late picking them up. Maybe in his rush, he just forgot. Or maybe he absentmindedly turned the key the wrong way. That had happened before.

He didn't know why, but something told him to turn the handle and push the door open slowly and quietly. He slipped into the gloomy entrance, softly closing the door behind him. As was his habit, he turned the latch when he closed the door, sealing himself inside. Later, with the clarity of hindsight, he realized he made a potentially fatal error, and only luck, or providence or whatever, saved him.

His eyes slowly adjusted to the dark, aided by a light reflecting from his office. The light startled him. Did he leave it on *and* forget to lock the door? Was he losing it altogether? Unnerved, Jake reached for the hall light switch, but he paused as he figured out the source of the light. It wasn't the overhead fixture or even the desk lamp in the office lighting the hall. The light was bouncing. The reflection jumped and rebounded off the office walls. Jake realized with a start it was the beam of a flashlight! The conclusion was undeniable and terrifying. Suddenly, his heart thundered in his chest, trying desperately to leap into his throat. Someone was in the house and they were rummaging around in his office.

What to do? He could confront the person in the office, but they might have a weapon. Jake looked around frantically for something, anything, within reach he could use to protect himself. Whoever was in the office could be the person who murdered Matthew and Melissa.

Then he thought how ridiculous this was. He needed to leave and let the police handle it. He was no hero and if the murderer was in his office . . .

It had to be *him*. Why else would anyone break into his house? Then his mind wildly switched gears. It could just be a crazed junkie seeking money for a score. But what if he had a weapon? *Jake had to get out of there.*

He reached for the door handle with one hand as he retrieved his phone from his pocket with the other. The resistance of the unyielding door sent a jolt through him, and his phone slipped from his shaking gloved hand, tumbling to the floor. It clattered on the ceramic tile, the sound echoing through the hallway like an explosion to Jake's ears.

He paused, listening. Had the intruder heard? He tried to see the phone in the dark, but it wasn't visible. *Dammit! It must have slipped under the bench!* He bent to search for it, but he would have to drop to his hands and knees to retrieve it. It was too late for that. Every sense was on full alert. Something crashed to the floor in the office. It sounded like a drawer from his desk. At least it meant the person didn't know he was home yet. He had time to get out. The phone would stay where it was.

The intruder could burst from the office at any minute. Then Jake made his second mistake. He eased the closet door open and reached around the corner until his fingers closed on something solid. The move ate up precious seconds he could have used to leave. The object he sought was a stick he used to play street hockey with the neighborhood kids when Mia was still alive. He meant to give it to the kids long ago, but never found the time. Now, at least, he could use it to protect himself if he couldn't get out fast enough. He left the closet door wide open as a barrier between him and the intruder.

Everything went black as Jake awkwardly fumbled for the lock with one hand while holding the stick with the other. The burglar had extinguished the flashlight. Jake held the stick in front of him as he reached behind his back for the lock. Gently diffused light lit the hallway through thin filmy material covering the sidelight beside the door, painting ghostly shadows on the walls and floor. Panic beckoned. Jake fought it off, but he couldn't slow down the runaway freight train that was his heart. His eyes flew open when the intruder, head down and his eyes watchful for obstructions in the dark, turned the corner.

Jake stood face to face with a possible killer.

His pupils had dilated sufficiently that he could make out the man's shape. He was tall and slender and scarcely visible with black attire from head to toe. A black ski mask completely obscured his face. Same height as Ryan but difficult to tell the weight because of the black winter clothing.

Jake found his voice. "Ryan, is that you?" He hoped to sound authoritative, but to him, his voice sounded shaky, barely above a squeak. His body vibrated as adrenaline pumped through his veins. Fight or flight? The man stopped dead in his tracks and looked up. Jake thought how absurd it must look. Two men standing fifteen feet apart, partially separated by an open closet door. One brandished a hockey stick like a saber. The other, a menacing apparition dressed in black carrying a silver rectangular object under his arm.

My laptop! Jake straightened and with both gloved hands on the stick, he summoned whatever courage he had left to thrust it out toward the intruder. "It's over, Ryan. Leave the laptop and I'll let you go." The words had no effect on the man as he inched forward. "STOP," Jake yelled at the top of his lungs as he jabbed the stick at the advancing intruder's midriff. The intruder was close enough now to slam the closet door shut and brush the stick aside with his arm while aiming a Taekwondo-style kick at Jake's ribs. The pain erupted along with a whoosh of air from Jake's lungs as the toe of the man's boot connected. Fortunately, Jake's arm, covered by his thick winter coat absorbed the brunt of the attack, but the kick caught enough of his midsection to wind him and the jolt slammed him back against the locked door. He slumped to a sitting position, gasping for air, pain and shock racing through his nerve endings. The stick clattered to the floor, bouncing to the entrance of the kitchen. Jake's position against the door blocked his attacker from leaving. The man grabbed his feet, attempting to haul him from the door, but Jake kicked at the burglar's hand. He connected and heard a satisfying grunt.

Jake's head began to clear from the shock of the kick, and he realized the laptop the man safeguarded under his arm restricted his movements. Otherwise, Jake realized, the intruder could have beaten him to a pulp by now. He pushed himself to his feet. "Who . . . who are you? Are you Ryan? Why are you doing this? Take off your mask, you coward." He desperately wanted to rip the mask off the guy's face.

As Jake rose, the man slammed into him like a linebacker with a blow that sent Jake sprawling sideways into the kitchen. Now the thief had clear access to the door. He was escaping. Still winded, Jake sensed a hard object pressing against his back. He pushed himself up on one elbow and reached underneath. He found the hockey stick and sat up, his head swirling. The man made it partway through the open door when Jake whipped the stick sideways in a two-handed baseball-style swing. While his position didn't allow him to swing with full force, his aim was true as he caught the man just above his boot-covered ankle with the blade of the stick. It wouldn't break the ankle, or even slow the man's escape, but it would leave a welt.

There was another discernible grunt as the man limped into the night.

Jake pulled himself to his feet, shaking his head to dislodge the cobwebs from his brain. He staggered through the door, hockey stick in hand, attempting to follow his attacker. All that was visible was a blurry shadow limping around the corner.

Any attempt to follow would be futile. Jake returned inside, propped the stick against the doorframe, and painfully squatted to retrieve his phone. He locked the door again, sat down, and shakily dialed 911.

CHAPTER THIRTY-EIGHT

J AKE SAT AT the kitchen table answering a police officer's questions when the doorbell rang. He didn't have time to move, so his eyes widened when Dani and Emilie unexpectedly walked in. Dani bent down with her hands on his shoulders to ask if he was okay. Jake's mind overflowed with questions as he assured her that he was. His foggy brain couldn't make sense of it. *Why are they at my house when they should be at dinner and a movie?*

Dani nodded to the constable who was wrapping up the interrogation. Paramedics had just left after confirming Jake's injuries were not serious. He assumed he had no major damage, aside from the skating stiffness, the usual aches and pains wrought by the personal trainer, and his arthritic knee. He felt about a hundred years old.

Dani and Emilie took off their coats and Jake soaked in the sight, completely forgetting his ordeal for a moment. Dani wore her hair pulled back from her face and tied into a knot at the top. She wore a white blouse and blue jeans that melded with her slender legs. The thought of Jennifer Lopez flitted through his head. Emilie's hair glistened like a waterfall down to her shoulders. She wore a tee shirt under a sweater and leggings that, well, melded with her lithe legs. Jake couldn't detect any holes in the leggings, a sight he had become accustomed to with her blue jeans. She wore a series of beaded leather bracelets. Both wore makeup for their girls' night out and Jake thought Dani looked youthful enough and Emilie old enough to be sisters. To Jake, they looked stunning, like they had just walked off a fashion runway.

The constable grinned, "Wow, you don't look the way you typically do, Staff Sergeant Perez. Must be ladies' night out."

Dani remained formal in her response, saying, "Indeed, it is, Constable Davidson. This is my daughter, Emilie. Thanks for letting me know about this."

As the constable nodded, Dani turned to Jake.

"Constable Davidson and I have worked together for a long time. He saw us in the restaurant and recognized you when he arrived. He realized I would want to know you were involved in an incident tonight, so he called me. I'm glad he did. Are you okay?"

No wonder the constable looked familiar Jake thought as Davidson got up to leave. He advised Jake he would call if he had further questions and let himself out.

Dani turned to Jake with concern etched on her face. She said, "Okay, you can tell me now. Are you okay? Be honest. What happened here?"

Jake nodded and said he was fine. He pointed at the kettle that boiled just before the police and paramedics arrived. He asked Dani if she would restart it and promised he would tell her the whole story.

She readily agreed. "Of course, you and Emilie go into the sunroom and I'll bring the coffee and hot chocolate as soon as it's ready. I want to hear everything so don't start without me."

As Jake slumped into his recliner with a groan and saw Emilie leaning forward in her chair opposite him, he noticed the same concern in the girl's face that Dani had displayed. He marveled at how much she looked like her mom. Even her facial expressions were similar. He started the fireplace with the remote and attempted to cheer her up.

"Oh, come on, Em, it's not that serious. Just a few bruises."

"Not that bad! Jake, he could have killed you. Some random druggie breaks into your house. It could've been terrible. I'm glad you're not hurt."

He winced and apologized to the girl for making her miss the movie. She shrugged it off.

She said, "My mom likes you. It upset her when she got the call. There's no way we were going to the movie after she found out about the robbery."

Jake was never certain which direction Emilie's conversation was going to come from, and he was learning to appreciate that about her. "I'm glad you came, Em. I like your mom, too. We get along well together and I'm enjoying getting to know you."

"You're different from my dad. I can talk to you and joke around. He's got a new girlfriend, and she doesn't like me." Her words were matter of fact, but her eyes reflected bitterness at her dad's choices as she reminded Jake about the new fiancée. "Mom is a different person around you. She's a hardass around the other police officers, but around you, she's relaxed. Totally different. I like that."

Jake winked, hoping to lighten the mood. He liked what he heard. He said, "Em, I'll let you in on a little secret. I have to treat your mom well, because I know if I didn't, she could kick my as . . . His voice trailed off as he heard Dani's footsteps coming down the hall. Emilie giggled, pretending to examine her phone.

"Alright, what are you two co-conspirators talking about behind my back?" Dani carried a tray with steaming mugs of coffee for her and Jake and hot chocolate for Emilie. Cookies Jake had stashed in the pantry had found their way to the tray. Dani distributed the cups and sat in a chair opposite Jake. She leaned forward, her hands clasped on her knees, and despite the makeup and her apparel, the formal policewoman took charge as her eyes locked on Jake's.

"Okay, let's hear it."

Jake apologized again for ruining their evening, which met with the same reaction he received from Emilie. He relayed the story as best he could, including his initial suspicion that he thought he must have left the front door unlocked. Leaving out that part of the story would raise questions about why anyone of sound mind would enter a house knowing an intruder lurked inside. Dani still asked why he didn't leave immediately after noticing the light in the office. He described the attacker emerging from the office as he tried to open the door which resulted in the fight.

Dani huffed they needed to have a serious conversation about taking unnecessary risks, and it relieved Jake to know he was off the hook for now. Then she said, "Do you think it was a random break-in?"

Jake sipped his coffee. As he set the cup down, he said, "I wish I knew, Dani. The man appeared to be Ryan's height and weight. He said nothing. I haven't been in a fight since grade three, so he got by me easily. Ryan has had hockey fights, but the kick seemed like it was martial arts style. Constable Davidson told me the office is a mess, and he said something about writing on the wall, but I haven't looked. Maybe I interrupted the thief before he could take anything else, but I'm hoping he just took the computer."

Dani absorbed the implication. "He must know about the book unless it was some random burglar hoping to sell the computer. Did you back it up?"

Jake recalled Davidson asking him similar questions. "Yes, fortunately, Nick, my daughter's boyfriend, suggested I do that. I only did it a couple of days ago. It sounded like a drawer hit the floor, so the guy might have been trying to find the backup or my notes or something."

Dani left to check the office. Her voice was muffled as she said, "There's stuff all over the floor in here. There's something else you should see, too."

Jake rose painfully from his chair and walked to the office with Emilie trailing right behind him. He turned the corner and Emilie bumped into him as he halted in the doorway. An explosion wouldn't have done much worse. Papers, file folders, pens, and paper clips lay scattered across the floor. The desk drawer was upside down on the floor and the gaping cabinet drawers threatened to topple it. He entered the office, avoiding shattered glass from a literary award he had received for his writing that had sat on his desk. Jake grimaced at the thought of cleaning up. He slammed the top drawer of the filing cabinet and glanced at Dani, who stood staring at the wall with her hands on her hips.

Jake turned to a sight that caused his stomach to flip. The words, LEAVE IT ALONE OR SOMEONE WILL GET HURT, had been scrawled with a black marker across the wall in large, jagged lettering.

Dani said, "I think we can discount a random theft. I take it your backup wasn't in here?"

Emilie stood beside Jake, her mouth agape.

It took him a few seconds to find his voice. "Uh, no, Nick told me to keep it someplace safe, so I did."

Dani walked out of the office, saying, "I know, it's in the oven."

Jake laughed mirthlessly. He said, "Close, it's in the casserole dish in the cupboard above the stove."

Jake and Emilie followed Oliver back into the sunroom. "There you are," he said to the cat. "You're some watch cat. You're supposed to warn me when there are intruders in the house and prevent them from leaving. But you disappeared like a coward."

The cat ignored Jake and sought refuge from Emilie, where he knew he would receive the attention he deserved. She hoisted him up on her lap where he settled in and began purring. Emilie said, "You were taking names, weren't you? I know you would have fought that wicked man to protect Jake. You can come home with me if you'd like."

Jake smiled at the one-sided conversation. The cat simply acknowledged by enjoying the attention and pressing his head firmly against Emilie's hand.

When Dani returned after checking the casserole dish, she confirmed the backup was still there. Jake asked if she would keep it after he reinstalled it on a new computer and she agreed. He said, "That's something else Nick suggested. I'll give it to you before something else happens."

After a few minutes of silence, Dani said, "Constable Davidson will lead the investigation into the break-in, but I'm going to speak with Ryan Cambridge. Enough of you playing detective. That's at least the second warning. Be careful. Keep your doors locked and if you see anyone suspicious or something unusual happens, anything at all, I want you to call me. Get a security system. Understand?"

"Yes, Dani, I understand. I don't want you to get in trouble with your boss either, though. Will you be okay talking to Ryan? Maybe I should do that."

"Did you not hear me? Or did you not understand? *I'm* going to talk to him. There are too many things adding up. He arrived first on the scene after the attack on Sarah. Coincidence? Maybe. Matthew and Sarah suspected something illegal was going on in the office. There's Ryan's apparent gambling problem. And why would someone steal your computer *this evening*? Maybe because he heard us talking about skating? I think I have plenty that I won't get my head blown off by the boss."

Jake nodded. He said, "There's one more thing, Dani. The intruder will have a king-sized welt on his leg and hopefully, a sore hand where I kicked him. He was wearing gloves, though. When he left, I saw him turn the corner, and he was having a little trouble walking. If you act quickly, you just might find out Ryan has a limp."

CHAPTER THIRTY-NINE

JAKE WOKE IN the morning with the fog of sleep and the previous night's experience still cluttering his brain. He moved his legs and felt the stiffness in his butt muscles where he landed after the attacker shoved him. His ribs protested with every breath, but the paramedic said there was nothing broken. If it persevered, he would have it checked again. It was an unsettled sleep, not the kind his body needed to heal. Black-cloaked men chased him throughout the night. Jake woke in a cold sweat just before one carrying an unidentifiable silver object under his arm reached to grab him. Although he didn't need to go, a trip to the bathroom helped him reset, but he was besieged by giant ants with silver heads when he fell back asleep.

He shoved everything aside by ticking off the mental list of items he wanted to accomplish during the day. It was incredible how they piled up now and his new lists included things he had neglected or put off since Mia died. He thought about postponing the day's session with the trainer, but he convinced himself that stretching and working the muscles would doubtless help. Plus, he planned to take advantage of the sauna.

He didn't feel so awful when he pushed himself out of bed and wandered to the kitchen in his blue pajamas. Oliver greeted him the minute he opened the bedroom door. He could never read the inscrutable cat's expression, but he thought if he could, it would be one of disappointment that he wasn't Emilie. Oliver arched his back when he petted him and immediately scarfed down the diminished portion of food Jake poured into his bowl. Jake suspected Oliver hated his diet even more than he did his.

The next order of business was to put the coffee pot on. A blast of icy air greeted him when he opened the door to retrieve the newspaper. The polar vortex was coming, and the damned paper carrier always dropped the paper just out of reach. He stepped out on the doorstep in his slippers. *Now* he was awake! He realized that the cold and any more aches and pains could put him in the running for the grumpiest man on the street award.

As he closed the door and locked it, he wondered how the intruder had broken in. Constable Davidson and Dani had asked the same question. Avery had the only spare key. He had thought of giving Dani one, for emergencies of course, but it was too soon. The gesture might give her the wrong idea, so he hadn't followed through. He saw no evidence of a break-in. No damage to the latch. No scratches on the door frame. Jake was convinced now he had locked the door. Either the guy had a key somehow, or, as Davidson speculated, he knew how to jimmy a lock without leaving a mark. If the intruder jimmied the lock without leaving a trace, it might help explain how Gary Thomas's gun got into the wrong hands.

He set the paper on the table and prepared his coffee and two slices of toast with peanut butter. It used to be his favorite time of the day. Getting up before Mia and sitting serenely in front of the fire while he enjoyed his breakfast and read the paper. He enjoyed the tranquil time, but he always looked forward to Mia emerging from the bedroom. Until recently, the silent time with his newspaper didn't mean as much. It was another routine and the precursor to more quiet time to follow.

Jake devoted the morning to gather up the papers scattered across the floor in his workspace. He stared at the writing on the wall. The well-formed, thick letters showed the burglar had taken his time and gone over them repeatedly. Only paint would erase them, and he resolved to do that soon. He couldn't stand being reminded that someone had invaded his domain, his sanctuary, every time he walked in the room.

As he bent to pick up his papers, he realized some of his notes were missing. The intruder must have stuffed them in his pocket. It was of no concern since Jake thought he had done a decent job of summarizing them on the laptop. He planned to flesh the notes out later anyway and his backup drive, which he reconfirmed was still in the casserole dish, would have everything he needed when he replaced his computer.

He wanted to talk to Avery, so he would ask Nick about the computer. The call should have happened last night, but exhaustion intervened, and he fell asleep soon after Dani and Emilie left. Avery picked up on the second ring and they chatted about her week for a few minutes. Then he described the break-in.

"WHAT? Are you okay? Were you there when it happened?"

"I walked in on him. Thankfully, he just wanted to get out, and I couldn't stop him." Jake felt guilty about leaving out most of what happened. He and Mia made Avery understand that omitting or misrepresenting the truth was the same as lying. He rationalized it by telling himself the complete story would only alarm her unnecessarily.

She was also curious about the lock. She asked, "How did he get in?"

"I don't know, honey. The police think he picked the lock. There's no damage to the door."

"Oh my God, Dad, that's terrible. Our neighborhood used to be so safe. You need to get an alarm installed."

"I haven't heard of other break-ins on the street, but an alarm is a great idea. Dani thinks so, too. I think it was a one-off, but he stole my computer, so I need to speak with Nick. Is he around?"

"The burglar probably wanted to sell it to buy drugs. No, Nick went into the office today. The only reason you caught me is that I'm working from home. Do you want him to call you?"

"Yes, please, I need the specs he used for my computer so I can replace it. Life will be simpler if I buy the same kind."

He realized he hadn't told Avery about the wording printed on the wall. He had no plans to as he heard her footsteps over the phone.

"Just a second." She was silent for a few seconds and then she returned and announced she had it. "He scribbled it down on a piece of paper. I can scan it and email it to you, but don't you have the packing slip? It should have the information you need."

"I never even thought of that. It's probably still in the box. I was probably so eager when it arrived, I didn't even look. I'll look for it but send the order information anyway and please say 'hi' to Nick. Now I have to go. Busy day today. It's torture day."

"Ah, you're going to see your personal trainer. Good for you, Dad. I'm so proud of you. Love you. Talk to you soon."

"I love you too, honey. Bye for now."

Jake found the packing slip and also checked his insurance policy to see if he could make a claim, but his deductible nixed that.

He spent the rest of the morning cleaning his office, a chore that took until after noon to finish. He understood now when people said they felt violated after a robbery. It wasn't just the robbery. It was that someone was in *his* household, invading *his* privacy, going through *his* stuff. What if it was the murderer? Would he come back? And what about the threats? *Someone could get hurt.* What did *that* mean? Jake concluded he was going to stop pursuing it and let the police figure it out. The book could come later. He was done.

He tried to push it out of his mind as he washed some masks in a basin in the kitchen. After hanging them up, he threw his workout clothes in his gym bag and drove to his session to meet with Attila, the name he had given his trainer at the beginning. He looked forward to the sessions now. He wasn't nearly as sore after each one, and he felt he was making progress.

The friendly receptionist at the counter greeted him by name when he walked in. There were still limits on the number of people allowed into the gym, so legging-clad young women and mostly buff young men occupied every second machine. A thump on the floor above told him some macho dude was probably lifting more free weights than he could handle.

His trainer congratulated him on his week, only mildly chastising him for the minor missteps with his diet. A three-pound weight loss put them both in a good mood. The session went by quickly and he spent a few glorious minutes warming his muscles in the sauna. It was time well spent.

He purchased the same brand of laptop loaded with the identical software at Best Buy. Loading his notes from the backup drive and the rest of the pizza from last night awaited him. Since he had lost weight, a further reward of a beer couldn't hurt either. He looked forward to it, especially after last night's events. He wanted to know about Dani's conversation with Ryan, although he was certain she would let him know sooner rather than later.

When he arrived home, he unpacked the laptop and plugged it in. While the battery recharged, he set the pizza on a plate and shoved it in the microwave. He was about to press the timer when the doorbell rang. Probably Dani, he thought.

But it wasn't Dani.

The sight on the doorstep made his stomach drop. He nudged the door closed again, so it was only open a crack, and held his shoulder against it.

Ryan Cambridge stood on the doorstep.

The sun shone a spotlight on a disheartened, downtrodden man. He had the collar of his coat pulled up, leaving his face in shadows, but it looked like he had a black eye.

Could the black eye have happened during the scuffle when Ryan tried to leave the house? Had he come for the computer backup?

Ryan stood back far enough that Jake felt comfortable he could slam the door if he had to.

Jake leaned toward the crack in the door. He said, "What are you doing here, Ryan?"

Ryan said, "I need to talk to you. Danielle Perez has been trying to reach me all day. She called a few times, but I didn't pick up. I saw her name on the display. She came to the house too, but I didn't answer the door. I want to talk to you first. I need you to understand so you can help. Can I come in?"

"What do you want to talk about?"

"I know you have suspicions about me. I want to clear things up."

Ryan moved toward the door, but Jake closed it tighter.

"Stay back, Ryan. Where did you get the black eye? Were you here yesterday?"

Ryan stopped with his hands in the air. A frown creased his forehead, knitting his eyebrows together. He said, "Yesterday? No, I was at a hockey tournament. Remember, I told you at breakfast I was going to a tournament? It was a one-and-done tournament in Cornwall. We lost, so we came home. What's wrong with you? Are you scared of me? I don't understand why you're acting this way. Come on, Jake, it's freezing out here."

Jake wanted to believe his friend. Did he have this all wrong? Questions tumbled in his head, but Ryan seemed sincere and somewhat desperate. He decided a meeting in public could work.

"Seems like a long way to go for a one-loss-and-done tournament, but okay, let's talk. But not here. I'll meet you at Brew and Buns in fifteen minutes. After that, talk to Dani, uh Danielle. Agreed?"

Ryan shrugged, the confusion on his face reflected in the shadows as the sun disappeared behind a cloud. "Okay, whatever works for you. Thank you. I'll see you there in fifteen minutes."

Ryan Cambridge turned to leave the doorstep and Jake watched him limp to his car.

CHAPTER FORTY

JAKE KNEW HE would be in trouble if he didn't tell Dani, so he dialed her immediately after Ryan left. She answered with a lively "Hello" and asked Jake how he was doing. He bought time for himself by telling her he had cleaned up the office and assuring her he was feeling much better.

She said, "I've been trying to reach Ryan. I even went to his house. He must still be at the hockey tournament he was talking about."

Jake inhaled deeply before he said, "I know you've been trying to reach him, and he isn't at the tournament. He was here."

Silence hung at the other end of the line as if Dani needed time to absorb the news before erupting. Jake imagined the increase in earthquakes and tremors before volcanos blow. Then it happened.

"WHAT!? What do you mean he was at your house? What did he want? You didn't let him in, did you?"

Jake replied in an even voice, saying, "He knows you're looking for him, but he wants to talk to me, first. I don't know why.

I didn't let him in, but I agreed to meet him at Brew and Buns in a few minutes on the condition he talks to you when we're finished."

"Well, at least you used *some* common sense by asking for a meeting in public. Did he ask for anything else, like, I don't know, the backup to your computer?"

"Nothing like that, but there is something else. I think he had a black eye, and he walked away with a limp. He said he was playing hockey in Cornwall, but they lost so they came home last night. If he was, he couldn't have been at my place, but it's conceivable I gave him the black eye and I absolutely could have given him the limp. He seemed sincere though, Dani. Let me talk to him first, like he asked."

"Well, I'll verify he played in the hockey tournament. My gut tells me to follow you to the restaurant and arrest him as a person of interest but go and talk to him first. Make sure he calls me while you're sitting there. I don't want him leaving town after he talks to you. There's one other thing. I'll be waiting at your house while you're talking to him."

It was Jake's turn to hesitate. Then, he said, "I don't have a problem with that, but why wait at my house?"

Dani spoke deliberately as if trying to impress something on her daughter. "First, I'm going to watch you walk to the restaurant, so you don't get jumped on the way. Second, did it occur to you he's trying to get you away so someone can ransack your house to locate the backup?"

Jake expelled air through his nose as the specter of Dani's suggestion settled on him like a canopy. It was a legitimate possibility and one that hadn't occurred to him. He said, "You're right of course, I never thought of that. Maybe I'm too willing to give him the benefit of the doubt. Can you come to the house now? I told him I would meet him in fifteen minutes and that was 10 minutes ago. I don't want to spook him, so he takes off *before* I talk to him."

"Wait. I'll be right there. I'm not saying he's guilty. You're right to talk to him, but please make sure he calls me right after. Sorry if I came on a little heavy, but if something happened to you, I wouldn't forgive myself. This case is making me a little crazy." A rustling sound drifted across the ether. "I'm putting my coat on now. See you in a couple of minutes."

Jake waited with his coat and boots on until Dani roared into his driveway, and after a brief hug, he left for the restaurant. The hug was so natural. They had hardly touched other than the fall on the canal, but Dani threw her arms around him like the most natural thing in the world. Was he making too much of it? Friends hug all the time, but this felt special, and Jake reveled in it the entire walk to Brew and Buns.

Ryan was waiting when he arrived, and Jake mused to himself it was the same table at the back used for all his clandestine meetings lately. Jake thought Ryan was fortunate to find a spot considering diners occupied most of the tables. Amanda poured coffee for Jake soon after he arrived.

Ryan opened the conversation. "I imagine you talked to Danielle before you came over."

Jake examined the purple and yellow bruising around Ryan's eye, clear in the restaurant's light. He decided he needed sugar in his coffee for this conversation, so he added a generous amount as he spoke. He said, "Yes, I did. She insisted you call her in front of me when we finish our conversation. If you don't agree, I'll call her to come over right now. There are many things I don't understand. You wanted this conversation, but I have questions, starting with the black eye. How did you get that?"

Surprise flitted across Ryan's face. He said, "I didn't think that would be your biggest concern, but I was in a fight in last night's game. A guy slashed me on the back of the leg, and it pissed me off, so we dropped the gloves. I got in a couple of licks, but he caught me with one just before the ref stepped in." The corner of his mouth lifted, and he chuckled wryly before saying, "Now I have a sore leg and a sore eye."

Jake said, "Dani's going to corroborate that you were at the game while we talk."

Ryan stiffened. Jake considered the reason for the concern, but his friend clarified it when he said, "Of course, but I don't understand all this concern about the hockey tournament. I wanted to talk about what's going on at my firm, and all you're interested in is my hockey game. Why is that?"

Jake wasn't in the mood to explain anything, but he wanted Ryan's reaction, so he told him about the break-in and ensuing fight.

Ryan's eyes widened and his mouth fell open at Jake's recollection of the incident. Finally, he said, "I understand now, and I assure you I was playing hockey in Cornwall when someone broke into your house, Jake. Dani will confirm I was there. I'm glad you weren't hurt. You actually think they were after your laptop?"

Jake drained his cup, surprised at how quickly the coffee disappeared, so he raised it to show Amanda he wanted a refill. He glanced around, startled to see that most tables had emptied. "That's all the guy took. I assume that's what he was after, but I interrupted him. If it was, it's someone who knows we're looking into Gary Thomas's case. It's a narrow list." He examined Ryan's face across the table. "Anyone who knows what I'm doing could have hired someone to break in."

Jake wasn't an expert at reading expressions, but all he saw on Ryan's face was concern. But concern for what? Concern for Jake's wellbeing or concern that they were closing in on him? Jake repeated his suggestion. "The intruder wouldn't have to be in town to make something like that happen."

Ryan exploded. "For Christ's sake, Jake, I had nothing to do with the murder nor with breaking into your house. That's why I wanted to talk to you. Let me explain what's going on, and hopefully, you'll understand why I had nothing to do with it. I'll be right back." He got up to use the bathroom.

Amanda arrived with a freshly brewed pot of coffee and watched Ryan disappear down the hall. "Everything okay over here? He seems upset."

Jake nodded, "Yeah, he's just a little stressed. Hard day at work." He forced a chuckle, saying, "I don't know whether another coffee will make it better or worse but fill his up too, please."

While he waited, Jake dialed Dani. When she picked up, he said, "Everything's fine, but I think we'll be here a while."

CHAPTER FORTY-ONE

RYAN WAS CALMER when he returned. The front of his hair was damp where he had obviously splashed water on his face. He began his story.

"Our firm is in trouble. It started well before the murders happened. I'm not even sure when it started exactly, but my partner, Luc Tremblay, discovered a discrepancy in a trust account he administered. He didn't tell any of us until afterward. He tried to fix the problem himself, but he just made it worse."

Ryan stared into the distance, apparently summoning the pieces of the story. His eyes glistened.

Jake pressed him. "What problem did he turn up?"

Ryan's gaze swiveled back to Jake. "I don't know how much you know about trust accounts, but they're established when we're required to hold funds on behalf of a client. To keep everything clean, we set up a separate bank account for each trust fund. My partner set one up for the proceeds on the sale of a house for a particularly wealthy client as we commonly do. Around the time he would have expected it, Tremblay received a request from the client or someone he thought to be the client, to withdraw the money. Luc approved the withdrawal like normal.

"We have an internal control procedure in place whereby a staff member has the authority to co-sign a requisition so that a partner isn't the only person signing. It's designed to protect the partners and the firm. By law, a non-licensed employee can't initiate a transaction, but they can co-sign, so, my partner initiated the requisition, the employee co-signed, and Luc transferred the money to the client electronically. Everything seemed normal at that point." Ryan's hands trembled as he picked up his cup.

Pieces clicked into place in Jake's mind—a puzzle becoming a picture. He said, "I'm assuming the employee you're talking about was Matthew Pawsloski."

Ryan's cup rattled on the table as he set it down. His eyebrows angled upward, forming an inverted 'V,' as the corners of his mouth turned down. He nodded and said, "The client who originally instructed the firm was legitimate, of course, but the person who requested the money was a fraudster. He hacked our client's account and emailed the instruction to e-transfer the money. In case you're interested, the technical term for someone pretending to be another person is 'spoofing,' and that's what this was."

Another pause. Jake took the opportunity to say, "Did you go to the police?"

Ryan sighed. "I still didn't know about it at this point. My partner, Tremblay, was worried about the firm's reputation and his own if the word got out. He said later the bogus client fooled him so easily, no one would ever trust us with their money again. The whole thing embarrassed him, so he tried to fix it himself. It was a stupid thing to do, but I might've done the same thing, I don't know. I don't hold him responsible." He shook his head before saying, "He sold his house to pay off the amount we lost."

Jake interjected. "How much money are we talking about?"

"Close to a million dollars."

Enough to kill for, Jake thought as he exhaled noisily. But who? The partner? He had motive, but by Ryan's face, there was more to the story.

Ryan said, "It gets worse. Luc did another stupid thing. He started gambling, hoping to win enough to buy a new house. That's when I noticed something was wrong. He wasn't himself. He would come to work looking like a tractor ran over him. His eyes were bloodshot, his hair was a mess, and he often wore the same clothes two days in a row like he hadn't been home overnight. He told me his marriage was falling apart. I couldn't believe it. We socialized some and he and his wife were the perfect couple, holding hands and enjoying each other's company. He told his wife we were expanding the firm, and he needed to put more money in, so that's why they had to sell the house. She discovered his gambling addiction. I called him into my office one day and asked what was going on. He avoided the question for a while, but suddenly he broke down and blamed everything on his marriage breakdown. It was awful, but it seemed like a rational explanation. I still didn't realize how bad it was at this point.

"Then one day Matthew came to me. He said he'd found discrepancies in the trust funds. I didn't realize it at the time, but he thought I was stealing money. It looked like someone was circumventing our control procedures and taking funds from the accounts. I looked into it and discovered it was Luc. It was obvious he was borrowing from one fund and covering it with money from another. I could see it was spiraling out of control. He was depleting the trust funds, and we were going to go under, owing millions of dollars if it didn't stop. I confronted Luc about it, and this time, he confessed everything. The fraud, his gambling debts, everything. It started with someone who purported to be our client defrauding the firm of the original money and it got worse from there with his gambling addiction."

Jake stared across the table at Ryan. He said, "Jason at Brew and Buns told us he overheard you and Matthew in a heated argument. He said you had coffee and then took the argument outside. Yet, you said the other day you barely knew Matthew. What's that about?"

Ryan sighed heavily. He said, "As I said, Matthew thought it was me who was stealing from the firm. He invited me for coffee and accused me of theft. At first, I thought he was making things up. His accusations made me mad. I've always put my clients first. I was on the verge of firing him, but I discovered he was right. Only it was Luc who was responsible. I knew if I told you about the argument with Matthew, it would look even worse for me. I've been so wrong about everything."

Jake waited quietly as Ryan seemed to fold into himself at the memory of everything that happened. He said, "Ryan, you seemed so calm at our breakfasts. I had no idea you had these issues."

"Those breakfasts and my hockey were all that kept me going. It was a sense of normalcy. I couldn't even tell my wife about it. She would have been too worried. I tried to help Luc with his gambling addiction. He and I went to the casino twice so I could try to help him control the money he spent, sort of to wean him off, but he just went other nights without me. I finally got him to enter the self-exclusion program. They take the person's picture and it's entered into an electronic database, so he's restricted from every casino in the province. It helped for a while, but there's still online gambling. A person has to want to help themselves."

"Yes, I can see that. I have a question though, Ryan. The night that Dani and I went to watch Eric's band play, I distinctly remember you saying it was too late for you—that you are in bed by ten so you wouldn't be going. Around midnight, when we were on our way home, we saw you in a big hurry to go somewhere. Since you said Eric's show was too late for you, we were concerned about you and followed. You ended up at the casino. Are you sure it isn't you who has a gambling addiction? Dani said she'd seen you go to the casino more than once. You said Tremblay's problems were before the murders. It's been three years. Why are you still going?"

Ryan's eyes were pleading, concern notched into his chiseled features. "Everything I've told you is true, Jake. I can see why you might think that I have a problem, but I sponsored Luc with his self-exclusion. I went there as a friend when he signed the document excluding him from the casino. That was before the murders. I thought I could help wean him off gambling, but it was no use. It bothered me all this time. I met with Casino management since then to tell them about the effect gambling had on Luc. They gave me zero satisfaction the first time I went, so I returned a second time to meet with more senior people. That was the night Eric played at the bar.

"I'm ready to tell Danielle everything I've told you. It's probably too late for the police to investigate the hacking incident, but if they want to send in a forensic team to verify everything I've said, I'm prepared for that. I've been doing my best to stay afloat, but I'm on the verge of declaring bankruptcy."

Jake gave up any pretense that he and Dani weren't close and referred to her by her shortened name. "I think it's time you called Dani, Ryan. I just have one more question. Do you think your partner might have killed Melissa Thomas and Matthew Pawsloski?"

Ryan bit his lip before answering. Finally, he said, "The reason I went to the casino besides talking to their management was to tell them they could remove Luc from the exclusion list. It took me all this time to work up the strength to do it. It's something I should have done long ago. Luc couldn't have killed Melissa and Matthew. He's dead. He committed suicide before the murders happened."

CHAPTER FORTY-TWO

JAKE NOTICED AS they walked to his house how relaxed Ryan seemed. He was a changed person, as if telling the story lifted a massive weight from his shoulders. Still curious, Jake said, "Why is the firm still Cambridge and Tremblay if your partner killed himself three years ago?"

Ryan shoved his hands deep into his pockets. He didn't look at Jake as he replied. "His widow asked that I leave his name on the firm until they settled the estate. I kind of liked having his name there, anyway. Luc and I went through law school together and we worked well as a team. The estate is settled now, so I'll remove his name."

"Okay, so why avoid Dani to talk to me first? She needs to know everything you've told me. She has suspicions about you and the murders. Why not go straight to her?"

"Yes, I could have, but I wanted you to hear firsthand what happened. Even though we only see each other on Saturday mornings, our friendship is important to me. You said nothing specific at our breakfasts, but I sensed you had your suspicions about me. It might have been my imagination, but your demeanor toward me seemed to change. After everything I've been through, I need friends more than ever." He glanced at Jake and smiled. "Besides, I think you and Dani are seeing each other, so having you in my corner can't hurt."

They reached the end of the driveway leading to the house. Jake said. "I'm not positive we're seeing each other, but we get along well. I don't think I have any sway over Danielle Perez or ever will. She's as professional as they come. Be straightforward with her, Ryan. If you miss something, I'll fill in any blanks as I remember them."

Jake unlocked the door and announced their arrival as they stepped inside.

Dani emerged from the kitchen. She was cordial but professional as Jake said she would be. She had brewed coffee while she waited and offered Ryan and Jake a cup. Both declined, saying they had drunk enough at Brew and Buns to float a couple of ships.

Darkness shrouded the house, other than the kitchen where Dani waited, so Jake clicked on the living room's lights. Once they settled comfortably, and Dani tapped on the recorder on her phone, Ryan began. He displayed only a hint of the emotion that previously filled his face as he told the story matter-of-factly.

Jake worried the first telling was a dry run. The word 'rehearsal' floated through his brain. He watched Dani study Ryan's face as the story unfolded. He knew she was looking for deception in the eyes, tics in the face, tells that he was being less than forthright. Jake knew Dani would investigate every bit of Ryan's story. He thought how surprising it would be if she hadn't already verified whether Ryan was at the hockey tournament in Cornwall.

Silence hung in the air for a few minutes until Dani asked, "Aren't there specific accounting and audit requirements for trust funds? Why wouldn't an auditor have identified the problem before you did?"

"There are very specific requirements. The funds have to be reconciled every month, we must provide statements to the client, all the supporting documents have to be kept on file. We engage an outside accountant, but they can only work with the information we provide. Luc was adept at keeping a second set of books. It would have caught up to him eventually if Matt hadn't stumbled across it. Our accountant has known everything since I found out, and he's helping me with the bankruptcy proceedings."

Then Dani brought up a subject that had completely slipped Jake's mind. She said, "Sarah Brown told us you drove her to the hospital the night someone attacked her. It's interesting that you just happened to come along. Did you attack her?"

"WHAT? No. I didn't attack her. When I arrived in the garage, she was lying on the floor, bleeding. She was semi-conscious. I decided it would be better to take her to the hospital than wait for an ambulance."

"Was her purse missing?"

"There was nothing around her. It was just her lying on the floor. I took her to the hospital, got someone to see her, and left."

Dani asked a few more questions, leaving Ryan looking spent when she finished. His eyes drooped and his shoulders sagged, but the lines in his face had eased. Apparently, recalling everything took its toll, but as it had with Jake, unburdening to Dani seemed to offer relief. He even teased Dani at the end about dating Jake. Dani, still in investigator mode, didn't react. Instead, she said, "What are your plans, Ryan? It sounds like you have things to sort out."

"I have *many* things to sort out, but I feel considerably better. The positive news is that declaring bankruptcy doesn't mean disbarment from practicing law. I have done nothing illegal or unethical. I tried to help my friend and business associate save the firm, and that was my only goal. Even if I haven't saved the firm, I can still practice. The bad news is that clients will be reluctant to hire me to safeguard their money. Our firm has a word-of-mouth reputation now for not doing that very well, and once this story gets out, it will be worse. I'll practice out of my home for a while and specialize in something else besides real estate, but that's okay. I'll have to downsize the staff, but I should be able to keep Sarah and one or two others busy. My wife has been very understanding through the whole thing and she's all for me starting fresh on a smaller scale. It sucks, but it is what it is."

Jake glanced at Dani and walked Ryan to the door. "I'm sorry it had to come to this, Ryan. Let me know if there's anything you need. I hope you will still come to the breakfasts."

Ryan put on his coat before turning to Jake. "Thanks, my friend. Your support means a lot. I'm sure I'll be at the breakfasts soon. As I said, it's part of my support mechanism." He threw his arms around Jake. "Thanks again. Take care."

Jake closed the door and wandered back to the living room to find Dani sitting with her legs crossed, staring at a Benjamin Chee Chee print on the wall. His arrival broke her trance. He sat in the chair, throwing his stockinged feet up on the hassock and leaning his elbows on the arms with his hands clasped across his stomach. He said, "Well, what do you think? Is he telling the truth?"

"I'm pretty sure he is. It's a fascinating story. He's carrying the guilt of not recognizing the problem sooner, but he did the best he could under the circumstances. I verified he was with his teammates in Cornwall and got into a fight with another player during the game. I tracked down the referee who confirmed the slashing incident that led to the fight. The referee corroborated it was a vicious slash, and it surprised him that Ryan continued playing. He kicked the other guy out of the game after the fight. I'll get one of my constables to follow up on the other stuff Ryan told us."

Jake tilted his head, saying, "You must have known about Tremblay's suicide. Was it investigated?"

"I knew. The police are always among the first responders at a death scene. His wife told the investigators about his financial difficulties and their marriage breakdown. It wasn't given much thought after the murder weapon surfaced. Everything turned on that. I'll be investigating Tremblay's situation more now that the pieces are falling into place. I'm sad about everything Ryan's gone through, but I'm happy we can all but eliminate him from having anything to do with the double homicide."

Jake furrowed his brow and waved his hand in the air as he said, "Where does that leave us? Do you think Gary Thomas should be in prison?"

"Maybe he should. If he's not guilty, then who? Maybe I should do what my boss says and just drop the case."

"Maybe so. The break-in adds another dimension to the investigation, but there's so much that still points to Gary. The gun. Motive. The opportunity. He could be orchestrating this whole thing from prison, although he doesn't seem to have many visitors or make phone calls. Who else could it be? What would give someone the motive to do something like that? What about covering up the hacking of close to a million dollars? That could be it. What else could be a motive? What about Sarah Brown's crush on Matthew Pawsloski? And why is she still working at the firm? That seems strange. Did she feel strongly enough about

Matthew to commit murder? If so, why not just get Melissa out of the way, so she could have Matthew to herself? Damon Brooks dated Melissa and said that he was jealous of Gary. Was he jealous enough to murder Melissa and frame Gary? Then there's the way Pierre Chevrier reacted about the book. Way over-the-top if you ask me. Why? Maybe Luc Tremblay's death wasn't a suicide. I just think there are avenues to pursue yet, Dani." He deliberately left Dani's former partner off his list of suspects. He didn't think she would take kindly to the suggestion.

Dani sighed. "I'm so tired of it all, Jake. You're right, there are people with motive. You're my biggest supporter and I appreciate it. Some of my colleagues will investigate Ryan's story, and then there're the notes warning you off and the break-in. We're just missing something. I need to focus on my work and Emilie. Speaking of my daughter, did I tell you her language has improved?"

Jake laughed. "No, did you finally get through to her? My mother always threatened me with a bar of soap in my mouth if I swore."

Dani shook her head. "Not me. Her new boyfriend Lucas comes from a strict family and they don't tolerate swearing. So, as long as he's in the picture, there will be a moratorium on the four-letter words."

They shared a hearty laugh at the thought and spent another hour trading stories about their past. The conversation continued until the light snapped off at 11 o'clock, plunging the house into darkness.

Dani snickered and said, "Is that a hint?"

Jake reached over and turned it back on.

"No, sorry, it's on a timer. I'm usually in bed before now."

Dani said, "Well, speaking of bed, it's time for me to head home. Promise me one thing before I go, Jake."

Jake's face lit up in an innocent smile. "I know, you want me to be careful."

As they walked arm-in-arm to the entrance, Dani agreed. "Well, there's that, but I don't need to tell you again. I think you have finally figured that part out. No, I would like to finish our date since the last one ended abruptly with the trip to the hospital. I was enjoying myself and I'd like to try it again if you're agreeable. Let's wait a few days to see where this case goes and then go back to the same restaurant. If you don't object and I can fit it into my schedule, that is."

Jake's smiled widened. He said, "You know what? I can think of nothing better."

CHAPTER FORTY-THREE

THE NEXT MORNING, Jake enjoyed a long soak in the tub after which he sought out the paint supplies from the basement where they sat on a shelf in his workshop since before Mia's death. He and his wife had plans to paint the house, but it never happened. As he searched for the supplies, he noticed mouse droppings in a corner of the basement. He guessed it was even too cold for the mice and, while Oliver would no doubt gleefully deal with that problem, Jake didn't want them in the house, period. He bought steel wool along with the additional paint supplies at Preston Hardware so he could temporarily plug any holes until he could seal them properly when it got warmer.

The lettering on the wall faded to memory as Jake rolled the cool gray paint, covering the last of the words. Some still showed through. It would take two coats, but the lettering would soon no longer be detectable to anyone. The walls soaked up the paint as he contemplated the passage of time since the last sprucing up, or even preventative maintenance, to the house. Maybe, he thought, the intruder did him a favor by using the laundry marker Sharpie from his desk to write the shocking words.

In a daring move, he wore the same khaki pants he had on when he took Dani to watch Eric's band at the Rainbow. It spelled the death knell for the pants as they were now paint-splattered and forever destined for work. The new clothes he bought with Dani and Emilie added to his renewed energy and he resolved to buy more. It was another step up the ladder from the doldrums that entombed him for the last few years. As he dipped his angle brush to paint the corner, he appreciated the simple things that bring a person joy and satisfaction.

Painting took his mind off the case, but he had resolved to leave it alone, anyway. He would start writing something else. Maybe even a thriller. Something with police procedures in it. It would be a challenge, but why not give it a shot? He had time, enjoyed the research and writing aspects, and it would be a learning experience. If recent events taught him one thing, it was that he needed something to do. Otherwise, he decided, he would just fade away.

He finished the last corner and leaned against the desk in the middle of the floor to observe his handiwork. *Not bad!* The wording was legible only because he knew what it said. He liked the new soothing gray color recommended by the salesclerk at the hardware store.

He was in a great mood, mostly thanks to the memory of Dani's parting words the night before. She wanted another date. He would have to be patient until her schedule cleared, but it was exciting. She was an extraordinary lady, and he was comfortable that Mia would approve. He thought the two women would have enjoyed each other's company. And Jake was becoming fond of Emilie. They had come a long way since their first meeting when

Jake struck out miserably. He felt like he had been reborn, and Dani and Emilie were a big part of the rejuvenation.

The plastic drop sheet rustled as he high-stepped across it and around the furniture he had shoved to the middle of the room. He removed his bedroom slippers when he reached the closed door, concerned that he had accidentally stepped on wet paint drippings off the roller. The hardwood floor felt cool on his stockinged feet as he padded down the hall. Oliver greeted him with a loud meow, and Jake assumed the cat was grumpy because the closed door blocked him from any opportunity to step in the paint.

Jake strode to the kitchen, opened the door to the fridge, and extracted a container of vanilla yogurt. If anyone had asked a year ago whether he would eat yogurt, he would have laughed. Now it was part of his daily snack as he spooned a generous helping into a bowl, added granola, and headed for his favorite chair in the sunroom. He clicked the remote to the weather channel and listened to dire warnings about the polar vortex. The forecast indicated that the temperature would plummet to minus 32 that night. Rather than work it out in his head, he tapped on the new conversion app Avery had suggested, which told him it would be almost minus 26 Fahrenheit. Yup, cold, he agreed. The old house would creak and pop tonight as the building materials expanded and contracted in the cold. It didn't matter; he had no plans to go anywhere for the next few days. He flipped through the channels to an old episode of CSI. Maybe they would give him some ideas for a novel.

Oliver wandered in and decided after scanning the room that Jake's was the only lap available, so he climbed aboard and settled in. Jake became engrossed in the show while he scratched the white spot under the cat's chin. The vibrating phone in his pocket startled the cat, whose nerves may have been frayed already from the events of the other night. Oliver jumped to the floor and hightailed it down the hall at Oliver speed, while Jake pushed the lever to set his chair upright and clicked on the answer button. Janice Richardson, Jake's friend from the *Ottawa Citizen*, was on the other end.

"Janice, it's wonderful to hear from you. We don't talk for two years and now twice in a week. How's it going?"

"It's going great, thanks. I wanted to schedule that luncheon date with you but, also, I'm curious to know how your investigation into the Gary Thomas case is going. Got any fact-based news for me?"

Jake chuckled at the reference as he knew it was Janice's little dig at those outlets trafficking in lies and misinformation. He told her about the threats and that the police were about to reopen the investigation. "Other than that, Janice, I'm moving on. It's a police matter, so I think any news you gather will have to come from official sources at Ottawa Police Services."

"What about your book? You seemed excited about that. Are you giving up on it?"

"I'm going to wait to see what happens with the case." He hesitated, but then he thought there would be no harm in telling her. "Maybe I'll try my hand at writing a novel. I have a couple of ideas that could make an interesting book. I don't know, I've never tried that before. Writing fiction would be something different, that's for sure."

Janice said, "Yeah, well, if you get great at writing fiction, I'm sure you could start a second career with some news outlets whose names shall remain unmentioned. Do you still think Gary Thomas is innocent?"

Jake said, "The warnings I've received certainly imply that. Someone seems to think I was getting close to something. Close enough that they deemed it necessary to warn me to back off. It's weird because they seem to think I'm closer than I think I am, that I know something I don't. Somebody has gone to great lengths to scare me off. The visitor the other night rattled me enough to stay away. I'm going to install an alarm system, too. They didn't get the backup for my computer, and I documented everything, so I still have all my notes."

"There must be something in your notes that concerns someone. A casual conversation that seemed like nothing. Have you gone through your notes again to see if something twigs?"

Jake said, "Not in any detail, but I keep thinking of Sarah Brown's feelings for Matthew Pawsloski. It seems to me there was another love triangle that nobody considered."

"I don't know Jake; it seems pretty weak. From what you've told me, Sarah Brown might carry around a broken heart, but murder? Not unless she's not playing with a full deck. It sounds like the person doing this knows what they're doing. It's more likely the perp would be the person who hacked into the computer system."

"You're probably right. I plan to document everything and fix it later, but I'll reread it to see if I missed something."

"I think you should, Jake. Remember what you always used to tell me when we were investigating a story? You always told me to follow the money. You might find out it leads right to the murderer."

CHAPTER FORTY-FOUR

JAKE AND JANICE concluded their discussion by organizing a lunch date for the following Wednesday. Janice's office was near Big Rig's Kitchen and Brewery, so it would give Jake a chance to meet some of his former colleagues either before or after the luncheon.

He thought as he prepared to cover the wall with a second coat of paint that Janice was possibly on to something about following the money. The fact she remembered his mantra from their days working together pleased him. He could take it two ways: with pride that she learned and remembered, or with shame for not devoting more time to following his own advice. He wasn't sure why he had spent so much time considering Sarah Brown. Ryan Cambridge was another matter. He still wouldn't discount Sarah completely, but now that Cambridge seemed to be innocent, the police investigation would undoubtedly concentrate somewhere else.

As Jake rolled the second coat on the wall, he reflected on his notes. Something niggled in the deepest reaches of his brain. One of those shadowy thoughts that dance just out of reach with its tongue out, its thumbs in its ears, waggling its fingers. Thankfully, one lesson *his* boss taught him and that he passed on to Janice was to take fastidious notes and to preserve them. In the news business, one could never anticipate challenges that could arise or from whom. Notes and the sources to whom quotes were attributable were crucial in the event of challenges from editors, bosses, the public, or law firms. He had also made a habit of typing his notes as soon as he could after taking them. His writing was problematic even for him to decipher, and it would be impossible for anyone else, so typing his notes immediately had developed into a habit.

He reminded himself that the case was a police force matter, so he resolved to tell Dani if he found anything worthwhile. Something still nagged at him. *What was it? A conversation? A comment? Someone's attitude or gesture?* Jake realized he had passed over the same spot with the brush three times as he mulled over his thoughts. A sound drew him from his reverie. A soft meow preceded the door opening just enough to allow an oversized furry body to enter. Jake set the roller in the tray and dashed to the door to stop Oliver in his tracks.

He picked up the cat with an admonishment. "Oh no, you don't buddy. Nice try, but you've seen the new color, so it's time to leave." He carried the feline to the cat tree in the kitchen and set him on the top ledge. In the front yard, a blue jay leaned forward on a branch, scolding a squirrel that was hanging from the bird feeder, calmly cleaning out the rest of the seed. Jake's tapping on the window had little effect. While the squirrel scampered away the first time, lately it couldn't care less. The leather-lunged jay continued screeching, and the squirrel carried on robbing the feeder undeterred. It reminded Jake of the invasion the other night. The outcome was the same. The jay objected while the thief took what he wanted. Jake gave Oliver one last rub and informed him it was up to him to guard the front yard now. The cat watched him retreat down the hallway before turning his attention back to the melodrama unfolding outside.

Jake desperately wanted to stop what he was doing to research his notes, but the painting project was nearing completion. Another tedious hour passed as he finished the work. He wracked his brain, thinking about his conversations and who might have a connection to the crime. He pondered the hacking at Ryan's firm. Something still nagged at him. *Was it something Ryan said? Had Sarah mentioned something? What about Damon Brooks?* Dammit, he just couldn't grasp it.

He scrutinized the room for spots that needed touch-up, and satisfied, he washed the brushes in the basement and stowed the supplies. He muscled the desk back into place and hung the pictures and plaques. Oliver, evidently tired of the drama unfolding in the front yard, enjoyed his renewed access to the office. Jake felt a sense of accomplishment at having finished the job as he plugged in his laptop and all the related paraphernalia.

He anxiously sat in his chair and called up his notes, totally ignoring the draft manuscript. It was the notes that could divulge the secret. He stored them in folders chronologically, so he started with the breakfast at which Eric Jacobson suggested he should write a book. His lips curved upward in amusement at the simple suggestion that changed his life. It gave him something to do, but more importantly, it had brought him and Dani closer. That may have happened anyway, but who knows?

He spent the next while reading and rereading his notes. Oliver came and went, but Jake barely noticed. The room darkened as the cloudy day turned to night, but he continued reading in the blue glare from the computer monitor. It was as if nothing else in the world existed.

Finally, it struck with the suddenness of running into a doorframe in the middle of the night. The thing that had been rattling around in his brain since Janice reminded him to follow the money. It forced him back in his chair as he inhaled a slow, deep breath. A sudden chill wrapped the room as the enormity shook his very being. He recalled the day referred to in his notes. The discussion meant nothing then but made so much sense now when he knitted everything together. It was in front of his face the whole time.

He printed the relevant pages from his notes and carried them to the sunroom where he laid them beside his chair. Oliver followed, begging for food, and Jake realized guiltily he hadn't fed the cat for a while.

He dumped the food pellets in the bowl, some of which bounced off Oliver's head, scattering across the floor as the hungry cat rushed to eat. Jake gave Oliver an extra treat to ask for forgiveness for ignoring him all day.

Jake wandered back to the sunroom and picked up the printed pages, examining them again, trying various scenarios to poke holes in his theory. He didn't want it to be true, but it seemed undeniable. Everything pointed to one person as the murderer. A person he had trusted.

He had to make a phone call, but when he reached in his pocket, his phone wasn't there. It sat on the nightstand in the bedroom where he left it when he changed out of his painting clothes. He retrieved it and carried it to the sunroom where he studied his notes one last time to verify his thinking. There couldn't be any mistakes. It was beyond doubt. He was sure he was right.

He dialed the number, but it rang and rang before going to voice mail.

CHAPTER FORTY-FIVE

JAKE LEFT A message, laying out his thoughts and quoting from his notes. There wasn't much more to do. He would not confront the person on his own. That would be foolhardy. It was definitely time for police department involvement. He carried his phone into the bedroom ensuite and turned the volume to the maximum before stepping into the shower. He didn't want to miss the call when it came.

The scorching water pelted down on his aching muscles as he stood under the showerhead. Muscles that had received their share of abuse in the last few weeks. The fitness trainer, the attack by the intruder, even painting had all set fire to muscles and ligaments he didn't even know existed. After a protracted stay, he emerged, toweled off, and checked the phone. Nothing. That's odd. He should have heard something by now.

The thought of pulling on his pajamas and robe and chilling for the rest of the evening had some appeal, but his body vibrated with uneasiness, so he was in no mood to sit yet. He pulled on his blue jeans and a sweater instead. He needed the phone to ring, so he could talk about his discovery.

Instead, a loud rap sounded at the door. Not a knock. Three urgent taps. The sound startled Jake, and he realized it must have landed on his last frayed nerve, instantly speeding up his heart rate. Freezing on the spot would have been preferable to his next decision. He raced into the hall to see who was at the door.

As he rushed down the hall, he wished he had installed the security camera he had promised his daughter and Dani, but he hadn't taken the time to buy one. He peered through the sidelight beside the door, but only a shadowy figure was discernible. Someone tall. He called out, "Who is it?" No answer. He scanned the street, but there were no cars he recognized. All he saw was smoke from neighborhood chimneys rising straight into the air, a sign of the bone-chilling temperatures. *It could be someone whose car has broken down.*

He called out again. "Who's there?" No answer.

He touched his pocket, and his heart sank as he realized he had left his phone in the bedroom ensuite. He turned to retrieve it and was halfway down the hall when the raspy scratching of a metallic object at the door grabbed his attention. The person on the doorstep was fiddling with the lock.

The handle is turning!

Jake raced back and tried to twist the lock shut, but it was too late. The door shot open with such force, it propelled him backward. He nearly lost his footing. A half-stifled yell rose from Jake's lips as a sharp pain pierced through his shoulder. He bounced off the wall and used the momentum to spin on his heel back toward the bedroom. *He had to retrieve his phone.* Jake was about to turn the corner when the door slammed shut and a distinct, resonant voice stopped him in his tracks.

"Give it up, Jake. I'll shoot you if you take one more step."

Jake's heart pounded against his ribcage. He turned slowly until he was face to face with the person he had identified as responsible for everything. The one person he knew with the skills to hack into a computer system. Jason Pruitt, the affable owner of Brew and Buns, advanced toward him with a gun aimed at his chest.

Pruitt growled, "You just couldn't leave it alone, could you, Jake? I thought you might after my warnings, but then I hacked into your computer and realized you could figure it out from our conversation about my past. It was too late for warnings. If only I hadn't told you I had a degree in computer science. At first, I thought Gary Thomas was the perfect fall guy, but you had to put your nose into it. Then, with Ryan getting more attention, I thought I was home free again. Now, you've ruined everything. I made one mistake, and that was telling you I knew something about computers. Now, I'm afraid there's no other way out."

Jake's mind raced. *Had Dani received his voice mail? Will she be here any second?* Needing to buy time, he took slow deep breaths, trying to marshal the strength to prolong this as much as possible. He said, "You made another mistake, Jason. When you kicked me in the chest, I thought it must be someone with martial arts training. I checked your social media accounts. The profile picture with you holding the trophy from some competition confirmed it. I reported everything to the authorities. They'll be here any second."

Pruitt laughed. "What authorities? Danielle? She can't do anything without evidence. Speaking of that, I need the backup for your notes."

"It isn't here. It's stored offsite. You're done, Pruitt. You might as well give up."

Pruitt rushed closer to Jake, grabbed the front of his sweater, and pressed the gun into his forehead hard enough to leave a round dent in the skin. He hissed, "I swear to God, I will kill you first and then Danielle and that daughter of hers. Tell me where the backup is."

Jake's stomach churned. Sweat droplets beaded on his forehead and in his armpits and trickled down his back. *This is the way I'm going to die.* He closed his eyes and waited for the inevitable.

It didn't come. He opened his eyes narrowly to see Pruitt's smirking face. Smirking, yes, but there was also desperation.

"I won't kill you just yet, Scott. We're going on a trip. I've planned everything and I'm one step ahead of you. You wouldn't be stupid enough to keep the backup here, not after the break-in. I can tell by your face you're telling the truth. I suspect you gave it to Danielle. Or is it Dani?" He sneered, "I know you two have been working together on this all along. Who else would you give it to? Get your coat. We're going to visit her. Oh, before you give me all that other crap about telling the authorities, I also know the only one at Ottawa Police Services interested in this case is Danielle. You can save your breath. It's amazing how much I hear at the restaurant. People keep talking when I'm standing there pouring coffee." He chuckled and said, "I could write a book. Now move. Get your coat."

Jake did as he was told while looking for opportunities to disarm Pruitt. While he pulled on his winter clothes, he stared at the gun being aimed at him. He debated about attempting to leap forward to disarm the man to save Dani and her daughter, but Pruitt was bigger, stronger, and younger, so it would more than likely be death for nothing. The best option to overcome his adversary would be with Dani's help.

Jake said, "We were ready to assume Gary Thomas was guilty if you hadn't left the warnings. We had run out of options. Leaving the warnings was your third mistake."

Pruitt slugged him in the head with the gun barrel. Not hard, but it hurt, nonetheless. He snarled through clenched teeth. "Dani wouldn't have stopped. She hasn't since the murders happened, and she has you wrapped around her little finger. I realized the two of you would have kept going, and especially after I opened my mouth about my computer degree. You would have eventually put two and two together. Too late now. Let's go."

As they left the house, the arctic air hit Jake like an electric shock. It was like walking into a refrigerator. House lights glistened through the designs painted on windows by the frost. Gossamer trails of breath drifted behind the two men as they walked down the street toward Pruitt's car. Snow crunched under their feet. Pruitt motioned that Jake should climb in the driver's side of the Mercedes while he hustled to the passenger side. The seat was hard and cold to the touch. Jake looked for anything to defend himself, but there was nothing. An old car battery sat on a towel in the back seat, but he couldn't get to that in time or even lift it from his sitting position. He filed it away for later.

Once inside, Pruitt handed Jake the keys and told him to drive to Dani's condo as soon as the windows cleared. The car engine turned over hesitantly at first, stiff from the freezing temperatures. When it started, the roar of the heater fan in the car seemed to heighten Jake's anxiety. He drove the entire distance with the gun pointed at his midsection.

Jake's stomach rolled and churned like it was a few seconds from launching its contents at the windshield. He felt horrible about taking this criminal to Dani's doorstep. As he pulled into a visitor's parking spot, he hoped that between himself and Dani they could overcome this monster before it was too late.

He prayed Emilie was with her dad.

CHAPTER FORTY-SIX

JAKE BUZZED UP to Dani's condo. He hoped she wouldn't be home, but when she answered he repeated what Pruitt told him to say. His voice sounded hollow.

"Hi Dani, it's Jake. Sorry to bother you, but I have some urgent information to discuss with you about the case. Can I come up?"

"Uh, sure, Jake." Dani's next words sent a chill to the bottom of Jake's very soul. "Em and I were just playing board games. Come on up."

The buzzer sounded to open the door and Jake and Jason entered, the pressure of the gun barrel jammed into Jake's back a persistent reminder of the gravity of the situation. Pruitt stepped to one side to shelter the gun as a young couple, wearing heavy coats, scarves, and hats for the cold Ottawa evening, stepped out of the elevator. They chatted and laughed loudly about a woman they had just met. By the decibel level of their laughter, it sounded like they had enjoyed one too many drinks before leaving a party.

Jake thought of screaming at them to run and call the police, but he feared Pruitt might be desperate enough to shoot all three of them and then go upstairs to kill Dani and Emilie. He refused to take the chance.

When they reached Dani's apartment, Jake tapped on the door. Pruitt remained to one side out of her sightline as the door swung wide to reveal Dani in a pink tracksuit. Apparently, she hadn't caught the distress in Jake's voice. Her brilliant smile lit up the doorway until Pruitt showed up behind Jake. It dissolved like a popped soap bubble when she saw the gunman.

"I'm so sorry, Dani," Jake said. He looked over her shoulder, disquieted to see Emilie sitting at a table with a board game spread in front of her. The sight would have brought him joy any other time, but now, under these circumstances, it made him nauseous. He thought how young and vulnerable she looked in a tee shirt and leggings. Two cell phones, their screens dark, sat on the table. Jake's stomach sank as Pruitt shoved him and he stumbled forward into Dani.

Dani said, "It's okay, Jake." Turning to Jason, she said, "So, it was you all along. It's all about the money, right?"

Pruitt gestured with the gun to order Dani and Jake to sit on the sofa. Then he motioned with his chin for Emilie to do the same. "Of course, it's about the money. I hacked into Ryan's client's computer and sent a bogus email, and Cambridge and Tremblay sent close to a million dollars to my account. They were so afraid of losing their business, they didn't even go to the cops when they discovered it. Then that partner committed suicide because he blamed himself. It was so easy. I'm planning to hit another place once I deal with this problem, meaning you three. The only problem was that Pawsloski guy. He knew too much."

Pruitt stopped short of admitting he killed Matthew and Melissa. He chuckled and then said, "So smooth until you two got involved. We're going to take a ride, but I need the backup for Jake's notes first. Danielle, I understand you have it."

Jake examined the unrecognizable person in front of them. He searched for the Jason Pruitt he knew, but this new, ugly, despicable version had replaced the congenial owner of Brew and Buns.

While Jake's muscles felt incredibly weak, Dani remained steady and strong by all outward appearances. She said, "I have one copy, but I made an extra one in case something like this happened. It's not here. You're welcome to the one I have."

A vein pulsed on Pruitt's forehead as his face reddened. He rushed over and grabbed Emilie by the arm, roughly dragging her to her feet. She screamed as he pressed the gun to the side of her head. His voice was loud and threatening.

"I'm sick of all this. I could kill you all right here. Give me the backup NOW or your precious daughter is going to die first in front of your eyes."

Emilie's face drained of its color as her bottom lip trembled and tears squirted from her eyes. The contrast beside Pruitt's bright red countenance was staggering.

Dani put up her hands. "Okay, okay. I lied. There's only one backup. I'll get it and give it to you, and then you can leave us alone. We won't have any evidence to charge you with. Gary Thomas will stay in jail and you can go about your business. Leave town. Move with your money to Bermuda or someplace. No one will look for you."

She got up and hurried down the hall to retrieve the backup.

Jason called out to her retreating back, "Come back with just the backup or your daughter dies. Understand? Don't do anything foolish."

Dani returned holding the USB drive in her hand in front of her, but Jason told her to stop halfway down the hall. "Turn around. I don't want to see a gun tucked in your waistband or something." When she did, it was clear she couldn't hide a weapon in her snug-fitting tracksuit. It dismayed Jake but relieved him at the same time she hadn't taken the risk.

Pruitt called her closer, and she complied. His demeanor was grim as he ran his hands roughly over her body. He did the same to Emilie and reiterated they were leaving soon.

Dani's calm exterior amazed Jake. His stomach rocked and rolled like a ship being tossed on the ocean in a hurricane. Her resigned look said it all as she gave up the drive.

She said, "Mind if Emilie and I put on something warmer? We aren't exactly dressed for minus thirty weather."

"You'll be fine where you're going," Jason replied.

Jake couldn't imagine where he would take them, but he was certain they wouldn't like it.

Pruitt searched Dani's and Emilie's coat pockets before he let them put them on. He did the same with Jake's, apparently having forgotten to do it when they left his house. "What's this?" He pulled a plastic bag with the Preston Hardware logo from the pocket.

"It's just some steel wool and masking tape. I needed the steel wool to stop mice from coming into the house and the masking tape in case I ran out while I was painting. I had to cover up the writing you put on the wall. Thanks for that."

The attempted bravado fell short.

Pruitt grunted, shoved the bag with its contents back into the pocket, and threw Jake's coat at him. He said, "Here's what we're going to do. We're taking two cars. Danielle, you drive yours and take Scott with you. I'm taking the girl. You'll follow me and if you do anything stupid, Emilie dies. Got it?"

Dani tried to dissuade him again. "Why not just let us go? Leave town. I don't know what your plan is, but if you kill us, my colleagues will hunt you down. They'll find out who did it and you'll never be safe."

Pruitt ignored her and waved the gun again toward the door, a sign that it was time to leave the condo. "Let's go."

Jake grimaced at the terror in Emilie's wide eyes and her quick gasps of breath as she snuggled close to her mom. As they got into their cars, he knew they needed to find a way to disarm Jason Pruitt soon, or they were all going to die.

CHAPTER FORTY-SEVEN

A S THEY PULLED behind Jason's car, Jake considered the seriousness of their situation. They were following a murderer who was holding Dani's daughter hostage, driving to some unknown location on the coldest night of the year to face death—unless they did something about it. But what?

He glanced at Dani, whose hardened face glowered in the gleam of the dashboard lights. She followed Jason's car as if connected by a chain, slowing when he slowed, speeding up when he sped up. Silence hung suspended in the vehicle like a morning fog. Jake's nerves tingled, his body vibrating, partly from the chill in the car that hadn't completely warmed yet, but more from indescribable fear as terror stabbed at his heart. He knew Dani must feel the same, but her professionalism had taken over.

Wind buffeted the car as they reached Highway 417 and drove west. Jake glanced at the dashboard thermometer and wished he hadn't. Minus 34 degrees! He mentally converted the number to minus 29 Fahrenheit. With the wind, it would feel like close to minus 50 degrees. He shuddered at the prospect. Dani, in her tracksuit, and Emilie in her tee-shirt and leggings, were not dressed warmly enough for the conditions, even with their winter coats. At least they were in the car.

He couldn't take the silence any longer. He tried to sound calm, but the nervous voice escaping his lips betrayed his fear.

"I guess you didn't receive the message I left on your phone."

Dani glanced sideways. "Message? No, I didn't receive a message. Did you try to warn me?"

"I wanted to tell you I discovered who the murderer was or at least the person with the skills to hack the system. I went through my notes and found a discussion Jason and I had at the restaurant when he told me about his computer degree. I thought nothing of it when it happened, but when I reread my notes, I realized the significance. He would be capable of hacking Ryan's client's computer and sending the fake email to defraud the firm. Then I checked his social media, and he bragged about some martial arts trophy he won. That explains the kick to my chest the night of the theft. It all seemed to come together. I wanted to know your thoughts. I was sure I had unearthed the murderer's name. Now we know for sure."

Dani nodded. She said, "I challenged Em to leave her cell phone alone while we played the board game. She said she would if I would." Dani's voice broke, a tiny fissure in the veneer she was employing to hide her fear. "She's such a great kid. We agreed to leave the phones shut off. I challenged her to last two hours without touching it and, of course, I had to do the same. That must have been when you called." She stared straight forward as the mesmerizing snow drifted across the road in waves. The blizzard occasionally obscured the taillights of Jason's car as wind gusts caused them to blink in and out as if a giant hand played peekaboo with them.

Jake wanted to keep her talking. Partly for her sake, but also so his mind didn't veer to dark places he couldn't afford it to go. "Where do you think we're going?"

The stoic side of Dani returned. "I think he's taking us someplace to kill us. That will not happen without a fight. The thought of my daughter anywhere near him and especially in that car with him makes me sick. The first chance we get, you and I are going to flank him. He can't get both of us. He's terrified about the discussion you had about his techie background. It would have led to more investigation, and he knows that. That's why he's doing this. He thinks if he gets rid of all your notes and us, that will be the end. He's taking us somewhere where he thinks no one will find our bodies, at least until spring." Dani took her eyes off the road for a few seconds to regard Jake. She said, "We will NOT let that happen, Jake."

It was a command. No hint of a question. No pleading. A command. This would be a fight for his life. Could he do it? Did he have what it would take? He was soon going to find out. He said, "Do you have anything we can use for weapons?"

Danie was pensive and said nothing, which confirmed to Jake that she didn't. Still hoping, he opened the glove box. His heart sank when he saw the owner's manual and a small flashlight. The side console revealed an iPod plugged into a USB port and an old Tim Hortons cup with the scratch and win tag lifted to reveal eligibility for a complimentary coffee. Jake searched in his pockets, but all he found was the plastic bag with the masking tape and steel wool. He hadn't even had time to grab his keys. He sat glumly as they turned south off the highway onto a regional road.

Dani finally spoke, saying, "Here's what we're going to do. We'll use the keys as a weapon. I'll give you the house key off the ring. Hold it in your hand between your fingers and when he gets close enough, jab it in his eye or throat. I'll do the same if he comes close to me. We'll have one chance, so make sure he's near enough to do maximum damage. When one of us distracts him, the other will hit him with everything we've got."

Jake's lips pursed at the thought. He abhorred violence. He never watched it on TV. Avoided reading about it. The times he reported on the aftermath of a shooting nearly made him physically ill. But he could do this. The lives of two people he cared about depended on him. Suppose Avery was in the car with that monster?

He could do this.

He *would* do this.

They turned onto a side road that was barely more than a laneway. Jake peered through the frosted windows into the darkness. All he saw past the blowing snow was the inky foreboding shadow of trees along the roadside. There was no sign of surrounding yards. If any houses existed, they were well hidden by the woods. The road merged with the snow-filled ditches on both sides. The cars jounced on the snowbanks piled randomly on the road by the wind like boats navigating waves. Dani followed in Pruitt's tracks. Jake wondered how Jason could see the little-traveled road as no traffic had passed recently.

Pruitt stopped and Dani followed suit. She squinted through the windshield as she leaned over the steering wheel, fiddling with the keys. Pruitt got out of the car, dragging Emilie with him. She struggled, but the grip on her arm was too strong. Jake watched him drag the girl toward Dani's car as Emilie launched her free fist at Jason's face. Through the window, Jake and Dani saw Jason laugh as he easily dodged the blow. It hardened their resolve.

Dani handed Jake the key she had extracted from the ring, and he closed his fist on it, placing it between his fingers as instructed.

As Dani watched Pruitt drag her struggling daughter toward her car, a determined whisper escaped through clenched teeth as she opened the door.

"Get ready, Jake. Remember, one chance. Make it count. This is it."

CHAPTER FORTY-EIGHT

THE CHANCE NEVER came. Pruitt launched Emilie toward Dani's car, sending her sprawling in the snow. He stayed well back; his gun aimed at Emilie. "Stay right there, Danielle. Toss me the keys and you and your daughter can climb in the back seat, along with Jake. Pop the hood before you do."

Dani hurled the keys at Pruitt as she threw herself out of the car toward their adversary. Jake, expecting Dani's move, did the same on his side, but Pruitt was too quick. While he let the keys sail past and land in the snow, he anticipated the move and swung the gun at the onrushing Dani. The barrel struck her on the top of her head, and she collapsed in a sliding heap at his feet. He swung the gun toward Jake, who came to a standstill.

"Mom!" Emilie yelled as she scrambled to her feet and slid to a stop beside her stunned mother, crouching to ensure she was okay. A trickle of blood dripped down the side of Dani's face.

With the gun pointed at his chest, a sense of dread settled heavily on Jake.

Pruitt said calmly, "Okay, now everyone let's settle down." He started barking commands like a drill sergeant. "Jake, pop the hood of Danielle's vehicle. Emilie, help your mom into the back seat and then come back to me. Jake, when Emilie comes back, you get the car battery and toolbox from my car and bring them back here. This won't take long." A moist chuckle emerged from his lips. Then he said. "I'll soon be out of your hair."

Everyone did as they were told. What choice did they have? Dani groaned softly as a trembling Emilie helped her into the back seat. Jake opened the hood on Dani's car and waited until Emilie returned. When she did, Pruitt grabbed her from behind and held the gun to her temple, watching as Jake retrieved the battery and toolbox.

Pruitt said, "Okay, now replace the battery in Dani's car with this one."

The bone-numbing cold leaked through Jake's coat and his fingers burned from the frigid night air. A terrifying thought bubbled to the surface of his mind. Pruitt had no intention of shooting them. He was going to leave them here to freeze to death.

Jake yanked a wrench from the toolbox scattering other tools on the ground. It was all he could do to hold it with his numb fingers. He said, "Why go to all this trouble, Pruitt? Why not just kill us?"

"Because three bodies with holes in them would prompt an investigation. I don't want that. But, if your battery died when you were out driving around and you froze to death, the police will consider it an unfortunate mishap."

Jake had to admit there was some logic to Pruitt's thinking, and he much preferred their chances of surviving an Ontario winter night than bullets, although neither option was attractive. With no light, he had to feel what he was doing. At least the movements warmed his fingers. Emilie had to be freezing, and he worried about Dani in the back seat. *Was she okay?* As he tightened the last bolt, he prayed there would be enough juice in the battery that he could blow the horn at least. He knew nothing about car batteries, but maybe moving it would somehow regenerate some of its life. He suspected Jason had already made sure that wouldn't the case.

Pruitt told Jake to gather up the tools he had spilled on the ground and put the toolbox and Dani's battery back into his Mercedes. Jake thought of trying to throw everything at him, but Pruitt still held Emilie with the gun at her head. He couldn't risk it. Pruitt fixed Jake with a feral stare, stepping back and dragging Emilie with him when he passed. As Jake complied and threw everything in the back seat, he noticed Pruitt leaning down and scratching the surface of the snow. He found the keys Dani had thrown at him and handed them to Emilie. Jake wondered what keys she might have left on the ring since he had put her condo key in his pocket, and she probably dropped the car key when Pruitt hit her.

The gunman told Emilie and Jake to climb into the back seat with Dani and trotted to his car. Dani sat upright holding her head, her face tight in a scowl.

Emilie's body shook, and she cried out through chattering teeth. "Are. You. Okay. Mom? I'm so scared."

Dani murmured, "I know, honey. We'll be okay."

Jake knew from the catch in her voice that Dani didn't believe it.

Jake watched as Pruitt pulled a U-turn on the road and stopped with his passenger window opposite their back seat window. He was so cold he could barely hear what Pruitt said, but he made it out through the closed window in Dani's car, and it wasn't worth hearing.

Pruitt said, "Stay warm," laughed, rolled up his window, and sped away.

CHAPTER FORTY-NINE

JAKE TOOK THE keyring from Emilie's quivering hand before remembering Dani had removed the car key. He leaned across Emilie so he could see Dani, and the sight of her head tilted back against the seat and the blood on her coat alarmed him. His eyes dropped to see her chest rising and falling in shallow, ragged breaths. He shouted. "Dani, can you hear me?"

Dani didn't acknowledge. Emilie pushed her mom's shoulder and Jake shouted again. Dani finally awoke with a start.

Jake's tone was still loud as if talking to someone with a hearing impairment, but his words were choppy as his body temperature dropped. "Dani—do you have the k-k-key?"

Dani's voice was scarcely above a murmur. She said, "It's in my pocket. I have such a headache and I'm so cold. What's happening?"

Emilie reached into Dani's pocket as Jake said, "Dani, stay awake. We're stranded and we need to figure out what to do. I'll try to start the car. Emilie, after you find your mom's key, cuddle with her. Your body heat will keep both of you warm until we figure out what to do. Put on your Covid facemask if you have it, ball up your hands in the palms of your gloves. Use whatever body heat you can." He understood their shared warmth wouldn't maintain them for long. When the car's interior reached closer to outside temperatures, frostbite was inevitable, followed by hypothermia and finally, death. They would never survive the night.

A dense blanket of frost coated every window of the car, hiding whatever was going on outside. Emilie tried both of Dani's pockets before she found the key and handed it to Jake. His body was too stiff to climb over the seat into the front. The door groaned as he opened it to a blast of frigid air. It was like walking into an icebox. He hastened to the driver's door. Frost blanketed the side of the car and door handle, but he yanked it open quickly and clambered into the front seat. Hope sank when he realized the overhead light had not come on when he opened the doors. Not a good sign. With quivering hands, he shoved the key into the ignition and turned it.

Click.

He tried again.

Click.

He turned the light switch.

Nothing.

He pressed the horn. Not even a squeak.

He smacked the steering wheel with his palm in frustration.

Another depressing thought occurred to him. *How long could they breathe the air in an enclosed car?* They couldn't lower the windows with the battery dead. *Was an automobile so airtight that breathing their exhalations would kill them?* He thought car manufacturers designed the seals to be waterproof, not airtight, so some air should seep through. He opened the vents just in case.

Although cold air might enter through the vents, it was better than succumbing to poisoning from their breathing. Or was it? Fading away from poisoning might be preferable to freezing to death.

He fought off the hopelessness weighing on his shoulders. The overpowering sense of responsibility for two women he cared about compounded the burden. But what could he do? A burst of icy air slapped him again as he opened the door and surveyed the surroundings. Either the wind had calmed down, or the trees facing the road on both sides sheltered them. No lights shone through the trees in any direction. No chimney smoke rose above the trees. There was no suggestion of life anywhere. Pruitt had evidently prepared carefully, making certain no miracle rescue would happen.

Jake leaned into the car to open the glove compartment. Even in his foggy state, he still remembered seeing a flashlight. As he leaned forward, he shouted, "Everybody okay back there?"

Dani and Emilie both muttered they were.

The flashlight was cold to the touch, and when he pushed the switch, the dim gleam was barely visible, as if someone draped tissue over it. He directed the meager light under the dash, where he found the latch to open the SUV's hatch. The flashlight flickered, so he shut it off, got out, and closed the driver's door. He rushed to the rear of the car to peer inside the yawning space. Turning on the dreary flashlight again, he found empty grocery bags strewn about and a box with what appeared to be winter survival gear. It was a shred of hope until he saw the contents. Black and red booster cables lay coiled in the box, the jagged brass jaws at either end clamped shut in a mocking grin. A small red plastic can with a black cap sloshed with liquid when he picked it up. He smelled gas when he unscrewed the top. There was a collapsible shovel. The irony nearly made him burst into tears. The jumper cables would be helpful if another car came along. Jake noticed on the drive that the gas gauge registered over half. Gas wasn't the problem, even *if* the car would start. The shovel could be useful *if* the car was stuck in a snowbank. His frustration mounted again.

It was all useless!

He tried to shove the thought aside as he dug deeper into the box to discover a folded blanket. Finally, something they could use. It fell from his numb fingers as he tried to carry it to the back door. His hands, feet, nose, and ears were beyond desensitized. Pain set in. It was a sure sign of frostbite. His arthritic knee joined the chorus.

Jake stooped to pick up the blanket and pulled open the back door. He climbed in, tossed the blanket over himself, Dani and Emilie, and threw his arms around them as much as he could to draw them close. Emilie wore her mask under the scarf she had pulled over her nose, but she shook uncontrollably with her hands tucked between her knees as she huddled under Dani's arm. While Dani was fully conscious, the moonlight peeking through the clouds and frosted windows revealed a face that was white with exhaustion and pain.

Jake decided. They were all going to die unless he did something. Once he warmed a little, he planned to roll the dice, pick a direction, and walk, hoping to find a farmhouse.

He said nothing, saving his breath for his plan. He rested his head against Emilie's and touched Dani's hair with his hand. This might be the last time he would see them, so he wanted to engrave their features on his memory banks. He was going to break the cardinal rule of winter survival when stranded in a car. Simply sitting here while they all perished was not an option. He removed his arm from behind the two women and kissed Emilie on the cheek. He touched his fingers to his lips and leaned across Emilie, pressing them against Dani's face. Then he reached for the door.

Emilie spoke softly. "Jake, do you think someone would see a fire?"

It was a strange question. Negative thoughts flooded into Jake's brain. They had no matches, no kindling, wet wood wouldn't burn, the wind would blow a fire out... *Why would we build a fire? It's too late for that. Is Emilie delirious?* He didn't want to discourage her, so he said, "Maybe, but we have no matches, sweetie."

Her answer startled him. "Let's try. Can I have the bag in your pocket?"

CHAPTER FIFTY

JAKE WAS PUZZLED and seriously concerned about Emilie's state of mind, but he reached into his pocket, withdrew the Preston Hardware bag, and handed it to her. She pulled her hands from between her knees and said as she rubbed them together, "Can I have the flashlight?"

Dani sat up and shot a questioning look at Jake. Suddenly, they were both pulled from their lethargy by Emilie's curious behavior. Neither said anything as they watched the girl remove the batteries from the flashlight and attempt to tape them together with the masking tape. It was a slow process as her young fingers, stiffened by the cold, fumbled in the darkness. Jake realized what she was doing and without saying a word, took the batteries from her and held them so she could finish her tape job.

"I haven't tried this," she intoned as she ripped off a narrow piece of steel wool and touched it to the negative post on one battery and the positive post on the other. For a brief second, a tiny spark was visible in the dark interior of the car. Emilie drew deep breaths; her speech was deliberate as she fought the cold. As she spoke, her breath formed clouds of vapor in the air.

"After that night in the park, I asked our science teacher how people survive if they are stranded in winter. He did a project about starting a fire and showed us this trick with the clip from a ballpoint pen. I remember him talking about other methods and I'm positive one he mentioned was steel wool. It will burn until all the iron is oxidized. He said it's practically impossible to start a fire in the snow, though. He said the cold also affects it." She added despondently, "We need tinder and something to accelerate it. What can we do with this?"

Dani and Jake answered simultaneously. "There's gas in the trunk."

They fell silent again, each lost in the challenges of starting a fire in the wilderness in the middle of winter. Jake said, "There's a shovel too. We can go into the trees and pack down a sheltered spot. We can break off branches and twigs to get it started and use the shovel to hack off some larger pieces to keep it going." He glanced at his watch. "It's another five hours until daylight. Maybe we can keep it going until morning. We'll have to take turns, though. One works while the others stay in the car."

Dani seemed to have forgotten her headache and added, "We can use the gas for accelerant once we find enough kindling. We need fine shavings for tinder. What about using the floor mats as a base? If we get a fire going, we can huddle beside it with the blanket."

They talked through their plan further and Jake insisted on going first, ignoring protests from Dani and Emilie. They had hope, however slim. The euphoria of having a plan seemed to raise the temperature, but negative thoughts crept in again as Jake braced himself to leave the car for the biting cold. *Will this work or is it just a fool's errand? Could they actually start a fire in the winter? Was his first plan of walking to find help the better one?* He decided the hope of starting the fire would keep them alive a little longer if nothing else. They had a purpose. It was better than sitting in one place waiting for death. Besides, moving around would warm their body temperatures at least a little.

He pulled his scarf over his chin and nose, moved to the front seat, and unlatched the trunk. He retrieved the shovel and gas tank and began trudging toward the ditch. It was difficult enough lifting one leg and placing it in front of the other without the extra weight. The load of the shovel and gas container was nearly too much to bear.

Reaching the ditch, he pressed down with one foot. The snow was level with the road, but if he sank to his waist in the ditch, he wondered if he could summon the strength to pull himself out. The other two wouldn't be much help either. His arthritic knee howled in agony, overcoming the numbness in the rest of his joints. The wind had formed an icy crust over the snow, but he still sank up to his ankle. He deliberately took a second step with the same effect. He struggled to yank his foot out and the snow's jagged crust felt like knives against his legs, but he slowly, treacherously, made his way toward the tree line, stopping repeatedly to rest. It was like walking in drying cement while the glacial air bit through his toque and face covering as if they were gauze.

It took ten agonizing minutes to reach the short distance between the trees and the road. He planted himself on a stump and glanced back at the frost-draped car. He perceived eyes peering through a clear spot someone had scraped on the window, but he couldn't be sure who they belonged to. It seemed marginally warmer in the trees, but maybe it was just exertion that heated his body temperature. He felt like pitching forward from the stump and falling asleep, but two precious people in the car counted on him.

He scanned his surroundings. Jake recognized a cluster of ash trees co-mingled with cedars. At least he suspected they were ash trees because many of them were dead, probably victims of the ash borer beetle that had ravaged the vegetation in the Ottawa valley. He thought it could work to their advantage. He pushed himself off the stump and lethargically chipped at dead trees with the shovel until he had to rest. His lungs burned as chunks of snow plopped down on him from the branches above, but he worked until he had a pile of branches of varying sizes. He leaned against the tree with his head down and his eyes closed until an abrupt noise caused him to look. He would have been shocked to know he had only been working for ten minutes. When he looked up, Emilie said through gasping breaths, "It's my turn. Go to the car. Mom said I should pack down some snow here."

Jake dropped the shovel and trudged back to the car using the same tracks he and Emilie had made entering the woods. When he got inside, Dani threw the blanket and her arms around him and drew him close. The temperature in the car was close to the outside now.

They continued working in short shifts for the next half hour, growing more and more exhausted with each passing minute. Dani lugged two floor mats with her on her journey into the woods, and Jake carried the other two when it was his turn again. Emilie stomped down the area where they would try to start the fire. Jake and Dani used the shovel to chop and scrape as much wood and kindling from the dead trees as they could with their waning energy. They knew the floor mats would melt if they ever got the fire going, but at least they temporarily separated the wet wood from the snow.

It was time to try this wild and crazy idea. If the fire didn't start, they had run out of options. Emilie wrapped the thinnest strands of wood around a strip of steel wool and held it and the batteries under the mound of sticks they had piled in a teepee arrangement. Sparks flew in Emilie's trembling hands as they hoped, and the tinder sizzled and popped—and died. She tried again, with the same result. High hopes and anticipation faded fast among the group. The sparks were less visible each time she tried as the batteries, already weakened by the cold, were on the verge of dying altogether. She tried one more time and nothing happened. No spark at all. The taped batteries slipped from her hands and tumbled to the snow. Jake's heart sank as he saw the tears instantly freezing on Emile's cheeks and Dani's head bow in defeat. He tried unsuccessfully to keep his tone even. "Let's go back to the car," he said.

Their time had run out. At least they would die together.

CHAPTER FIFTY-ONE

D ANI AND EMILIE rose dejectedly and turned to meet their fate in the car. Jake was slower to move, totally exhausted by the cold, his physical exertion, and the realization they had failed. He wanted to be with them in the car, so he attempted to follow, but he stumbled, sprawling to the ground in a bone-tired, dejected heap.

Dani and Emilie didn't notice, lost as they were in their thoughts and efforts to make it to their icy tomb.

Jake closed his eyes. The cold seemed to melt away as numbness overtook him. Death could have him. He had done his best for Dani and Emilie. He pried one eye open, but instead of seeing Dani and Emilie, a red object caught his eye. His mind told him it was something important. He summoned the strength to tilt his head. A red plastic container lay on its side at his feet. The gas can! In their hazy state, they had forgotten all about it. How stupid, he thought. He lifted his head to shout, but he couldn't muster the energy. Why were they walking away? Oh yes, the batteries Emilie taped together died. *The batteries!* Was there any hope of getting one last spark?

He had to try.

He pushed himself to his feet and found the batteries in the snow, picked them up, and reached beneath his coat to shove them in his underwear where he thought they would be the warmest. He brushed the snow from his face and the crusted ice from his eyelids and nose. As he did, he watched the scene unfold in slow motion as Dani and Emilie sluggishly approached the car. He tried again to call out, but only a weak rasp left his throat.

He willed himself to rip a thin strip from the steel wool, twisted it together, and lay it on the stump along with the remaining fine strands of matted steel. In what seemed like an eternity, he struggled to loosen the cap from the gas container until it finally spun free into the snow. He splashed the gas first on the strip, then on the clump of steel wool, and finally on the stack of kindling and bigger pieces of wood, spilling some on his leather gloves.

There would be one shot at this.

The gas fumes drifted up his nostrils, tugging the last remnants of his energy to the surface. Another glance toward the car told him Dani and Emilie made it and were about to climb inside. He thought irrationally they would be safe, even though an inner voice yelled it wasn't the case. They wouldn't be safe in that icy grave. He saw Emilie glance back, but she turned and sluggishly climbed inside after her mom. Somewhere in Jake's subconscious, he was still glad they were in the vehicle. His school science education was long behind him, so he didn't know whether the gas could explode if the batteries somehow produced one last spark. He didn't wish them anywhere near if an explosion occurred, even though they were probably already doomed.

He set the wad of gas-soaked steel wool under the kindling and removed the batteries from his underwear. It's showtime, he thought as an unnatural laugh he didn't recognize erupted from his blistered lips.

He painfully sunk to his hands and knees, leaned in, and touched the strip of steel wool to the opposite poles of the batteries. No spark. Maybe he missed the mark. He hazily touched the two poles again. A pinprick of a spark flashed in the darkness. Or was his mind playing tricks on him? It felt like he was watching the scene play out from above. He could see himself leaning over the sodden wood, fiercely willing the batteries to produce just one more spark. His hands were dead weights, sticks at the end of the arms. With no sense of feeling, his eyes guided the steel wool toward the batteries.

Everything happened quickly. The batteries sparked, igniting the tiny strands of steel wool, which in turn lit the larger clump. It sparkled red, generating flashes of fire. A tiny flame began chewing at the tinder and thin pieces of kindling they had chopped and scraped with the shovel. Jake laughed, on the verge of hysterics, as he couldn't remove his hands quickly enough and his gloves caught on fire. He bent to blow on the burgeoning blaze as he scraped his hands on the snow to douse the flames licking at his gas-soaked gloves. He added larger pieces to the tiny fire and dragged the remaining wood pieces they had cut closer so they could dry in the warmth.

The wet wood sizzled, sending white smoke curling into the air. Would the flames generate sufficient heat to overcome the dampness of the wood? He stacked another larger piece on, but it was too much. The flames crackled, faded, and disappeared. Only smoke poured from the pile. Nooo! Jake's shoulders slumped, and he felt like his heart would stop. He yanked a piece of wood from the bottom, so more oxygen could reach the flames, and blew on the glowing pile. The wet wood smoldered agonizingly for a few seconds, teasing him like some warped joke, before leaping to life again.

From the corner of his eye, he noticed the car door open and the shadowy forms of Dani and Emilie moving through the ditch with renewed energy. When they reached the warmth of the sputtering fire, a single word fell out of Dani's mouth. "How?" She was too exhausted to continue, and Jake too fatigued to answer.

They huddled under the blanket, reveling in the heat, meager as it was. Even the heavy, pungent smoke drifting their way couldn't budge them. They just closed their eyes and let it waft over them.

Dani remembered a mat on the floor of the trunk, and Emilie volunteered to retrieve it. Jake peered at the holes in his frayed gloves. He thought he should feel pain from the darkened burned skin, but he didn't. He slowly pushed up his sleeve and squinted at his watch. Still over four hours until daylight. He rolled his neck, his muscles and ligaments emitting a sickening grinding sound. The peculiar thought of crinkling Christmas wrapping floated through his mind. As he held Dani close, the fire warmed his aching body, but he was just so tired. The sight of the dwindling pile of wood through his bleary eyes deflated him. The pile would not last four hours. They had to cut more. The battered shovel beckoned, but could he summon the strength to use it?

Emilie dragged the heavy mat through the snow to their spot by the dying fire and threw it on the ground. They collapsed on it, their bodies falling like marionettes with their strings cut. Jake's cloudy mind registered that the fire was dying. The faltering flames were barely noticeable now through the ashy smoke curling into the air.

Jake thought he should do something, but exhaustion weighed him down as if a 400-pound man was sitting on him. A shadowy figure beckoned to him from the woods. Was Mia urging him to join her? He tried to point, but he was too weak to lift his arm. He had to tell Dani and Emilie they needed more wood. The words wouldn't come. His bone-weary mind registered a light beyond the fire just before his chin dropped to his chest.

CHAPTER FIFTY-TWO

WHEN JAKE WOKE, he was in the back seat of a moving vehicle with his head resting on Dani's lap. His shivering had ceased as the warmth of the car heater settled over his body. A searing sensation in his ears, fingers, nose, and toes greeted him as the fog gradually lifted from his brain. His left hand stung like hell. He looked up to see Dani's head leaning on the headrest; her eyes closed. This time was different. The look on her face was one of serenity, although even from Jake's vantage point he could see her frostbitten nose and ears. He struggled to sit and realized a heavy fleece blanket lay draped over him.

When he extracted himself from the blanket, sat up, and studied his surroundings, he realized someone unfamiliar occupied the driver's seat. Emilie slept soundly on the passenger side with her head braced against the window. Another blanket lay draped over her, and she used part of it to insulate her head from the glass. Jake noticed the driver sat on his coat, having apparently removed it at some point. Jake sensed perspiration beading on his own forehead, but he welcomed the warmth pouring into the car from the roaring heater fan.

"Welcome back, Jake. Meet Mr. Macklin." The words came from Dani, whose eyes remained closed. She continued, the slowness of her speech a reminder of the ordeal they had been through. "He's a manager at the ski hill down the road. He was worried about the pipes in the lodge freezing, so he was driving to check when he spotted the fire. Thankfully, he found us. He's taking us to the Queensway Carleton Hospital."

Jake sat back in his seat as his thoughts slowly coalesced into something he could understand. He recalled seeing a light, but he thought it wasn't real. He also remembered someone's arm under him, supporting and guiding him through the ditch to a waiting vehicle, but he assumed the fire had gone out and they were going to their ultimate resting place. A sudden sense of relief washed over him. They were okay. They actually survived!

He said to Dani, "How's your head?"

"Hurts a little."

His thoughts immediately swiveled to the monster who left them behind to die in the cold.

"What about Jason Pruitt? Do you have sufficient evidence to send him to prison?"

Dani's eyes remained closed, but she said, "We have kidnapping, attempted murder, break and enter, and theft, to name a few. There's enough to incriminate him, but it won't free Gary Thomas from jail."

"That's not acceptable, Dani. We have to get Gary out. We know he didn't commit the murders. Pruitt admitted to us he killed Melissa and Matthew. We can testify." He stopped, replaying the conversation in his mind. *Did Pruitt admit to killing them?*

Dani answered his unspoken question.

"He didn't admit he killed them, Jake. Not to me, anyway. But there's something else. How did Pruitt know about Melissa's affair with Pawsloski? How did he know about the client's trust fund? Did he know the client? How did he know about Gary's gun? There is still a piece missing. I'm so tired." She yawned without opening her eyes. "Wake me up when we get to the hospital."

There was little traffic, and the driver wasted no time, but he carefully avoided slick icy patches polished by the ghostly swirling snow. Jake realized now it was the trees that protected them from the wind gusts and safeguarded their fire. Curious, he leaned forward in the car. The driver appeared to be in his forties, although it was hard to be certain with his gray knit toque tugged down to his eyes. The puffy orange nylon coat behind him rustled with each turn of the wheel.

"Sir, my name's Jake Scott and I can't tell you how much we appreciate you stopping to help us. Was it the roaring fire you spotted?"

"Nice to meet you, Jake. I'm Dan Macklin." He chuckled and said, "I expect 'roaring' might be a bit of an exaggeration. You had a nice little fire, but it was faltering as I approached and it died completely when I got there. Just a lot of smoke. The wet wood killed it. It was substantial enough while it lasted to attract my attention through the trees, though. Never higher than a small bonfire. But, as I said, it was enough. Pretty resourceful and a lot of luck. I guess someone was watching over you to get it going at all in these conditions. Hardly anyone uses that road, but they keep it plowed for the few cars that do travel on it. Sit back and relax. We'll be at the hospital in five minutes."

Jake leaned back in his seat again. In his mind's eye, the fire was blazing. Interesting how perspectives change depending on

292   Barry Finlay

the situation. He closed his eyes, but sleep wouldn't come. He was certain Mia was the person watching over them. Then his mind switched gears again. *There's a piece missing.* Dani's comment swirled in his head. What connected all this?

Macklin pulled his car into the driveway in front of Emergency at the hospital as Jake nudged Dani and Emilie to wake them. They sleepily thanked Macklin and Dani asked for his phone number with a promise to compensate him for his gas and time when they recovered. Macklin replied it was nothing and was on his way.

Jake thought they must look like a threesome of the walking dead as they slowly and painfully made their way to the front desk. An inventory of his body awarded the pain in his right hand and toes the win by the thinnest of margins over his ears and nose. His arthritic knee came third.

Nurses hustled them into the Intensive Care Unit the minute they entered, much to the chagrin of a large group of people who had undoubtedly been waiting their turn for hours.

The doctor gave Jake the good news that he wouldn't lose any appendages after an X-ray of his fingers and toes. It wasn't even something Jake had considered. The doctor frowned at the severity of the frostbite and advised Jake he had come within about fifteen minutes of being an amputation victim. The nurse stuffed cotton balls between his toes to keep them separated. Then she treated his hand for the burn he received from the fire and applied sterile bandages to his nose. The doctor prescribed an extra strength medication for the pain and gave him a bottle with a handful of pills to keep him going. He added that he would need to see his family doctor in a month to assess the necessity for surgery to remove any damaged tissue.

As the doctor completed his treatment, Jake received a text from Dani announcing that she and Emilie were okay and sitting in the waiting room.

Jake emerged from the ICU and spotted Dani with Emilie asleep on her shoulder. Unhappy and just plain sick-looking people surrounded them. Emilie sat up and out of respect for the others in the room and the pain from injured facial muscles, they stifled giggles at the site of the collection of bandages each wore. With their assortment of bandages and discolored skin, they could have walked off the screen of a horror flick.

Dani surprised Jake in the taxi ride home when she announced she had been thinking all the way to the hospital. She hadn't been sleeping at all. She said, "While we were waiting on you, I asked Constable Davidson to monitor Jason Pruitt to make sure he doesn't leave town. I'm going to visit him tomorrow. I think it will be a shock when he sees me. Oh, and I'm pretty sure he won't be alone."

Jake's eyes widened as Dani explained her theory.

"It makes sense, Dani. I would love to be there when you take him and his accomplice down."

Dani was pensive for a minute. "I can probably arrange that, but are you sure, Jake? You look like you're in a lot of pain and it will be worse tomorrow when the shock wears off."

Jake pulled the bottle of capsules from his pocket and rattled it to show Dani. "This and watching the arrest will pull me through. Nothing could keep me away."

CHAPTER FIFTY-THREE

A DISTANT, MUTED sound registered in Jake's brain. It became more relentless as the cobwebs in his head cleared. He pried one eye open to see Oliver staring at him from the end of the bed and realized the cat was urging him to get up. Satisfied, the cat thumped down to the floor and Jake dragged his less damaged hand from the warmth of the covers, dangling it so Oliver could press his rounded back into it. Even the cat's fur caused Jake to wince. A peek at the clock on the bedside table told him it was 11:58 a.m. Now that he was awake, so were his nerve endings. His frostbitten appendages and the burn on his left hand told him it was pain medication o'clock.

He threw the covers aside and limped to the bathroom. The cat meowed loudly this time.

"Just give me a minute, Oliver. I need to do some things first. You need a little more patience." Jake used the facilities and swallowed two pills with a glass of water. He checked the mirror quickly, but the bandages on his nose and ears forced him to look aside. He needed no reminders of the night before. When he peeled the dressings back on his hand, the skin was red, swollen, and blistering, but he wasn't sure where the frostbite ended, and the burn began. He applied the cream the doctor provided, recalling him saying it was something with aloe vera. It had a welcome, soothing effect, but the doctor warned him that time and rest were the best healers. He reapplied the wrappings awkwardly with his other hand. It wasn't the job the doctor's professional hands had done.

When Jake arrived in the kitchen. Oliver circled his bowls impatiently.

"I can see your diet is making you grumpy old chum," Jake said as he poured a reduced quantity of food and milk. "Your vet and my trainer follow the same script."

Jake heated water on the stove and was about to drop in two eggs when his phone rang. He glanced at the screen to see Avery's name. Too soon. He wasn't ready to relate the story of last night, and he couldn't lie to her. He let it go to voice mail, resolving to call her later.

After lunch, he stretched out on his chair with Oliver on his lap, called his trainer to postpone his upcoming sessions citing a hand injury, and promptly fell asleep. The sound of his ringing phone jarred him awake. Oliver, recognizing Jake would move, jumped down and haughtily left the room. Jake instinctively reached for the phone with his injured hand, but abruptly changed his mind when the white bandage came into view. This time, the screen registered Dani's name. He answered with a drowsy, "Hi, how are you?"

"Better than last night," she said. Jake recognized by the tone that policewoman Dani was calling. She said, "I hope you are too. There isn't much time. I just got a call from Constable Davidson.

Jason Pruitt is at his house with the friend we talked about. I thought I would pay him a visit. Are you up to coming along?"

Jake put the phone on speaker, rose from his chair, and hobbled to the front door to retrieve his winter attire.

"Like I said last night, I wouldn't miss this for anything. I can be ready in two minutes."

It was more like five minutes when Dani wheeled into Jake's driveway in an unmarked Ottawa Police Services' issue Ford Explorer. The sight of Emilie in the back seat surprised him. Dani shrugged at Jake's inquisitive look.

She said, "Her reaction was the same as yours. She wasn't going to school today anyhow, and her dad is busy."

Jake noted that Dani and her daughter survived the night in better shape than he had. They wore an assortment of bandages, but Dani's hands, nose, and ears, although rough and red, looked to be relatively unscathed. Blisters were already forming on Emilie's nose and bandages covered frostbitten areas on her right ear and hand. Jake said, "By the look of our bandages, we could get free admission to the mummy convention."

That brought a chuckle from the back seat. Emilie said, "Don't. It hurts to laugh."

The adrenaline rushing through Jake's veins masked the pain from his various bruises, frostbitten parts, and burned hand. That and the heavy dosage of pain killer.

They traveled in silence past quirky shops on Bank Street and turned onto a tree-lined street just south of the downtown core. Dani's unyielding gaze held the road. They stopped in front of a house in an area of Ottawa called the Glebe, the sight of Pruitt's car bringing terrible memories flooding back for Jake and a flush of anger reddening his face.

Dani turned to Emilie and said, "You stay here. This won't take long."

Emilie retorted by saying, "No way. I want to see this. I was there last night too, don't forget."

"Okay, but you two stay outside until I tell you to come in. Understand?"

Jake and Emilie agreed as the threesome completely forgot about their injuries, undid their seat belts, got out of the car, and marched toward the large two-story brick building with a side-to-side porch. Dani rang the doorbell, and they all stepped to one side, out of sight.

The door swung open. Pruitt stuck his head out and, spotting the onrushing Dani with her gun drawn, tried to slam the door. Dani shouldered it open, pushing Pruitt ahead of her.

Jake and Emilie could see the action through the window. Pruitt's face was ashen.

Dani had the gun in both hands, aimed at Pruitt. Her growling voice came through the yawning doorway as she said, "Are you seeing a ghost, Jason? Your game's over. You're under arrest." In one move, she holstered the gun and whirled him around, efficiently restraining his hands with flex cuffs while rhyming off a list of charges.

Jake heard no reference to the murder of Melissa Thomas and Matthew Pawsloski. Had he missed it? He watched as Dani guided Pruitt to a chair and roughly shoved him into it.

She shouted, "You can come out now," her voice echoing through the large house.

Jake grabbed Emilie's arm as she started for the door. "That wasn't for us, Em. Wait."

There was no response to Dani's challenge.

Pruitt's eyes remained fixated on Dani. His teeth clenched, he said, "T-t-there's no one else here. How did you survive?"

"That's our little secret." She raised her voice. "If you don't come out, I'll bring SWAT in to hunt you down. You won't like what they are likely to do. There's no escape."

Seconds ticked by in absolute silence until a sound drifted from the rear of the house. The unmistakable creak of a door echoed to Jake and Emilie's location at the front. Jake expected Dani to rush down the hall and he panicked at the thought of the martial arts expert who sat scowling in his chair, his face beet red, making a break for it through the open front door. Even in handcuffs, Pruitt could do a lot of damage with his skills. He and Emilie continued to observe from a distance. And that's how he wanted it to stay.

Suddenly, shouts erupted from the rear of the house, shattering the silence. Everyone listened. Pruitt scowled, his tied hands forcing him to sit upright awkwardly in the navy fabric chair. Dani focused on him with laser intensity, holding her gun in a classic two-handed grip aimed squarely at the center of his chest. The beet-red blotches on her unwavering hands were plainly noticeable. Her face was stone-like. Jake and Emilie stood outside the open front door, staring wide-eyed.

The shouting stopped as shuffling footsteps made their way down the hall.

Sarah Brown emerged, her hair disheveled, her jeans covered in snow, a red bump thickening into a welt on her forehead, and her hands tied behind her back with plastic cuffs. She had not taken the time to put on a coat before trying to escape, and one shoulder of her tan sweater was halfway down her arm, exposing a white blouse. She wasn't the mousy individual Jake had encountered. Her wild-eyed appearance reminded Jake of a trapped animal.

Constable Davidson followed close behind.

Dani said to Davidson, "Any trouble?"

"She tried to run, but the boys and I subdued her." He nudged Sarah toward an unoccupied leather chair in the living room.

Three squad cars rolled to the front of the house where they slid to a stop, angled to block the street. Jake assumed they had been behind the house waiting to rush in if required. He and Emilie walked through the open door to stand in the entrance. Jake noticed Pruitt glance up, frown, and return his gaze to the floor.

Dani said, "Okay Sarah, we'll add resisting arrest to the double homicide we'll charge you with." She pointed to Pruitt. "We've got him on kidnapping, attempted murder, and a few other charges."

Sarah's mouth dropped in shock. She stuttered, "*Double homicide*? What are you talking about? I didn't kill those two. It was him." She pointed her chin sharply toward Pruitt. "What do you mean *attempted* murder?"

Jason snarled, "Sarah, shut up."

Dani said, "He left us in the country to freeze to death last night, so that's where the attempted murder charge comes from. We got lucky or he would have been responsible for three murders along with the two you committed. You two are a piece of work. Constable Davidson, read them their rights."

Sarah wasn't to be denied. "Wait, I said I didn't kill Matthew and Melissa." She pointed her chin at Pruitt again, saying, "It was him. After I told him about the trust fund, he planned everything. At first, it was just to get money to help him with his business and so we could start our lives together. I never thought it would end up with people dying. Matthew discovered something was wrong, so Jason killed him. Matthew told me about this friend of his whose husband liked to go to the shooting range and that he kept a gun at his house. It turned out to be Gary Thomas. I wanted no part of it, but I told Jason about the gun. It was a mistake. He broke into Gary's house and stole it, and then he killed Melissa and Matthew." She looked at Jake, saying, "Everything would have worked if you hadn't started investigating. Everything unraveled after that. I tried to make you think I was in love with Matthew."

As Jake shifted his eyes to Pruitt, who still sat with his head bowed, he thought how he had believed her about falling for Matthew. He had been wrong about her suspected love affair with Matthew, but his gut instinct had been correct not to trust her.

Dani stated matter-of-factly, "So, you staged the robbery in the parking garage."

Sarah confirmed it with a nod of her head. She said, "Jason shoved me so hard I fell and hit my head on the car bumper. But that made it more convincing." She mumbled despondently, "At least we *thought* it made things look more realistic. I thought we did everything right. He didn't tell me he was going to let you freeze to death in the country. It's the first I've heard of that." Tears rolled down her cheeks, darkening her jeans. "The murders and now this. That's not the Jason I fell in love with."

Dani turned to Davidson, saying, "It's time. Take them away."

CHAPTER FIFTY-FOUR

JAKE TIPPED HIS hot chocolate-filled cup toward Dani as they sat in front of the fire in his sunroom. They had returned after officers led the two criminals away from Pruitt's house and started the evidence gathering process.

"Here's to you for the way you handled Sarah and made her incriminate Jason. She sang like a canary. I wondered if you would chase her down the hall and leave Emilie and me to tackle Pruitt if he made a run for it, though." He winked at Emilie. "I know Em could have handled him and protected me, but still."

Dani's laugh turned into a wince as her frostbitten nose wrinkled at the thought. "If I hadn't had backup, you two wouldn't have been anywhere close to the house. The backyard was crawling with officers. SWAT was on standby seconds away. You were never in danger. As for Sarah, I hoped that the threat of a murder charge might make her talk. Davidson said she's still talking.

"Pruitt probably learned lock-picking skills from the good old internet. He proved he could do it by breaking into your place without leaving a mark on the door. Since Gary left the gun lying around, it was easy. Pruitt wore gloves when he handled the gun, so Gary's were the only prints that showed up. You were right to be bothered by the gun.

"As it is, Sarah will be charged with accessory to murder. She knew about the murders and willingly helped Pruitt cover them up. She probably doesn't realize it, but if convicted, the consequences are the same as if she committed the murders herself."

Jake said, "Well, Sarah had me fooled. I thought she might be connected to the murders because she loved Matthew. She played her part well. I'll be haunted by that day she spun the yarn about the theft in the office and staying late to investigate. And the story about the computer password. I would give her credit if she wasn't such a lying, uh, criminal." He glanced at Emilie, relieved he hadn't called Sarah what he wanted to.

Dani reached out to put her hand on Jake's arm.

"Your instincts told you she had some involvement. I just looked at it from a different angle. Pretty good sleuthing on your part. We solved the crime, and that's what matters. I couldn't have done it without your help."

"Well, we flushed the murderer out. It could have been bad for us if Emilie hadn't talked to her science teacher about winter survival. That saved the day. So many people had a motive. Even Eric got upset about me writing a book. I guess that was just Eric being Eric. Do you still think Ryan's partner, Tremblay, committed suicide?"

"Yes, I think that was the sad way he chose to end his problems. We'll ask Jason and Sarah about it, of course."

Silence hung over the room until Jake said, "What about Gary Thomas?"

"His case will go before a Federal Review Board. There might be compensation if he pursues it, but it won't give him his time or reputation back. He's been in prison since they arrested him. I recorded the conversation at Pruitt's house. Hopefully, that will speed up the process."

Emilie had been leaning forward, her elbow resting on her knee with her fist supporting her chin. Oliver rested his hefty body snugly between her crooked arm and her chest. She sat back without disturbing the slumbering cat. She said, "Mom, isn't that illegal?"

"No, sweetie, not in certain circumstances. There's something called 'one-party' consent, but Constable Davidson got a warrant to ensure the defense lawyers couldn't challenge it. Are you finished your hot chocolate? We need to get you to your dad's."

Emilie grunted as she picked up Oliver's large furry body and gently placed him on the floor. She took a large, noisy sip of her hot chocolate as a satisfied "Ahhh" escaped her lips. She wiped a brown mustache off her top lip with her sleeve and set her cup on the coffee table.

"You make the best hot chocolate, Jake. Yup, I'm ready." She pushed herself off the chair and hustled down the hall with Oliver's eyes following her every move.

Jake marveled at her unrestricted movements as if nothing had happened to her. It must be nice to be young, he thought.

Dani and Jake got up and she wound her arm around his as they sauntered down the hall, careful not to touch each other's injuries. There was barely room for both as they walked side-by-side, but they managed since it brought them closer.

Jake said quietly, "She seems happy to be going to her dad's."

"They had a pleasant conversation and came to an understanding. Besides, she has a story to tell."

Emilie stood facing the door, and without turning as she pulled on her coat, she said, "I heard that. Sound travels, you know."

Dani and Jake glanced at each other. Dani half smiled and shook her head. Jake grinned. He was pretty sure the teenager had heard that comment from her mom a few times.

Dani said, "You owe me something, Mr. Scott."

The recently familiar rush of excitement hit Jake as he knew what she was referring to. He said, "I owe you a great deal for changing my life in a lot of ways. The last few days have been quite the ride. Would you be willing to join me for dinner on Saturday? Can you stand two enormous meals in a day? I assume you're going to breakfast."

She didn't hesitate as she said, "Yes, to both. I would love to have dinner with you and also enjoy a nice breakfast with friends without an agenda for once." She hugged Jake and put on her coat.

Emilie threw her arms around Jake as well, pressing her face into his chest before pulling back in agony, touching her nose. "Ugh, that hurt! See you again soon, Jake. Have fun at dinner with my mom." She winked as they left.

All the aches returned as Jake dragged his body back to the sunroom. Oliver waited until he settled in his chair before hoisting himself onto his lap. The cat responded to Jake scratching his head with a deep, satisfied thrumming sound.

Jake said, "Time to relax, huh Oliver? We've had enough excitement for a few days."

Jake felt like falling asleep on the spot, but he had two phone calls to make. The first was to his friend, Janice Richardson, at the *Ottawa Citizen*. He told her enough that she could publish it as a "developing story with details to follow." Dani could fill in the rest.

Next, he sent Avery a text. He knew his use of technology would surprise her. The wording was simple enough: "I have a story to tell you." She called immediately. She wanted to visit her dad the next day but agreed to wait ten days with Jake's promise that she would meet Dani and her daughter when she arrived.

The phone calls eliminated any thought of sleep, so he woke Oliver and nudged the cat off his lap. He rose from his chair and walked toward the picture on the wall. He regarded the photo of him with Mia for a few minutes before saying, "You would like Dani, sweetie. She's like you in a lot of ways." He kissed his index and middle fingers and placed them on the picture. "Everything's going to be alright."

He stopped at the bathroom to swallow more pain medication before ambling into his freshly painted office. Careful to avoid putting pressure on the fingers of his left hand, he clicked the file for his manuscript, which opened to the first page. He sat back examining the opening sentence until finally, he moved the cursor behind the period. The sentence vanished as he pressed the "backspace" key. Using the one-finger technique with his right hand, he hunted and pecked until he had the opening sentence that he wanted in capital letters. He leaned back in his chair, folding his hands behind his head. His lips curled at the corners with a look of satisfaction as he read.

IT ALL STARTED WITH BREAKFAST.

Thank you for reading *Searching For Truth*. If you like what you read, please consider leaving a review at your favorite online book retailer.

QUESTIONS TO START YOUR BOOK CLUB DISCUSSION

1. How did you experience *Searching For Truth*? Were you immediately drawn into the story? How did the story make you feel?

2. What motivates Jake Scott? Dani Perez? Jason Pruitt?

3. How do the characters grow or change during the story?

4. Is the story plot or character driven? Do events unfold quickly or is more time spent developing characters' lives?

5. Do you think the cover reflects the storyline?

6. Were there any questions left unresolved in the story?

7. Have you read Barry Finlay's other books? Can you discern a similarity in theme or writing style between them? Or are they completely different?

ABOUT THE AUTHOR

Barry Finlay is the award-winning author of the inspirational travel adventure, *Kilimanjaro and Beyond — A Life-Changing Journey* (with his son Chris), the Amazon bestselling travel memoir, *I Guess We Missed The Boat* and five Amazon bestselling and award-winning thrillers comprising The Marcie Kane Thriller Collection: *The Vanishing Wife, A Perilous Question, Remote Access, Never So Alone,* and *The Burden of Darkness*. His new novel, *Searching For Truth,* introduces the Jake Scott Mystery Series. Barry was featured in the 2012-13 Authors Show's edition of "50 Great Writers You Should Be Reading." He is a recipient of the Queen Elizabeth Diamond Jubilee medal for his fundraising efforts to help kids in Tanzania, Africa. Barry lives with his wife Evelyn in Ottawa, Canada.

Contact Barry Finlay

Author Website: **www.barry-finlay.com**

Facebook Page: **https://www.facebook.com/AuthorBarryFinlay**

Twitter: **https://twitter.com/Karver2**

BOOKS BY BARRY FINLAY

THE MARCIE KANE THRILLER COLLECTION

The Vanishing Wife: An Action-Packed Crime Thriller (Marcie Kane Book 1)

A Perilous Question: An International Thriller & Crime Novel (Marcie Kane Book 2)

Remote Access: An International Political Thriller (Marcie Kane Book 3)

Never So Alone (Prequel novella to the Marcie Kane series – Book 4)

The Burden of Darkness: A Marcie Kane and Nathan Harris Thriller (Marcie Kane Book 5)

NON-FICTION TITLES

Kilimanjaro and Beyond: A Life-Changing Journey

I Guess We Missed the Boat

FIND THEM ONLINE OR AT YOUR FAVORITE BOOK STORE OR LIBRARY

How far will a man go when someone threatens his family? Mason Seaforth is about to find out. He is a mild-mannered accountant living a quiet, idyllic life in the small community of Gulfport, Florida with his wife, Samantha. That is until Sami, as she is known to her friends, vanishes the night of their 20th anniversary. With the help of his wife's brash friend, Marcie Kane, he follows clues uncovering secrets that lead them into a dark, dangerous world. One mistake could result in the death of Mason's entire family.

Please turn this page for an excerpt from

The Vanishing Wife

The first book in The Marcie Kane Thriller Collection

The Vanishing Wife

Chapter 1

MASON SEAFORTH WAS WAITING.
It was 6 o'clock in the morning, and the darkness in the suburbs had begun to ease. The sun would soon make its appearance for another day, causing the shadows to beat a hasty retreat. Mason was now restlessly sitting on the couch in the sunroom that belonged to him and his wife Samantha, or Sami as she was known to her friends. He was staring at the walls and thinking that if he smoked, now would be a good time to light one up.

He hated waiting. Mason was a very punctual man and had always had the attitude that everyone's time is precious. He never wanted to give the impression that his time was more valuable than anyone else's. His wife was no different. She had always had the same attitude as he did, and together they'd earned the reputation of being the "Early Seaforths." That's what made this so unusual and frightening at the same time.

Mason was waiting for Sami.

It had started out to be an amazing 24 hours. They had spent the day relaxing, exploring the area around St. Petersburg, Florida and enjoying each other's company. It was that delightfully peaceful time of year on the beach between the departure of the snowbirds back to the north and the invasion of the tourists from Europe. They had wandered around John's Pass at Madeira Beach, leisurely strolling in and out of the various shops lining the walkways. They had held hands as they walked along the beach, feeling the sun drenching their skin. As they did so, the wind rustled through the palm fronds, sending shivers through the tall grass that separates the beach from the traffic noise on the street. They'd looked into each other's eyes as they enjoyed crab-stuffed mushrooms washed down with Coronas at Sculley's, their favorite hangout.

It was their 20th wedding anniversary and Mason had never been happier. At 48, he was in the prime of his life. He was a mild-mannered accountant who had worked his way into the position of owning his own firm. He worked hard at his one-person operation, but that suited him just fine as it gave him the flexibility to come and go as he pleased. Since meeting Sami 22 years ago, she had become his entire world. She worked as a financial advisor in the bank where Mason kept his investments, but it wasn't until Mason decided he needed additional advice on his current fixed-interest rate instruments that their paths actually crossed. The attraction was instant and intense. As he walked through the door of her office, he couldn't help but notice how attractive Sami was. And when she spoke, Mason's heart skipped a beat. Her dark auburn hair was drawn back off her face, emphasizing her beautiful features. Her green eyes were large and seemed to draw him in as he advanced towards the chair. Her lips were full, a feature he had always found attractive. When she stood to greet him, he noticed her business attire of a pale yellow blouse and dark skirt on her shapely 5'5" frame. Business attire to anyone else, but to Mason it was beyond sexy.

Sami's confidence and professionalism, along with her beauty, won him over in a way no other woman ever had, and after making up excuses to go back and see her a few more times for financial advice, he worked up enough courage to invite her out. After a short courtship, they were married, and life for Mason had been wonderful with every passing year. At 46, Sami was two years younger than her husband, and still very attractive. Mason was only too aware of the admiring glances that inevitably came her way as they walked down the street. But he felt confident that she was more attracted to him than she could ever be to anyone else. Their anniversary had been perfect. They had agreed to celebrate the entire day together, and the hours had flown by as they drank too much wine and ate too much steak and lobster over a candlelight dinner at home. They'd laughed as they donned bibs and sprayed juice from the cooked lobster everywhere while cracking the hard shells. Reminiscences came easily, and they shared memories that would only be funny to them. As she loved to do, Sami teased Mason about how he'd run into the wall in the dark in their hotel room while they were on their honeymoon. She unsuccessfully tried to stifle the wine-soaked gales of laughter as she recalled the black eye that Mason sported for the rest of the trip.

When dinner was finished and the last of the wine consumed, they brought their anniversary to a close by heading into the bedroom early and making love passionately. As Mason reflected on that part of the evening, he recalled that their clothes had come off urgently on the way to the bed with an intensity that was unusual even for them. He also recalled that Sami seemed even more passionate than usual. When they were finished, she had tears in her eyes and her voice quavered slightly when she told him she loved him. But she'd assured him it was only because her feelings were so strong and she was only thinking about how happy she was.

Afterwards, they had both fallen into the deep sleep that only lovemaking brings. Around 4 a.m., Mason had awoken. He felt that something had awakened him. He felt confused and groggy, but he forced himself out of bed and staggered to the bathroom. He was sure his stupor was not only from sleep but strongly enhanced by the effects of the large quantities of wine they had consumed just hours earlier. He could still smell the lingering scent of Sami's perfume. As he stood naked in front of the mirror washing his hands, he smiled at the thought of the last 24 hours, and his tired reflection smiled back. Mason shut off the bathroom light before opening the door so as not to awaken the slumbering Sami. As he felt his way around the bottom of the bed in the blackness, he thought that she must be curled up on the far side because he only felt empty space where her feet should have been. As he climbed into bed, he suddenly sensed an eerie emptiness in the room that shouldn't have been. He reached across the bed to fold Sami into his arms. She wasn't there.

With a jolt, Mason got up again, battling the stupor that he was still feeling, and threw on the blue robe Sami had given him last Christmas. He unplugged his cell phone from the charger in the bedroom and glanced at it as he always did when he first got up. There had been no calls. He went downstairs to the living room. No Sami. Their daughter Jennifer had left for college earlier in the year, and they both missed her dearly so he went back upstairs to check her room. Maybe Sami was missing Jennifer a little more because of their anniversary and had decided to spend the last part of the night in Jennifer's bed. But she wasn't there, either. Mason padded down the hall to the room they had converted to an office, but again there was no sign of Sami. He called out nervously into the silence. "Sami? Sweetheart, where are you?" There was no response.

He decided to check their favorite room, a combination sunroom/entertainment area. They often spent their mornings there sipping coffee, or evenings together with Sami curled up beside him on the couch to watch something that they mutually agreed upon after much playful negotiation. They had splurged a while ago on a 60-inch TV and determined that the sunroom would be the place for it. Now, Mason wondered if maybe Sami couldn't sleep after all the wine and was watching TV quietly with the headphones on. He made his way into the room to check, hoping against hope to find her there. His heart sank when there was no glimpse of Sami.

A creeping uneasiness began mounting against Mason's will. He went to the back door, turned on the outside light, and stared out into the darkness of the back yard through the window. His hand shook slightly as he unlocked the door, hesitated, then called out for Sami into the night. There was no answer. Mason went back inside and opened the door leading from the front hall to the garage to see if she might have gone there for some reason. He switched on the light as his bare feet felt the coldness of the two steps to the grey concrete floor of the garage. He walked around his Audi, checking inside the vehicle as he went. There was barely room to walk between the tools hanging on the wall and the sides of his car, but he squeezed by to open the garage door to the driveway to ensure that her Miata sports car was still there. It stared back, mocking him.

After closing the garage door again, Mason returned back inside. He stood frozen, uncertain and increasingly tense. What was going on? Where was Sami? Where was his wife? Mason couldn't think. He still felt strange and detached, almost as if he was in a dangerous dream that wasn't real. Why couldn't he wake up?

And now it was 6 a.m. The sun would be coming up momentarily. There was no Sami and no question of going back to bed, so Mason finally went to the sunroom couch where he sat despondently, waiting and flipping distractedly through magazines. But he couldn't focus on the words in front of his eyes. The anniversary clock they had been given by his parents sat on the mantle ticking loudly, interrupting the silence that permeated the room. Each tick was a reminder that his wife was gone and he was alone. Then a moment of hope sprang forward: what if Sami hadn't been able to get back to sleep and had decided to go for a walk in their quiet residential neighborhood? It was, after all, a very safe community. She was in all likelihood just out for some fresh air to clear her head, especially if she'd felt as groggy as he did.

Sami never went anywhere without her cell phone, and if she had gone out for a walk, she would certainly have taken the phone with her. He reached for his own phone and dialed Sami's number. The number rang. And rang, and rang again. Mason held his breath. "Please, Sami, please, pick up," he whispered. On the sixth ring, he heard Sami's confident voice message. "You have reached Samantha Seaforth. Please leave a message, and I will call you back."

In a shaking voice, Mason heard himself doing as she asked. "Sweetie, it's Mason, I'm leaving a message. Where are you? Please call me back right away."

It had been two hours since he first noticed Sami was gone.